REDBIRD

IN THE

POPPIES

REDBIRD

IN THE

POPPIES

ANGELA GEER-GANN

atmosphere press

PREQUEL

Iowa

The setting sun shone over the west as the purple-flowered stalks flowed delicately over the fields. The harvest was coming soon, and the memories of the hay baler enthralled us. We bounded wildly within the waves of wispy drying grass, not knowing how precious the time had become.

We were small, but not hidden, always in sight of our mother. We knew to keep visible while we were with her. She didn't like to worry, and we knew the rules. We listened for her voice, as it would carry over the field, when she called us home.

"Andy! Lizzy! Time to come in! Daddy is on his way!"

We played till dusk outside every day. Not a care in the world. Looking back, I had to be five and Andrew six. The crackling foliage passed through our hands as we ran home. The drying flowers begged to be picked. We obliged by pulling a small handful daily to bring in for the dinner table.

Bumblebees wove within the blooms, raising ever so slightly when we raced past. They knew we were no threat. The pheasants who nested within the tall grasses were different. They were easily shaken and left the nest quickly to find sanctuary for themselves in the skies above. Giving them a scare was most entertaining—although from time to time, it would give us an unexpected scare as well.

The anticipation of possibly running across one hiding in the field kept our wits quick. It was always in the moments right before we got out of the field. The unhatched fowl were all too eagerly abandoned in the nest unattended. It was a wonder that any of their young made it to adulthood.

We snuck quietly beside the door to the kitchen, alfalfa flowers in hand. The sweet smell of roasted beef wafted through the air. Mother was preparing our plates. She always made sure they were cool enough to eat before we all sat down. Dad began to get closer to her with that look of loving adoration he gave her so often.

"So, what did they decide?" Mother inquired.

"Yes!" Dad declared, excitedly grabbing her waist. "I start as General Manager next month! With a little planning, we'll be out of here within a year! No more renting, baby! The sky's the limit! I knew if I worked hard enough, they would pay attention! A promise is a promise! It took a little longer than I'd like, but you stuck right by my side. I love you so much!" With that, he dipped her down for a kiss and we knew it was time to break it up.

Andrew and I came running in between them, offering our gift. We wanted to share in the excitement as well!

Mother backed away, smiled at Dad and began, "Let me put these in some water."

Her blue eyes seemed to absorb some of the purple from the flowers and somehow seem magical. She was the only one with blue eyes in the house.

She began to dispose of the day-old floral harvest and rinsed the small vase of the debris. As she set the fresh flowers on the table, she announced, "I know it's a little early, but I'll start looking for our forever home tomorrow! Oh, and I love you more!"

The reaper came for the hay only twice before we left the farmhouse.

The drive away from our sanctuary was left with dust. Gravel set free by the unsettled wind of an upcoming storm. There was no time for sad goodbyes. We were children too easily distracted by the promise of new adventures.

It began with a housewarming pool party with all their friends. Mother looked to be glowing in the sun. She finally had her place, and you could see it was where she truly belonged. Dressed in her sarong and sunglasses, she received the guests, showing adults only around the vast expanse that was now our house. Dad, beer in hand, was just happy to have some guy time. He worked some really long hours to get to where he was now.

We kids headed to the basement to check out the new playroom, then out to the pool. The evening seemed to bring us all the excitement we were promised all along. The farmhouse would have its sweet memories for the four of us, but this house was here to make memories with everybody. We were blissful inside our bubble. Laughing and playing exhausted us as the night went on.

"Come on!" Dad motioned. "I'll have to keep a vat of that pink stuff to treat all the mosquito bites!"

Although our complaints were few, he had a point. We seemed to have attracted them in our newly built house near an undeveloped field. All sorts of things can be stirred up when you disturb that which had been so long undisturbed.

We lasted there for eight years, unscathed. Until we didn't. We would soon find that there were more things out in the world that wanted to suck the life out of us than mosquitoes.

CHAPTER 1

Hysterics

It was early in the morning when I woke up and realized that something was very wrong. My parents were in the hallway. It was still dark. There was screaming and crying. I couldn't make out what they were saying. Mother sounded completely hysterical. Pure shrieks were coming from her lungs. They would have to burst soon. I knew that they would.

I was afraid to get out of bed. I was afraid of what I was going to see when I exited my solace and entered into whatever hell must be going on with the rest of my family. My brother wasn't in the room, so I decided that it was time that I go see what all the commotion was about.

As I entered their world as they knew it, I found out soon that it would have been better to stay put right where I was. The agony and anger in my mother's eyes were so exuberant that it scared me. I took a step back. I thought that she might attack me. Not that she ever had, but I wasn't sure what happened to get her this blindly hysterical.

In fact, in the few seconds that it took me to see her this way, I realized that the mood was catchy. It's like her emotion flowed so freely that it crossed right over to me and left me stunned and dazed. I realized, as I was trying to get some form of communication out of my mouth, that she looked at me and stopped screaming. It was like she saw herself in the mirror and it scared her too.

She came to hug me, but I just pulled away. I still felt like I wanted to be unreachable.

"W-what's going on?" I finally stuttered out of my trembling lips.

"It's ok. It's ok. Everything is going to be fine." That is all she seemed to be able to say.

"Where's Andrew?" I finally asked where my brother was.

"He won't be coming back home anymore," she replied.

I didn't even *want* to know what was going on after this.

"So *that* was the screaming? You kicked him out? I'm going to catch him! I won't let you make him leave!" I began toward the door.

"Elizabeth!" Mom screamed.

"Stop, Elizabeth!" Dad interjected. He came after me and grabbed my arm. It wasn't like him to physically manhandle me.

"Andrew is *gone*." Tears began to fall from his eyes in a most horrific way. Dads don't cry! It left everyone stunned for a moment.

My mind was racing, yet I couldn't react to what was happening.

Within the moments of awe and stillness, my dad slowly began to explain. "The police officer just left. Andrew was the passenger in Kyle's little car." He paused to ponder what more to say. "So much for *best* friends." He mumbled, and then continued. "Kyle was traveling too fast on a side road. When they got to Highway 69, they couldn't stop and literally ran right into a semitruck. The police said that they found drug paraphernalia and empty containers of alcohol around the crash scene. Knowing him, I'm sure there were drugs and alcohol in Kyle's system. They couldn't tell us if Andrew was under the influence yet either. Kyle was driving. Why was he driving?"

My mind began to race again, but with more clarity. I knew why we were all here. Times had been hard for our family. In recent times, with the economy and all, my parents gambled on buying their dream home in their early thirties. Now that they were both forty, they realized that it was the worst judgment call that they had ever made.

They really ruined everything. Our house got foreclosed on and they made us move fairly abruptly. Andrew had to leave some of his stuff because my parents wouldn't get the house cleared out in time. The mortgage company sure didn't care much about our current situation or our personal items.

It was after this that Andrew started drinking. He was only fourteen. When he went out with his new friends, it was the end of the Andrew that we had always known. It was like some zombie had taken his place. I heard from the grapevine that he was smoking pot and possibly other drugs by the time he was sixteen.

It never mattered if he had his own money or not. Even though he was finally old enough to get a job, he didn't need any money. His friends were always there to supply him with what he wanted.

I tried and tried to reason with him. I told him that it wasn't cool. I told him all about the dangers that they taught us in school about drugs. He just called me a kid and told me I didn't have a clue about suffering *'cause I was too young*. I was only a year younger than he was.

I always wondered why he thought of me as so young compared to him. I mean, he hung out with some kids from my class! It wasn't like I was too immature either. I was the most logical person in the house. The only one, including my parents, who had a good enough head on their shoulders to get somewhere in life and keep it.

I didn't just obliterate what *I* saved on inconsequential goods based on popularity. I thought Andrew was growing to be the same way I was. I wished right at that minute that he had. He would still be here, and we wouldn't be here having this horrible discussion all alone.

Yet here I was. Still stuck in this stupid, stupid hall between my room and my parents. I had no way of escape unless I once more retreated into the bedroom I was supposed to be temporarily sharing with Andrew. I was hoping that us staying in the same room would make us somehow closer. He never seemed to understand that I was on his side and that his whole life was—over.

Now it was. It was a chapter closed. It began with the first move from our old, rented farmhouse that wasn't good enough for my mother. It continued with the loss of our lux party house, and now ended with my brother. Over, everything was over.

It was like every worst nightmare had come true. Mother's hands once again reached out and embraced me slowly from the side. I wanted to gravitate to her for security. The security she once gave me. My mind raced back to when she would call us home. The shift within her parenting was insurmountable. So much so that her embrace was no more than a snowflake in the wind, cold and elusive.

I grew cold. Not only to her, but cold to the thought that I would ever have to enter that room again. I didn't want to be in there without Andrew. I started calling his name, over and over. I didn't know where the voice was coming from. It couldn't be from me. I would know, wouldn't I?

The need to hide was overwhelming. That is what I had always done in times of tragedy. I would go off and sulk until the time came that I had thought the problem over thoroughly.

When I got an answer from inside myself and could go on, I would come out of my hiding place, and I would be perfectly calm and rational. Before that time, however, look out!

It's not that I was an overly emotional person; I mean it took something really major to send me running. Like when my grandparents died. Again, when we got thrown out, rather publicly, from the big house. Every time, I ran for refuge to the farmhouse. It was only down the street a couple of miles, and an easy bike ride, so I would visit it often for perspective, not going up on the property, but rather sit by the fenceposts at the side of the road.

Only this time, there was no place of refuge. No place here, in this low-rent apartment building inside the city, that felt like it would be quiet enough to still the drumming of my heart. There was only one place I could think of: the communal laundry room.

I darted so fast that my mom yelped in pain when I ran through her arms and into the living area. I knew that I just had the need to get out quick enough to escape. I did escape down the stairs, down the dark corridor of the downstairs breezeway that headed straight to the laundry room. It was a communal laundry room, but what were the chances that someone at four in the morning would be out to do laundry?

I slammed the door shut behind me, wishing I could somehow lock the door. Then my solace would be complete. I stood in front of it, barring it just in case someone was to come.

I fell to the ground, right on my knees. I had not felt bare concrete to my knees since I was little and had a bike accident. The pain was so real. Everywhere.

I realized though that it wasn't pain from my knees, but the pain I felt all over. It was like I had been run over by a truck and I was a limping animal left to die. Death is what I wished for at that moment. I decided that I couldn't take one more thing to happen in my life. I was no longer whole.

The part of myself that was here when Andrew was alive

was now just a really big hole. It was gaping open and bleeding. My soul bled, along with my knees. I began to cry violently. I knew that only time could stop this. I knew that these emotions would pass if I could cry it out enough. As I sat weeping, I tried to focus on a happier time.

I closed my eyes and fought my mind to go back to the farmhouse. Even in exasperation, special memories never let go. Andrew had gone out into the meadow with me, beyond the hayfield.

It was early in the morning. As was usual, my only companion was my brother, my co-explorer. "Lizzy!" I could still hear Andrew's voice as if I were once again living in that moment. "Look what I found!" We were gathering wildflowers. There were so many varieties. Andrew noticed something far off in the field. It was odd to see it out in the middle of a meadow, but it was a lone rosebush with one single rose reaching towards the sky.

It was so beautiful. The flowers were begging to be picked. We once again obliged. I gathered the harmless bouquets as Andy bravely opted for the other.

"Be careful, Andy!" My wild notes of anticipation were thickened by my concern. No words could describe how happy I was when he chopped it down with his foot. Of course, I thought that he was brave, sticking his shoed foot to a thorny bush just for a flower for me.

A morbidity awoke within me. My final dedication for Andrew dawned on me, just as the sun too had risen in the early morning sky. That no matter what happened, my newly deceased brother would get his payment for his bravery.

I too would muster up the courage to find a single rose. I would place it on his casket myself. My head lifted as I came back to reality. I made it through my pain. As I made it back to our apartment, my dad held out his hands.

"Did you get enough time, Elizabeth?"

He knew where I was, even when I didn't know for sure

where I was going. He knew I needed my time and not to be smothered. My mom, on the other hand, always seemed surprised.

"I just want to go to my room and get some more sleep. I really feel tired now."

With that, I walked past my mother for the second time in the morning without acknowledging her.

"Feel better, Lizzy. We love you."

My father's voice was the last thing I heard as my head hit the pillow. It was four hours before I woke again.

As I awoke, I heard voices coming from the living room. I wanted to sink into a hole and just disappear. No one normal liked having a crowd before you could get up and around in the morning, especially me. That was something my brother lived for, a bunch of friends all congregating to see him.

How surreal that they would be doing just that for one last time. I began to weep. Not cry, just weep. It was like my body knew that it had lost something so precious that it was distributing tears on its own.

I got up slowly and got ready for my quick escape plan to the bathroom. I gathered clean clothes, all necessities, so I would be fully dressed when I got out of the shower. I crept quietly to the door. Tears traveled silently down my cheeks.

I looked back at the bed that he had slept in for the last couple of years. It seemed too empty. I wanted to run and lie down there, not move or be found. Just to disappear with him wherever he went. I knew that was impossible, and that it was time for me to face whatever was on the other side of the door.

It was worse than I expected. There were literally twenty people in our small apartment. People even congregated in the hall due to the lack of space. I couldn't hold it in. I didn't care that they were there for my parents and possibly for me. I didn't care because I wanted to be alone.

"MOTHER!"

I started screaming, just like I would have when I was younger, and I really needed her attention. Unfortunately, attention was no longer her strong suit. I always had to make a fuss if I wanted anything from her now. Everyone abruptly turned around. The people in the hall turned out to be my immediate neighbors. I couldn't even look at them. I just kept screaming until she came running.

It wasn't but about fifteen seconds before she made her way to me, yet it seemed like an eternity.

"We have company. Please come back in your room with me so we can talk." Of course, she would see her company as something detrimentally more important than her daughter. The only child she had left.

I backed up. I mean it was either that or throw a tantrum in front of everyone. I already felt like I caused a scene.

"I need to get a shower! There are too many people out there and I can't get a shower if they are in my way!" My voice more frantic with each word. "Make them leave! I want them all to go away!"

Smack!

She hit me across the face. She must have thought that I was in a panic and that I needed to be more sensible. She was wrong. We struggled against each other as I tried to leave the room. She was trying to restrain me, as if that would happen. It was like she must have felt that if we just didn't leave the room, no one would even know what had taken place.

It was amazing how quickly the apartment cleared out. Even if my mom didn't know what I needed, it seemed like the rest of our friends and family did. They knew that I hated close quarters, that I hated confrontation. My dad just smiled as I opened the door.

"Quick, get in the bathroom. There's no one in there now."

I could tell from his tone that he wasn't meaning it like my mom at all. He knew that I desperately needed my space. That even through everything that had happened to us in the past few years, nothing could have prepared me for what just did. I took exactly five steps, and I was in the bathroom.

The shower was hot. It was what I needed to calm down. Pools of warm salt water kept flowing from my eyes. It was as if there was some hidden faucet that my body had, and I wasn't in control of it. My knees stung as the water hit them. The fact that my pain was mainly interior couldn't vanquish the outer pain that occurred with my previous fall. I just stayed under the warmth of the water from the shower until my tears slowed.

As the water eventually cooled with time, so did the fire in my heart. My tears began to dry. It must have been about thirty minutes. It was time to get out and face the day the best that I could. After I bandaged my knees, I got dressed rather quickly. It seemed that a chill was about to set in my bones.

I started the hair drier and blew my hair with high heat until every single strand was bone dry. The heat felt so good. Suddenly I felt too warm. I knew that as soon as I was done with my hair, I would have to leave this security and venture into the world I never wanted again to see.

I slowly opened the door and to my relief, no one was there to get in my way or watch a show of grief. As I entered my room, I realized that I never looked back to see what my mom was doing when I retreated to the bathroom. It never occurred to me that she would do anything to my room while I was in the shower. That was wrong. I somehow miscalculated that she had my best interests at heart.

"W-what's going on?" I asked as I looked around.

This was the second time in a very short morning that I had to ask this question. She stripped his bed! His bedding was replaced with all of his clothes. She had taken them out of our shared closet and put them all over his bed. I stood confused, waiting for an answer.

"We have no life insurance for your brother. I know boutiques will pay top dollar for all of his things. He can't use them now, and we have a funeral to plan." She said it so matter-of-factly.

I was sure that she was the one in shock. That she'd just

lost it. She was now a certifiable loony. I went up to her and tried to give her a hug. She seemed to need one this morning, as she'd tried to give me one earlier. Instead, she backed away from me.

She looked me straight in the eyes and explained, "Your time is over, Elizabeth. I have had enough of your hysterics and mood swings for one morning. I am too busy!" She became belligerent. "I still have to go to the storage building. All of those things I've been meaning to sell have to go. NOW! Just get out of here and let me do what needs to be done! You know—*for the rest of the family?*"

I didn't even know what that meant. What rest of the family? Dad and I were all she had left. I knew all along that she had a different bond with my brother than she did to me, but to say that I wasn't an important part of her family was like another slap in the face. I did what she told me to do. I left my own room for her to pick through my brother's valuables and maybe even my own if my luck had run out completely.

A blank stare was shining through my eyes. It was as if, by being so mentally confused, all my focus just left. I became blank. Somehow, I got to my dad. He was standing by the front window, just staring out. It was as if we had become unable to handle what my mom had just put at us. I think that he was just glad everyone had gone. He lifted his arm and I tucked myself under it. We, at that moment, were simultaneously supporting each other. We had supported each other many times throughout the years. It would seem like Mother would go on binges and leave us in a lurch in lieu of some shopping spree or garden party at a friend's house. She never felt that she was good enough. My dad, no matter how hard he tried, was never enough for her. It was as if she had some score to settle with him at any moment for ruining her life and she had come to collect.

He was much like I was. We both didn't like the noise and couldn't take drama at all. It was funny because we were staring out the front window, but no matter what we did, we couldn't see farther than the glass itself. We were trapped in hell. The hell my mother caused in her own overbearing way of dealing with things. She knew that she failed. She knew that we were happy with where we were in the beginning. We loved the farmhouse. We moved for her. Dad took the promotion and worked longer hours for her. He tried to keep up with her newfound extravagance. Everything just spiraled out of control after that.

Eight years of false blissfulness. What I thought was worse is that when we had to move to this apartment, we moved away from everyone that we knew. I was always so alone. Not only alone, but broke and alone. Usually, one compensated for the other. Now, that loneliness was just part of me. It became who I was.

It was in that very moment I knew that my life would change. I didn't know how, but I knew that even with all the overwhelming money catastrophes, it would be nothing less of a miracle if we just didn't dissolve into sand and disappear in the wind. My brother was gone. My big brother Andrew was wiped off the face of the earth.

During the year after my brother died, so did we. My mother did sell many of his things before coming to the realization that she would never see him again. She had been in shock. She finally understood that with all of his things gone, she would never get to remember him by looking at his clothes or listening to any of his favorite CDs.

When it came to the funeral, I came to know that in times of grief, there were those waiting with unexpected compassion. It began with the rose that I promised in that lonely laundry room.

With love and compassion comes love and compassion.

This was attached to a purple rose with a handwritten note sent by the florist. My prayers had been answered. She had answered my call. I believe it was the prettiest rose that ever existed, with the exception of the very rose he picked for me. I knew immediately that as hard as this funeral was going to be, I would have the strength to make it through.

We stayed alone for about an hour. Just our little family in the reception room. It seemed so empty and full at the same time. Floral arrangements from what I could only have expected from the nicer neighborhood friends covered the walls. A spray with blue and white that Mother decided upon adorned the casket.

"It's time," the funeral director announced.

With that, I watched as the general public made their way in. I felt almost underdressed, as the people coming in seemed to have dress clothes to spare. I wondered what it felt like to get to go to church every Sunday and have different clothes each time. I'd outgrown all of my church clothes long ago and was put in a dress my mother had kept in case of just this kind of situation.

The compassion grew as the crowd multiplied. Distant family members, new neighbors, and strangers all processed through the line of bereavement. One girl caught my eye. It was her look of understanding that grabbed my attention.

"Hi," she announced as she was leaning over to give me a hug. "I'm Amelia. I am Tommy's sister."

Tommy had already passed by. It didn't surprise me that they weren't coming in together. There came an age where it seemed you split with your sibling companion and became a liability to their coolness.

"Can you come over here for a second?" Amelia asked. "I just had a few things I thought you might like to know about your brother."

Tommy was one of Andrew's newer friends, even though, as I found out, was not one that drank and partied. She was trying to straighten Andrew out too. When Andrew stayed the night with them, he evidently stayed up with Amelia and talked the night away.

The way that she expressed it gave me a new regard for

the people in this part of town. They weren't all as bad as they seemed. Her family wasn't rich either, but the difference was they never tried to act like they were. Nor did they try by illegal means to attain that wealth.

I asked her why she never introduced herself to me at school. "I was trying to get through to him. I thought that if he knew that I was talking to you, he would quit talking to me." Amelia explained.

It reminded me of what he had said just before he died, that I was a kid. I thought at that moment that he was right. I was just a kid who would have teamed up on him and made his life miserable.

Amelia continued, "I was getting through to him. He said that he was going to get away from the crowd that he had been hanging with. He said that he was tired of making his family more miserable than they already were. That there were too many other problems, and he wasn't going to be the one to add to them."

That sounded just like Andrew. Even though he was more into dramatics like my mother, he had known just how his behavior affected the rest of us. It never occurred to me that we were all getting through his thick skull. It was good to know that he was at least trying.

Unfortunately, bad friends seem to find you a lot quicker than good ones. They're always hanging out with nothing to do. They don't involve themselves in anything more in life than to bring others down with them. I wished so badly that Amelia could have done what she set out to do, what we all set out to do, before it was too late.

But now that it was too late, there was nothing that could be done but look ahead. She handed me a packet of pictures. They were of my brother. Just hanging out at her house. I couldn't believe it. He looked so normal. He looked happy, like he did when we lived at the farmhouse. I hugged her and told her how much they meant to me. She stayed right by my side for the rest of the funeral. The same rock that tried to hold my brother down was now doing the same thing for me.

The wind seemed to pick up at the cemetery. My grip on the purple rose tightened. I wasn't ready to let it go. I wasn't ready to let Andy go.

"Amen," said the pastor as he concluded the service. "If anyone would like to place flowers on the casket, now is the time."

"Come on, Lizzy. Right here." Dad motioned.

I had a hard time making my legs move. I felt like I would trip and fall in the hole by accident. I began to panic. But as he reached out and held my hand, once again we were there for each other. I placed the rose on the casket as the pallbearers did the same.

I wanted to run away and stay all at the same time. I wondered how Kyle's family felt. I wondered if they too had grief even though their son caused all of this for us. I never wanted to think of him again.

I started grief counseling that was provided by the school. All of the students that were affected by the loss could come and talk. I found it so strange that so many kids from school were affected. Who were they to him? To us? I barely knew any of them at all. Even as they reached out during the funeral with their condolences, I felt mostly alone.

After the initial counsel was over, the counselor tried to get my family set up with a local therapist. It seemed as if I wasn't the only one to think that we were dysfunctional. We were told that the bill could be written off. We were told that after you have a child that dies in a tragic accident, they all of a sudden want to extend their services. Before it started, my dad got quiet at home and spent most of his free time with the other men in the neighborhood. My mother started sleeping a lot. She didn't care about all of those 'friends' she had been so sure that she wanted one day to impress.

As far as my life went, Amelia remained my constant cheer team. She waited for me outside the school every day. I wondered at first if I had worn the right clothes, because she was smiling so happily. I thought I was so mismatched that I was somehow humorous. It turned out that she was just there to see if I was ok. She would never know how happy I was to see a friendly face there, especially after the couple of years of unfriendly. I had just put up a wall, one that wouldn't be taken down that easily.

When it came time to sit by her other friends, which she had plenty of, I wouldn't go anywhere near them. She was cool about it though. She sat where I was instead. She was giving me support once more where it wasn't deserved. I couldn't have made it through the next couple of weeks without that constant companionship.

It turned out that we had a lot in common. We both liked the same music, movies, and TV shows, and we both had brothers. One of us still did. We also wanted to go to college and had these crazy hopes and dreams for the future. No one needed to tell us that we were going to make something of ourselves. We knew for sure that we would.

As far as my family, it was unfortunate, but the therapist wouldn't do pro bono counseling after the first month. It only took two weeks before we found out that there was too much resentment between all of us, and basically, we stayed out of each other's way. The last thing my family needed was another reason to fight over money.

I really thought it was funny in the end, that she was so adamant that we come to see her, just to tell us we couldn't, especially after knowing the real reason for much of the discourse in our house as it was! Or what was told in the therapy sessions anyway. I remained grateful for my new friendship. It would see me through much more than false compassion and a bill.

CHAPTER 2

Sixteen

I was sixteen now, and it was just like I imagined. I woke up early to the magic of the day-supplied sunshine that never came through my west-facing bedroom. The soft glow warmed my face. I looked over and there he was.

Andrew was lying there under his covers. Safe and sound. He looked so peaceful. He looked so happy. I turned to look at the glow again from the window and realized that it was lights of a passing car. No, not a car, a truck, but a semitruck. It was coming right into my window.

I turned to look at Andrew. I wanted to scream, to tell him to watch out. I wanted to save him at that very moment. I was so close to him. I was desperate. I reached toward him. He looked at me and said in a calm voice, "I will see you on the other side." He smiled and then disappeared just when the truck was about to hit him. I woke with a jerk. I looked around the room, remembering that his bed was no longer there. This was my first birthday alone.

I realized that it was true. I had made it to my birthday. I was now the same age as my older brother. The same age he was always going to be. In fact, it kind of made me a little leery about being sixteen. Would there be a certain fate out there that would bring me the same ending?

I wiped that thought out of my mind along with the bad dream. I mean, at least I saw his face one more time. That was enough of a birthday present to me. I wondered what fate had in store for me.

I crept silently through my door, taking my five steps to the bathroom. There was no one up yet, or if they were, they were being awfully quiet. The shower went pretty quickly, as it did every day. I was glad that things, for now, were normal.

It was like nothing big was happening today. I wondered if my parents would even remember. I washed that thought down the drain. Of course, they would remember, they were my parents, and it wasn't every day that their daughter turned sixteen.

As I returned to the hall, I smelled something very good. It was waffles. My dad had this special waffle maker that he only brought out for special occasions. I knew from that moment that the day would be bearable.

I was excited to see what he had done. I really needed happy family times. I skipped, like a younger kid, to the kitchen. There he was, cheerfully making his famous dad's celebration waffles. He smiled.

"Happy birthday, Elizabeth. Or happy sixteenth birthday, should I say?"

"Oh! Thank you, Dad!" I was just so ecstatic that he remembered. I looked around and there was someone missing. The person that seemed to always be missing. My mother.

"Where's Mother now? Is she still asleep in bed?"

"She left early this morning. She said that she needed to

get something. She didn't say for what or when she'd be back. I just had to let her go like I always do," he explained.

"Well, I'm glad you were here to surprise me."

My morning would have totally been a bummer if it weren't for him. I gave him a quick peck on the cheek and sat down at the kitchen table and waited to be served a little magic. He knew that food, especially his sweet food, could do the trick to cheer me up about as well as hiding.

He was always considerate. Every day, it never ceased to amaze me that he kept me in his consideration for things. He never gave up on me. It was the same way he was with my mother. He always gave her everything that he could. He tried so hard to make us happy.

"Well, eat up, Lizzy. You have sixteen to eat!"

"Dad, you didn't!"

"Yep, sure did, but don't worry, they are silver-dollar-sized waffles. They were made with much more care than the normal ones I usually make! Your brother really tried to eat sixteen full-sized ones last year, but for all of our sakes, I decided to spare us a trip down the road to stomach misery."

It was so great, we just laughed and laughed. It was a full conversation about Andrew. Not one tear came, well except for when we laughed so hard that it brought tears to my eyes.

No matter what happened for the rest of the day, I knew that I would be able to take this small memory with me and I would make it through.

After finishing the last of my silver-dollar-sized waffles, my mother came running into the apartment. She had a look on her face that I didn't see very often. She was glowing with a beautiful smile. I was so happy to see it. It was like the clouds had lifted on my special day and brought bright sunshine into my life.

"Elizabeth, Elizabeth, Elizabeth! I have the greatest news!" My mother began to explain.

"I was watching TV early this morning, because I couldn't

sleep. The channel five news had a segment during their live at five. They were saying that if you were watching right now and were the fifteenth caller to the station, then you would win three hundred dollars! Oh Lizzy, I did it. I finally did something right! I was the fifteenth caller! Happy sixteenth birthday!"

She handed me a hundred-dollar bill, then pulled out two more, waving them in the air. Then she turned her head around toward the counter and I saw a small but wonderful little cake. All my dreams were coming true. There was a strange peace that came over all of us that morning.

I just knew that it must have been Andrew, looking down on us, watching over us, and taking care of us. Maybe all that had happened, as horrible as it was, would get us to where we would want to be. I almost cried, but I held it back as I ran to give hugs to both of my parents. I was witnessing a miracle, a birthday miracle.

"Can you take me to go shopping, Mother?"

This was truly the first time in almost two years that I had even tried to raise this subject with my mother. It's like she couldn't stand the thought of an impromptu shopping trip if it couldn't be a full-out shopping spree. But that was her trouble all along.

Her spending was so gratuitous that no matter the amount of money that was made, the money was gone, and the credit card companies began to call. She lost our money along with her dignity. It was so iffy with her that I found satisfaction when she would get tired of her clothes and would be willing to pass them down to me.

"Sure, Lizzy, it's Friday and as soon as school lets out, we'll go somewhere. Just you and me." She held up the rest of *her* money, fanning her face in delight.

I turned to look at her one more time before I went to meet the bus. They were both so happy looking. It was like it was six years ago, and we were in the heyday at the big house. I had so much hope for today. Only in the back of my mind was

I worried that something would change before I got home in the afternoon.

The day at school passed quickly. I told Amelia that I would be busy tonight with my mother for my birthday. She knew what that would mean to me. She wished me luck and said that she had a 'hot date' with Matt anyway. Sure enough, as soon as school was out, my mother was there waiting for me. We went straight to the mall. I was in the clothes shop looking for sales, as I knew one hundred dollars needed to get me a wardrobe.

As I was passing the endless racks of discounted clothing, I noticed someone staring at me. It was Rob, a friend of Andrew's, that I remembered from the funeral. I never knew if he was one of those friends that were for or against his recovery. It wasn't long before he approached me.

"Hey Liz, how've ya been doin'?"

"K," I quietly replied.

He just kept staring at me.

"You got a boyfriend?"

"No!"

It never occurred to me that I was sixteen, and that I was technically old enough to have a boyfriend to date. Most of my schoolmates had been dating since they were like fourteen. After we moved to this particular part of town, my parents were really strict with the rules. It was sixteen when independence came our way.

"Hey, you want to ditch your mom and go to the new miniature golf place?"

My face turned beet red with his directness. Why was he talking to me? Why did he want me to come with him? It was hard to have this conversation! Awkward wasn't even the word for what I felt! I somehow opened my mouth to mutter my reply.

"Now? I'm shopping for my birthday," I said as I kept my head down, appearing to peruse the clothing selections. "I doubt my mother would let me just go."

"Watch this." He turned around and gave me a wink.

"Um, Mrs. Redbird, hey, do you remember me? I was in Andy's class. I just found out that the new mini golf place is open. I just got off work and some of my other friends just ditched me. Would it be ok if Liz went with me? I would really appreciate it!"

"Well, Rob, I'm not sure. Let me speak to Liz for just a minute over here."

She pulled me over to the next rack of clothes.

I gave him a 'I told you so' smirk.

"Liz, are you almost done shopping or what? I mean, if you *wanted* to go out with this guy, you could have just asked. I thought that it was supposed to be our afternoon together!" She started acting frantic again, like I was the cause of ANY of this! "You got what you came for, for the most part, so why don't you just go! Your new friend is waiting, right?"

"Mother, I don't even know Rob!"

She lowered her tone and whispered, "Besides, as you know, you *are* now sixteen and I guess you're ready for some freedom. If you wanted to start dating, you could have just asked." She must have thought it was really MY idea and that I wanted to go out with Rob. Maybe she was trying to make up for all of the failed attempts at a relationship with me. Who knows?

I quietly replied. "I mean, I just see him around, but it's not like I planned this." *Did she just say I was allowed to be around boys on my own now? Then I'll go with him?*

I turned around, not believing what had just happened. TODAY really was MY day!

"Fine, but get home by no later than 7:30," she said in a fake parental voice. "Don't be late. Your *dad* really wanted to take you to dinner tonight, and he would really be disappointed if you skipped out on him." She rolled her eyes.

"That is not a problem, Mother, I promise!" With that, I gave her a big hug. It wasn't as if I was going out for a night on the town for a romantic first date. This wasn't even technically a date.

We returned to where Rob was standing.

"Ok. Elizabeth can stay to play golf, but that is it. Today is her birthday and her dad wants to take her to dinner. She has to be home at 7:30. Do you have a way to get her home, or should we just come to pick her up?"

"Actually, I just got a car," Rob assured. "I will make sure that she is home on time."

I watched her scamper off back into the store. I knew at that moment what was really going on. The other money she had this morning was too tempting and she wouldn't want an audience to her gluttonous spending. She knew if I were with her, she couldn't revert to her old habits. I just couldn't believe that she ditched me on my birthday.

I guessed that addictions, no matter how long ago, could rear their heads at any time. On the other hand, *freedom for me!* I thought her asking if she needed to find a way for me to get home was a bit excessive, as I knew that was not where she was headed—maybe the shopping center down the street, but not the apartment.

I said a quick goodbye to my mother and hurried toward the golf place with Rob. This birthday was just getting better and better all of the time. I did feel kinda weird being alone with Rob. I barely knew him, and it wasn't even like me to hang out with anyone besides Amelia. The way my mother reacted; it was as if I did this all the time just to drive her crazy.

We got to the *Dark Hole in One* golf place. It was so dark in there; it was glow in the dark golf. Ok, I can handle this. Cute guy, dark room, bunches of other people, playing games. I was amazed at how it felt when he accidentally got close to me in the dark.

My breathing quickened. I could tell that his did too. He

would glance my way with this big overconfident smile, and from time to time, give me golf tips by guiding my hands. It was the most unbelievable feeling that I ever had in my life.

I was on my first date! I hadn't had a boyfriend since I was in the third grade! I was sure that right now, that didn't even count. I got 'the talk' when I was twelve or thirteen, but it never applied to me. Those feelings just never came up. Not until now. It was as if he could feel how I felt. He could tell that I was nervously comfortable with his demeanor towards me, that I enjoyed every sly glance, every little touch.

It was 5:30 in the afternoon, no parental supervision and I was suddenly feeling very brave. He was feeling that very same way. It was as if he knew that he had me. He knew, because he must be experienced at this. He didn't get through my mother's teen awareness, but he was smooth about what he thought would work with her. It must be because he had used it before with some other girl at this same mall. Somehow, that just didn't matter.

I took into account all of that, yet I was the one receiving his affections. He chose me for some reason today. Maybe it was just fate, maybe it was my birthday wish for things to be happy the way that they were long ago. Either way, something was in the air. I could feel change coming.

It wasn't long before we were done with the first game. It was only 6:15, and I didn't have to leave the mall for about an hour. We deliberated about playing another game, but he said that he knew of a better place that he would like to show me before he brought me home. I wasn't totally naive about life, but I really gave him blind trust for some reason that day. We were actually holding hands before we left the mall. We were heading for his new car. The one that would safely get me home in just about an hour.

"Where are we going?"

"You'll see!"

I sat patiently while we drove down the road to another

mall. It wasn't until he parked the car that I realized that we were in a deserted parking lot of the old vacant mall complex. He shut off the engine and looked at me very seductively. He placed his hand on my knee and leaned in to kiss me.

Me, I couldn't believe it! I wasn't popular, and didn't have any reputation, good or bad. People just stayed away most of the time. I leaned in, even though I was astonished that I even knew what to do. The breeze picked up, just as our breathing did. Small raindrops began to hit the car. The sound was so interesting.

It drowned out the sound of the breath that was coming quicker and quicker as the afternoon began to unfold into evening. Before I knew it, we were almost lying in the car. I knew that it had to have been a long time that we had been there, and it must have been time to go. I really didn't want to disappoint anyone today, especially Dad.

I looked at the clock in the car. It said 7:28! We had been making out for a long time. I gasped, "I have to be home in two minutes!"

With that, all of our inspiration of the afternoon was gone. He knew I meant what I said, and that it was time for me to go.

"Well, have to do this again some time."

"Um, yeah."

With that, he said goodbye to me. I was fifteen minutes late, but I didn't regret one thing about that afternoon. I felt free. I felt really alive, like my life had just started for the first time.

My dad was waiting for me in the apartment. It was a quarter till eight, and I was late. It didn't occur to me that anyone would be worried about me. I mean, for all of these years, Andrew was the topic of worry. They knew that I was never up to no good. For the first time, he looked at me with those same suspicious eyes.

"Was 7:30 too hard to remember, Lizzy?"

"Yes, I mean no. I mean I told him we had to leave as soon

as I saw what time it was. We just lost track of time. I am so sorry."

Unfortunately, it was too late. The tide had turned and the joyous mood that once was in our space was no longer there.

"Sorry just isn't quite good enough, Elizabeth. Your mother told you a specific time. You were with a boy that we don't know very well. When you didn't come home right away, she figured that you didn't have a ride home. She left to go try and find you at the mall. Your mother made a judgment call without me, and now we see that split decisions just don't work."

This was unbelievable! I was out fifteen minutes late! They were already calling out for reinforcements, for Pete's sake!

"I guess I should have called you from his cell phone, but it was 7:28 when we realized what time it was, and I just thought that a few minutes wouldn't be that big of a deal. I'm so sorry! I had no idea that I would be a cause for concern. I mean, I never go anywhere."

"And it may be a while before we let you go again if this is the attitude that we get from you. After all, we were just concerned and worried for our only living child!"

"You know, that is where you are wrong! I am not a child anymore! Just like Andrew! He wasn't little either. You let him do anything that he wanted to do. You never let me do anything, and it has been a year since he died. Why do I have to pay for what happened to him? Mom understands. Why can't you?"

"It's not punishment or payment for anything when we expect certain things from you, Elizabeth. I am just trying really hard to make sure that you do make it till your seventeenth birthday! Is that so bad?"

I thought about what I dreamt about this morning almost immediately. It was like he was confirming that he was as worried about my fate as I was. The only difference was that I had enough good sense to know that what happens to one person has nothing to do with the fate of another.

"No, Dad, it isn't that bad at all! It's just that you should have waited until eight or something before you sent her out looking for me! You know how upset she'll be when she gets back home! It would almost be better if you just brought me back there and I could pretend that I was in the bathroom the whole time!"

"Elizabeth Annette, that will be enough!" My mother managed to come into the apartment unnoticed and unfortunately heard all that I had said to my dad. All of her apparent coolness towards the situation changed.

"Mother, I'm sorry, I didn't hear you come in. I didn't mean it. I was just saying that I hated to worry you, and hated that you wasted your time going to find me when I wasn't even there!"

"Wasn't even there? Yes, that would be exactly what the attendant at the golf place told me. He said that you and that boy hadn't been there since 6:30! What was it exactly that you were doing, and where?"

"Mother, he just decided to take me around the mall and show me a few of his favorite shopping places, and then we just drove around. We were driving around when I noticed what time it was. I told him that we had to go as soon as I saw the time!"

"Driving around with boys that we hardly know is not what I was talking about when I said that you could stay with him there! You know that if you say that you will be somewhere, we should be able to find you there right away. Is this what we will be dealing with just because you turned sixteen today?"

What did sixteen have to do with anything? How in the world could they think that just because I was one day older that I would completely change! I knew what happened in Andy's case, but that was different. He was a boy and he had tons of friends.

"No, Mother. I'm sorry I ruined everybody's night!"

"Well, it's almost too late to eat. What do you say, Ed, should we still go out, or just stay here, eat this cake, and make sand-wiches?"

I still couldn't believe what I was hearing! Sandwiches, on my birthday?

"No, I can't stand another sandwich. We can go to the piz-za place just down the street. I know that it isn't the best, but it is cheap and close," he replied.

"Cheap! That's all you ever think about!" she argued.

I couldn't believe what I was hearing! That was just great! It was a fitting end to a wonderful day. As usual, something had to ruin it. Just this time, I guess that it was my fault. Fate. Just like I thought. I might not be dead, but my chances of ever getting out of the house and enjoying my new year of being sixteen were somehow ending before they began.

This started a round of fights between my parents. Noth-ing was ever decided that night. I ended up retreating to my room and eating a piece of cake and a peanut butter sand-wich. Somehow, I found it ironic that this would have been the one kind of dinner I would have begged for when I was five. I wished that life was still that simple. Mother would have whipped something up and it would have been the best dinner ever.

Now it was the same old, same old. That money she had was gone. Somehow, she spent all the extra cash before 7:30 and hardly had anything to show for it. I wondered if she was drinking again.

It was always the same with her for my whole teen years. She would have people over and 'drink socially.' I could never fathom how much she must have spent to have that lifestyle. All the false friends that were no longer there once the money was gone.

Amelia called about 9:30. My parents got the call. They let me know that she called but wouldn't let me talk. I figured that it wasn't that they didn't want me to talk to her, but that they wouldn't quit arguing loudly.

Especially not long enough to let me carry on a conversation with someone who wasn't directly in the room. I knew that I could call her later when my parents decided to settle down and go to bed.

When I did call her, I told her about meeting up with Rob and how I thought that he really liked me. She told me to be careful of him. She knew him a lot better because her older brother was in his grade. I guessed that he *was* one of those friends of Andrew's that liked to party. I thought about that for a while and decided that maybe it was time for me to have a party in my own life. I wasn't going to be stupid like Andrew and end up dead, but I was going to live. Finally.

CHAPTER 3

Party Time

It was Saturday afternoon before Rob called, asking for me. My dad answered the phone. Man, did he give him the what-for! He told him basically that if I were to ever see him again, he would have to abide by his rules and follow any curfews. There was no telling what he thought about that, but he still got on the phone with me and was unexpectedly cheerful. It was evident that he had run into this problem before and knew just how to handle it.

He told them exactly what they wanted to hear, and by the time I got to speak to him, he was already promised another date without me even having to accept. I figured that my parents were convinced that I truly liked this really nice, polite young man already. That, and the fact that he was a smooth talker, got him way farther than expected.

"So, you wanna go out for another round of golf?"

"*Golf*, huh? Yeah sure, what time?"

"How about five o'clock? Last night, we went out before that, and we didn't have enough time to finish what we started!"

"Golfing? I thought we *did* finish that," I said mischievously.

"That wasn't what I was talking about. I hope you won't be too disappointed now. I mean, it has been a whole day since you saw me. What if you decided that I wasn't at all like you remembered?" He playfully chuckled.

"You do realize that it is already 4:30, don't you?"

"Yep. Hope you can get ready quickly."

"Where are we going, really?"

"Don't really know, to be perfectly honest. I thought we would go riding around, or something. There are movies playing that seem pretty decent. The golf place will be packed, but it would be fun too. We'll decide after I pick you up."

With that, our fate was written in stone. We would have a second date. Maybe even one that I would call a real date. This time, I would have a real time curfew: 10:00 pm. It wouldn't be like before, when I had to come home right after it got dark.

He was there in no time. He met me at the door and actually shook hands with my dad. I was so embarrassed. You never know what your father will think of your choice in friends. It takes a while, but it always gets let out later about what kind of influences they are and how they should be. I shuddered at the thought of a later conversation about this boy that had all but swallowed my face just yesterday.

We basically did exactly what he said we would. We went and played another round of golf and went to the early movies. By 8:15, our movie was over. We had a whole hour and forty-five minutes to do whatever we wanted to. So, just like he said before, we started to ride around.

This time, he told me that his parents were not home. They had to go out of town. He really wanted me to see his house. I told him a little about our house history and told him how much I missed our old house and the limitless fun we used to have.

He said that I would have to take him there to see it someday, that he would take me. I felt so secure thinking about sharing that with someone who thought it was important just because it was important to me. I could see why he wanted to show me his house.

As we stopped the car, I looked over to what must have been where he lived. I don't know why I expected a bigger house. I mean, we didn't go to the same school because he was rich and decided to slum a little. It wasn't like his parents must have wanted him to have a lesser education. It was nice enough though. It was a small one-story frame house with faded blue paint and slightly falling shutters. He led me up the driveway to the door at the side. It went directly into the kitchen.

"So, you want anything? My dad's got some beer in here. He'll never notice that it's gone!" he said as he opened the bottom of the refrigerator.

"No way. If I come home from my second date with you and smell like beer, my parents will never let me out of the house!"

"That's just a myth. I know ways of covering that smell up. I mean, at the least, you can brush your teeth here. I'll let you borrow my toothbrush. Come on, don't you want to celebrate your birthday?"

I really don't know much about what happened next. He was just such a smooth talker. I had never taken a drink before in my life. I never wanted to, for that matter. I mean, why? I guess that my tolerance for it wasn't very high either. I was swimming in a pool of happy before I knew it.

I couldn't think straight for anything. I guess that is when he decided to take advantage of that fact. It was one thing to be in a deserted parking lot somewhere in the middle of the bright day, and another to be in a boy's living room alone in the dark.

He just kind of crept up on me and before I knew it, I was partially unclothed and letting him touch my body. It was *definitely* not anything that I had planned would happen. I tried to tell him that it was getting late and that I had to go home. I said it with slurred speech, and kind of giggly too. He knew that he had me exactly where he wanted me.

It was so sobering when I was in the bathroom throwing up after I realized that he had taken total advantage of me. He did things that I didn't even know for sure that you could. Truth be told, birds and the bees, cable television and such could have never prepared me. It wasn't romantic the way that it should have been. It was nauseating. Sober as I was, I just looked once again at my watch. It was 9:30, and I was so ready to go home.

"Listen, I better go home. It would be better if my parents didn't have to worry."

"I told them I would have you back safe and sound, and besides, you still need to brush your teeth, remember?"

"I think the breath of the vomit should get rid of any smell that I have from beer!"

"Suit yourself, but don't be mad at me if your parents catch on."

I didn't know how to respond to that. I'd just lost my virginity. What would happen if they found out I'd just had a few beers? I mean, in the whole scheme of things, big deal!

If they found out what kind of influence he really was, at least I wouldn't have to endure this again.

It took altogether too long to get home that night. It was even worse on Sunday when he called, sounding so cheerful again. It was like life was one big party for him and I was just the clown making balloon animals, a lot of fun to have around and just for his amusement. I realized right after he agreed to take me home that night that I'd had enough of him.

I never wanted to lay eyes on him, let alone allow him to do that again. I was unwilling, and he knew it. He was just like

I thought, a smooth talker. Maybe I wasn't prepared to date yet. I mean, if this is what it meant, then I wasn't. I tried to explain to him on the phone that it wasn't such a great idea for us to keep going out.

"So, you just took advantage of me and now you don't want to see me anymore?" he asked slyly.

That was the way that he could just turn things around. He made it sound like I knew exactly what I wanted from him and that I was the one in the wrong for not wanting to see him again. When I finally got him off of the phone, I retreated once more to my bedroom. I didn't come out again till Monday morning.

School was something I was also unprepared for. He was standing there waiting for me when the bus let me off. I tried to walk away, but he just kept tugging on my shirt and begged me to let him have another chance. I didn't know why he was doing this. Did he really like me? I thought for sure that I was just another of his conquests. I just wasn't prepared to hear that he actually had feelings for me. It was so confusing.

"Fine, Robert, we are still together! Is that what you want to hear?"

"That's fine by me, baby, whatever you want!" His other friends had started gathering around us a bit more and his demeanor showed them just what he always wanted to show, that he was in control.

"Come here, Rob." I pulled him away from his friends into a corner so that we could have time to finish our strange conversation before the bell rang.

He had such a gigantic smile on his face, as if he'd heard a joke that only he understood, and the rest of us had to wait for someone to explain the punch line.

"You just need to quit smiling." I kept my voice low.

"No, baby, everything's cool." He said that rather loud; evidently, he was under the impression that he had some classmates to convince that he had no problems.

"What is *wrong* with you? I told you that I didn't think that it would work out between us, and you start showing me off to your friends as your new girl?"

"You are my new girl, Liz. Don't think for a minute that something happened on Saturday that you didn't want to happen. I've known all kinds of girls like you. You look all innocent, but in the end, you are just looking to be the life of the party."

"What are you talking about? I have never even been with another person in my life. Couldn't you tell that on Saturday? What do you want me to do, just pretend that everything with me is just fine? Well, it isn't! I didn't want to do those things yet. I barely know you! I wasn't ready!"

"Come on, baby, I love you. Can't you tell? I don't share that with everybody! Besides, I don't want to tell all of my friends about how you loved me and left me, now do you?"

That sounded too much like a threat. I didn't know what else to do, so I lifted my hand away from his grip and walked away with tears in my eyes. Luckily, Amelia was not far away.

"What happened with you two, Lizzy? You look all serious!"

"Don't worry about it. We are just having a *lovers'* quarrel." I looked her straight in the eyes when I said that. I believe that she knew what I meant immediately.

"Lovers' quarrel, huh? Well, if you need me to break it up by breaking him up, you just let me know. He knows better than to mess with me. My brother would take care of that in a minute."

If there were ever a time when I thought I could have used Andy, it would have been now. I needed him to protect me from Rob. Now, I would have to rely on Amelia's brother, Tommy. He wasn't anybody I really knew—just in passing at her house.

He was always doing his own thing and left Amelia and me alone for the most part. He was Andy's friend and Andy never let me hang around with any of his friends, so I didn't know any of them. I think that if I did, I would have known to stay away from Rob. That was for sure.

"I'm fine, Amelia. I just want to go to class."

I really thought that it was exactly what I would want to do. What I never realized before is that the classes were mixed with kids in different grades. I was going to have to sit through class with kids in *his* grade. I did that every day, but somehow, I thought that they would have sexdar (sex radar).

Like they could pick up the fact that I had a change in my virginity since last week, and they would know that Rob had me just where he wanted me, for all to display. I almost couldn't endure being in there. It was like everybody in his grade was all of a sudden nice to me for some reason. Like they suddenly found me to be interesting.

"So, Rob, huh?" Sara Ann asked casually.

"Huh? What do you mean?" I tried to stay calm and hoped that he didn't spread the news around to everyone already.

"You are dating Rob?" She said that matter-of-factly. "I saw you guys out on Friday night at the mini golf place. I guess you didn't see me. It was pretty dark in there and you guys did seem like you were in your own world."

I sighed. I was ecstatic that word hadn't spread about our relationship, but that we had just been seen out together. Out, not in the parking lot or going to his house, just out. What a relief!

"Yeah, I mean, I guess. We only went out a couple of times, and I just don't know."

My face grew so flushed; I knew that I was giving some-thing away. Like a clue about what had really happened.

"Yeah, just be careful. I hear that he wasn't too nice to his last girlfriend when she broke up with him. I mean he's nice and all, but going out and stuff is different, you know?" Man did I ever know! Now I really did feel trapped. What would he do if I ever convinced him that I didn't want to see him anymore?

This was the second person that had told me to be careful

with Rob. I decided to heed their warnings. I had the opportunity to have an obligation every afternoon at home and
somehow could never see him other than at school. I realized
why I'd never thought of him before he approached me at the
mall. We had no classes together, and we had different lunch
periods. I didn't have to face him at all unless we met each
other in the halls.

He started leaving me notes in my locker at least three
times a day. Some of them just said *I love you, baby!* Others
would be like three-page long letters. I wondered when he had
the time to write them. Surely the teachers would notice that
he wasn't paying any attention to what they were saying.

Either way, something strange and unexpected happened.
It was like he got to me. All of his conning and attention worked
some strange magic. All of the love letters just started to sink
in. It's like you can't help but like those who like you. Especially
when they write you love letters and poems and things. By the
time Friday came again, even though I had paid him almost no
attention all week, he met me in the hall, smiled his big smile,
and let me know that he would pick me up at 6:00.

I thought that it was good we would have one less hour
than last Saturday night. Maybe I could find something that
would take longer. Then I could limit our alone time together
again. I thought I could tell him that I wanted to see a movie.
I would find one that didn't start till 7:30. That way, we would
have to go to dinner right away, and then come home right
after the movies. Even though he was wearing on me, I still
knew somehow that I needed to keep my distance.

He arrived promptly at 6:00 pm. I made him come to the
door and knock before I came out. He didn't know that I was
looking for him and that I was trying to control our night.
Before we left, I asked him if he wanted anything to drink, and
suggested that we just hang out with my parents for a while.
That didn't deter him for a minute. He just told them he would
have me back by curfew, and off we were once again.

"Your parents ever get back home?" I wanted to know the answer; I needed to know if I was safe from a repeat of last week. He took it a little differently.

"Yeah, they're back. They're home all night. I'm sorry—I mean, if all you want is time with me alone, all of you have to do is tell me, baby. I can find another place."

Ugh, I couldn't believe that he would take it that way! Of all the nerve. He knew how I felt about all of that last week. I made it clear. Just because he talked me into another date didn't make me forget anything.

"That's not what I meant, thank you very much! I told you that I'm not ready for all of that yet!"

"Whoa, I was just kidding. I heard what you said loud and clear. I promise, I will not take you to my house."

"So, what *do* you have planned for us tonight?"

"You'll see." That's all he said. That stupid smile was back. It was cute now, really cute, and almost irresistible. He reached over, took my hand, and softly kissed it. He was being so kind and loving. Maybe he was just up to no good last week. Maybe he was taking it slow with me now.

We turned the corner and got onto the highway. He was heading for the good part of town.

"Dinner?"

"Yep!"

We stopped at this fancy Italian restaurant. I was impressed and very excited.

"This is your birthday dinner that I made you miss because I was taking all of your time last Friday."

Now, I was excited. Nobody ever gave me a birthday party like this before. It was so grown up. They seated us. He told me to get whatever I wanted off of the menu. The meal flew by. We even shared a dessert! Before I knew it, it was over and it was only 7:30. *Seven thirty, oh no.* That is when the last movie started. I sank in the seat with aggravation and anticipation of what he had planned.

"Are we going back to golf? I mean, that is 'our place.'"

"Nope, something much more fun!"

For some reason, I just didn't like the sound of that. I already knew that our definitions of fun were two different things. We got into the car. He opened the door for me. So far, we'd had a perfectly romantic night. We drove down a couple of streets over into the residential neighborhoods. He stopped outside a really big house. There were cars everywhere.

"Where are we?"

"My cousin's house. I promised that if he ever had a party, I would come. It'll be fine. No one will know us here. They all go to North Side High School. If you didn't notice, we did come to the better part of town."

"Yeah, I noticed. I just thought you were taking me this way for dinner. I guess that this is cool though."

Cool, yeah right. How could I express that I didn't want to go where there was drinking, and partying, and that I wasn't that type of person! I wasn't like my brother, even if that is what I decided just a few days ago that I was going to be. I changed my mind. I didn't like the way he explained how he pegged me for a party girl. Just how could he know how I was if I didn't even know yet?

"Par-ty man! Thanks for letting me in on this! This is sweet!"

He began to high-five some guy right inside the door.

"Hey man, this is Liz. She's the one I was telling you about." That mischievous smile was back.

"Hey, any friend of Rob's is a friend of mine. Come on in!"

"Thanks. You have a really nice house. We used to live a few streets over."

"You ever go to Singleton Middle School?"

"Actually, I went there for two years. I went to Farmville Elementary School when I was little. We just moved in the last couple of years or so."

"I'll have to look you up in my middle school yearbook!"

"I looked a bit different then. My brother Andrew would

44

have been in your grade though."

"Hey guys, are we going to talk about this all night, or are we going to party?"

I'd heard about these parties, and I knew that Andrew saw a good few of them when he used to go out. I guess that he had a point about me being his younger sister. He knew that I was never exposed to anything like this. I really was naive. People were dancing and talking and drinking and making out, some of them all at the same time. I thought that it must take skill to pull that off.

There were some girls just dancing by themselves. The guys were gawking at them. Probably wishing that they would be asked to join them. You could tell though that the party was just beginning. I looked at my watch. It was just 7:45.

Luckily, if I was to do anything, I would have a while for it to wear off, not that I was going to. I was just thinking. Also, since it took about twenty-five minutes to get back to my house, we would have to leave the party in just an hour and a half! What trouble could we get into in that little time?

I was being pulled to the kitchen. Rob had my hand and handed me some punch to try. I reluctantly took a sip. I noticed that it had a bite, but it didn't seem all that strong. I was wrong. In twenty minutes, I think I had drunk three drinks. It wasn't because I wanted to drink alcohol, it was just that I was nervous being around all of the older kids, and it seemed to make me feel more at ease.

I didn't realize the large amount of liquor I had consumed before it was too late. The girls that were dancing by themselves were no longer by themselves, I was with them. I began to dance seductively towards Rob. I called his name. He grabbed me and took me to another room. There were so many rooms. It was quiet. He began to kiss me again. He asked if I was ready. I was ready, ready for anything, or so I thought.

I looked around the room and noticed his cousin stood at the entrance to the room. He brought his friend too. Before I knew what was happening, I was in this unknown room being taken advantage of while people were watching.

"Why are they here too?"

"Oh, they are just watching out for other people. They are j-just guarding the door."

I accepted his answer. I was too drunk to know any better. For some reason, knowing they were there for protection made me unbothered by their presence.

It didn't last long, and I sat there waiting for him to let me get up and go to the bathroom. I suddenly felt the need to retreat. I turned as invisible as I could and headed out into the hall. There were others congregating near the door. I was beginning to wonder if I was being set up.

I was sobering up while I was in the bathroom. I splashed cool water on my face. At this point, I didn't care if it messed up my makeup. It would just make me appear like my life had become. On the other hand, I did have to go back home pretty soon, and I didn't want my parents to know that I was out doing anything that I shouldn't be.

I breathed in deeply, opened the door, and wobbled toward the staircase. I thought that if I could just get out of there then I would call Amelia or something and I could get home. I didn't get very far before my way was totally blocked. Rob, his cousin, and his friend were all there waiting for me to return. They were smiling like they'd just found the greatest thing since sliced bread, except I was the bread.

"Come on guys, can't you see that she's ready for a little down time? She's not used to all of this partying." Rob was actually coming to my rescue. "Are you ready to go now, or do you want to join the others for a while longer?" I was just stunned that I even had a choice in the matter.

"Go. Quiet. That would be nice."

I put my head down as not to be seen.

"Sure, baby, whatever you like."

I cringed. I began to hate when he called me that.

"Please quit calling me baby." That's all that I could manage to say all the way to his car. He knew that I was confused and mad, and that this wasn't anything that I had planned to do tonight. We got into his car and headed for 'our' part of town. I suddenly felt more at ease there than in that overly populated big party house. It was nice to know we were alone, and our 'date' was coming to an end.

"You know, Liz, I don't want to freak you out, but those guys were really into you too. In fact, we have been looking for a new girl to party with. Our last one moved, and you just really seem like you enjoyed what we did. You didn't seem to mind the audience." I didn't know how to respond. I mean, I was drunk. I would have never let that happen. Not sober.

"Just take me home, Rob. I have to get sober enough to even tell you what I want. Home is the only thing that I know for sure."

"Ok, ok, baby. I understand it's all a bit to take in. I'm just saying that you could make a lot of people happy, yourself included. I'm not trying to talk you into it, but there are no strings attached. We just want you to party with us and we'll all love you. It's about time you quit hiding! You're not a kid and I miss your brother and all, but he wouldn't ever let us near you. He always said 'hands off my sis.' I knew from then on that you'd never be allowed to really experience life. Well baby, this is life and we're willing to give you everything it has to offer!"

I remained silent for the rest of the trip home. I was a little fuzzy about what exactly had happened. It was like I had been dreaming the whole thing. As a matter of fact, I know that I dozed off two or three times on the ride home. I just kept hoping that it would wear off before I had to step in that small apartment.

I wondered how Andrew ever did it. I mean, he would go to these parties all the time and I knew that he was high or drunk two-thirds of the time, but you could never really prove it. He was really good at hiding it.

"Hey, is there anything that I should do to make myself less conspicuous to my parents when I get into the house?"

"First, I wouldn't get home early. That could tip them off. You always need to be right on time or show up a couple of minutes early and run in the door saying that you just knew you would be late. If they think that we were speeding to get home, they might be a little relaxed on your curfew. I mean, before you know it, we could be partying until eleven! You don't smell like alcohol if that is what you are worried about. We put Everclear in the punch. You can't smell that on people after they drink it, so no worries. I'll just drive us around the block a time or two, and it'll be ten till ten before you know it."

"Good to know, Rob. Hey, do you do this a lot? I mean, with a lot of other girls?"

"Why, you jealous? Don't worry about it, baby. Just been a few is all. You don't have anyone to be jealous about!"

I didn't respond. I just kept my mouth shut and was hoping that time would go more quickly. I was so relieved to see my apartment complex. I don't think that I ever felt so happy to see that place. He parked his car and reached over to give me a kiss goodnight. I leaned the other way.

"My dad is probably watching for me through the window. If he thinks that I'm out kissing boys, he'll never let me back out."

"Hee, hee." He chuckled menacingly. "What he doesn't know can't hurt him."

"Yeah, I'll see ya later."

"I love you, baby."

I leapt out of the car and ran up the stairs as fast as I could, but being inebriated didn't help. I entered the living room, and I was in luck. My parents had already gone to bed to watch TV. I stuck my head in their door and told them goodnight. I wondered why they didn't check me for drugs or alcohol. I mean, I was basically doing the same thing that my older brother did, and he died from his stupidity. Were they really that blind or did they really not care?

I went straight to the shower. I really needed a shower, especially after all that had happened. I felt like there was some invisible scum all over my body. The hot water held out, and I was able to soak my body and think things through. I had a lot to take in.

What kind of vibe did I give off to attract him to me in the first place? I mean, there had to be something, right? He said that he could tell it about me. He thought that I would enjoy it with all of his friends. What made him think that I enjoyed it at all now, with him? I almost felt like clawing his eyes out when he mentioned how my brother was protecting me from all of the bad out there.

I think that Andy knew all of the bad and decided to shield me from it. That is why he always said that I was little. It wasn't because he thought I wasn't as old as I was, it was just that he was older than his real age because of the things that he had experienced. He would have fought the world for me to keep me safe. He would be disappointed by what I was led into.

I wished that he would have had talked to me about what was really out there, instead of keeping me in the dark. If he would have just said in passing that this guy, that guy, or these people were up to no good. If he would have warned that he'd better never see me with them. Instead, he kept his knowledge to himself and shielded me by telling others to keep away from me. He made me a target, not on purpose, but who could resist someone that was supposed to be unreachable?

I quietly got out of the shower. I was overwhelmed by my thoughts. After I wrapped up in my towel, I headed straight into the kitchen to call Amelia. I knew that the help that she had offered would definitely come in handy in a time like this. She was lucky enough to know the bad that was going on around us and still had a big brother to take care of her. I was hoping that he could be like a big brother to me also.

"Amelia, I know that it's really late, but can you talk for just a minute? I have a problem."

"Yeah, sure, Lizzy. I just got home and am a little wound up anyway. I just went to see that new horror film and man was it spooky! I don't think I'll be able to sleep right now anyway, so what's up?"

"I don't want to get into it right now, but I went out with Rob, and he was everything that you warned me about. It turns out that I may need you to get your brother to pay him a visit. I mean, if you think he really wouldn't mind."

"Elizabeth, what happened? I mean, can you talk?"

"They're in bed, but I still don't want to talk on the phone. Can I come over to your house in the morning?"

"Yeah, of course you can. Just come over and if I'm still asleep, just wake me up."

"Oh, I really hate to bother you about all of this. I'm sorry, I'm just still a little tipsy."

"What do you mean, tipsy? Liz, you didn't drink or take drugs, did you? You know better!"

"We just went to a party. That is all that I'm saying till tomorrow. You can probably fill in the blanks for yourself."

"Go to bed, Elizabeth. I'll try to do the same. Get over here right away tomorrow. Oh, I wish that you could just come over right now!"

"Yeah, me too." Tears had started forming in my eyes as I said goodbye. It just seemed so much worse when I had no one to talk to.

I went to bed and passed out in a matter of seconds. The whole night had given my body more than it could handle, mentally and physically.

I had a miserable headache in the morning. I figured that was what I got for acting like a complete fool. I explained to my parents that I was going straight to Amelia's to talk to her about Rob. I didn't want to be totally lying about what was going on. Besides, they should know that he was most definitely not someone that they would want me to be hanging around with. I didn't want anyone to think that he was some boyfriend that I was just in love with.

In all reality, I wished that he had been that kind of guy. Warm and loving, and willing to give me space and like me when I was sober as much as I was when I wasn't. That was most definitely not Rob.

I got there really fast. I guess that you can walk pretty long distances very quickly when you are in a hurry to get there. It was either that or I was thinking so much to myself that I never noticed the time flying by. I reached out to knock on the door. Amelia was up. She answered the door before my hand touched it. She must have really made an effort to be up for me by the time I came. She had even taken her shower and looked one hundred percent presentable. I was impressed, as usual.

She was an amazing piece of work. I wished every day that I could have her knowledge about the people around us. I admired how she was always so comfortable around anyone. It didn't matter who they were. She was never afraid or intimidated. I wished that I wasn't so intimidated by Rob. I wouldn't even be here today if I could just stand up to him in the first place. There were so many times that I just wished I could have screamed "no." Even saying no at all would have been something. Instead, I let him use me twice, two miserable, demeaning times.

"Amelia, what is wrong with me?"

Tears just started streaming down my face. I knew that they had been building up, but I was trying to face the world hard and cold. It was seeing her face, being in her protective custody, that allowed me to finally let it all out. I sat there and explained everything, from the very first date, till now.

I told her that I should have told him no. I knew better than to drink in the first place. That I couldn't even remember everything about last night, the longer the time went by. How it was all like a bad dream. Tommy came into the open area of the living room. I didn't realize her brother was just in listening distance, hiding in the doorway to the kitchen. That was my old MO! Always look to see if someone is in the doorway! I never imagined that anyone else on earth would get to hear my sad little story. I never intended to have an audience, not last night, not now.

"Liz, now don't freak out, but I knew that you would never tell your story directly to him, and you said that you needed his help. He's not gonna fault you for what Rob talked you into. He knows all about his tricky ways. He's just here to help."

"Elizabeth, you know now that Andy tried everything that he could to keep you safe. I promised him all the time that if I saw one of those creeps around you that I would let him know so that he could take care of things. Now, I know that I can't go to him anymore and that he isn't here to help you, but Amelia is right. I will defend you if you want me to. It really sounds like you fell for his lines hook, line, and sinker. I'm just sorry that I didn't stop him in the beginning when you guys came to school last week looking all lovey-dovey. I should have known that it wasn't a two-way street. He had your name all over his notebooks and everything though, so I thought that this time might be different. I really thought that he cared about you. I mean, every few years they do to a few girls exactly what they did to you. I heard about it last year. I couldn't believe that it was happening. I always felt so sorry for the girls. I mean, I'm all for it if a girl is, but man, not while she's too drunk to know any better. How would you even know if she liked you when she was sober?"

Suddenly he changed his tone. "Hey, you know, I just got a good idea. You can just go up to him and say that you don't like him when you are sober. That he is only fun when you can't see straight. Maybe that would do the trick."

He laughed all the while he was saying that. I couldn't tell if he was serious or being condescending.

"Sorry, Tommy, but there is no way that I can just go up to him and say that!"

"Liz, I was just kidding. Sorry, I guess that this isn't the time. I just hate for things to get heavy like this. Naw, I will be more than happy to tell him that myself. I'll let him know that not only do you not like him, but I'll kick his ass if he as much as gets within one yard of you at school!"

"Thanks."

I started crying again. He reached out and gave me the most compassionate hug. He wasn't feeling me up. He wasn't doing it because he wanted something from me. He was there to take care of me. Just like he told Andrew he would. Such a warm peace came over me. I just knew that all this bad decision-making would finally be over, and I could start again.

It was time at Amelia's that saved me once again. She was the youngest in the family—just like me—but taught to be stronger. She had a big brother that she could turn to, but it never was needed. Her street smarts kept her out of trouble, and I knew that if I was around her longer, it might very well wear off on me. I was just happy I could borrow her brother. At least for now.

CHAPTER 4

Defense

Rob didn't try to contact me all weekend long. I thought for sure that he would at least try to call me on Saturday night, or Sunday, but not one call. I walked up to the school looking to see if he was waiting for me in the same spot that he always did. He was. Ugh! He motioned me to him. He still had that smug smile on his face. When would that stop? I reluctantly walked toward him.

"Hey, baby, what's the matter? Didn't you have as much fun as I did? You were the best party girl I'd had in a very long time. I'll tell you what. I won't go spreading anything around about you to those who don't already know."

He twisted my hair gently and pushed it behind my back. I shrugged his hand off my shoulder.

"Ah now," Rob continued. "I want you to think long and hard about all of this. We really had a good thing together.

I've got a lot of friends that would like to have that same good thing with you. Just think it over. Tommy talked to me, and I understand that he's just trying to play the hero. I figure that he just wants you for himself. I respect him though, and don't want any waves here."

I turned to walk off. He grabbed me by the sleeve.

"Everything's cool, baby. I'll be patient. I know that you'll come around and realize that you made a mistake. I'll be waiting, not by myself—I mean, I can't be alone—but I'll wait for you to come to your senses and when you do, I'll take you back."

I turned to face him.

"Rob, I didn't have a good time. You scared me. You used me. I just don't see us going anywhere from here." I channeled my inner Amelia.

That was the toughest thing I had ever said to anyone in my life. I didn't know why I was giving him an explanation. He sure didn't deserve it. I think that it was that I didn't want to cause a scene. I was already skeptical about his silence concerning our relationship. He just did what he was capable of, he leaned over to me, pulled me to him, gave me a kiss, and left. I didn't know what that was all about, but I sure was red when I turned to come out into the open area in front of the school.

Why didn't he just get it? I wasn't into him. I wasn't in love with him, I wasn't in like with him. I just wanted him to leave me alone. I wanted things to be the same way that they were on that magical sixteenth birthday. I wanted cute love. I wanted to feel like he liked me, not just lusted after me. These were such new emotions for me that I didn't know where to take them. Amelia noticed my dazed state.

"What happened? Did you tell him that he was a jerk? Did you slap him? What happened? You look like someone just ran over your cat. Well, except you don't have a cat." She chuckled.

I knew that although she was just trying to lighten up the

difficult conversation, she really wanted answers. I knew that she was trying to give me time to determine what exactly had happened. She knew how slow I could be about some things. She knew that I was a shut-in, inexperienced nobody who never knew what to do. I must be exhausting to be friends with. I felt exhausted all the time just by what I was doing to myself.

"You wouldn't believe it if I told you."

"Yes, yes, I would. Tell me right now!"

"He told me he would be waiting for me, basically that we were a good thing. I told him I didn't like him, and he kissed me goodbye!"

"What do you mean? He kissed you goodbye! Why on earth did you let him kiss you goodbye? You know that Tommy and I tried very hard to get it through to him that he wasn't allowed to be around you anymore. We pulled the Andrew card and everything! I told him that he'd probably be haunted if he kept on bothering you, that you didn't even like him, and that he was torturing you by carrying on like he had been."

"Oh, I can see that he's so worried. At least he said that he wasn't gonna spread rumors about me. I think he actually does like me, and maybe he will have enough respect to be nice."

"Respect? You have got to be kidding me. That was not respectful to kiss you after he was warned to stay away from you. He was telling all of us where to go. He must have decided that it would be more fun to go against the grain and keep trying to get you back. I told you before that he could be dangerous. Now you are like a conquest that he wants more than ever. I hope you're happy. Now, there is nothing more we can do. It was up to you to undo what you started. We began to unravel him, and you just twisted him right back into place!" Her tone changed from surprise to anger and frustration. "You want to start to double date? At least I could keep an eye on you two. He can't get you drunk and do things that you don't want if he's not alone with you. Oh, wait, yeah, he could. Maybe if I were there, he would at least control himself."

"Don't be mad at me!" I turned, thinking of what to say to defend my actions. I really am trying here. He's just smooth. I knew it from the moment that he started talking to me in the mall on my birthday. "For your information, I *will* stay away from him! So, if it's alright with you, I don't think that I'll be dating for a while. Plus, since I'm broke, that just means that I will be spending most of my time at home. He can't get to me there. If I'm not out, then I'm not out."

"You can't hide your life away, Lizzy!"

I didn't like the way she said my name. It sounded like she was talking to a little kid.

"Whatever! I wished that I never let you in on this. I should have just kept it to myself! I bet I could be pregnant or have some disease in a month with the way that I was going! I'm sorry that you just don't care about that!"

"I'm not your mother, Liz. I am just like you. Have some pride in yourself! You don't need me for that! You also don't need me for any other help that you thought you did."

The bell rang right on time. Amelia stormed off, knowing that she was not winning the losing battle that was my love life. I just wanted to leave school. I wanted to run and find my happy place. I wanted to just pretend that I never existed in this place. Like this place had just disappeared. I thought about it and did what my impulse told me to do. I ran.

I got off of campus and headed downtown. I didn't know where I was going; I just knew that it had to be away from here. I needed to fly off into the sky like the pheasants from long ago. Only, I was the one being startled, and I needed to retreat.

"Hey!"

I heard someone calling from down the street. I didn't know if they were talking to me or someone else. I also didn't know if it was a kid or an adult. I didn't turn around to look. I just kept running. There was a convenience store just around the corner. I knew that if I just got there, whomever it was that was following me would leave me alone. I would lose them. They wouldn't know to look for me in there.

I rounded the corner and leapt into the door of the store. I went to the furthest aisle and tried to act like I was looking around. I was there to hide just in case the 'hey' was meant for me. As I was standing looking towards nothing in particular, I was startled by his voice.

"Hey, baby."

The sound of the voice was low, but it still startled me. Ugh. When would he quit calling me that? I tried to ignore that he was talking to me. He was still over one aisle and I intended on not giving him any kind of reaction to go on.

"Psst. Lizzy, over here." I turned and faced the wall now. There was absolutely nothing to look at there.

"Oh, I see what you are doing, you were waiting for me. You wanted me to be here with you. You know we are really close to the bathroom, and I see what you have been looking at."

I turned around. I knew that me ignoring him while he was right beside me was so childish that it would just fuel his attention.

"What are you talking about?"

I turned around and saw what he was talking about, condoms and other toiletries. My face turned all shades of red and I almost ran for it.

"Ugh! You are so childish, Rob! Why are you here? Why did you follow me? Don't you know that skipping school can get you suspended? I wanted some time by myself! I didn't want to be around you, or anyone else from school, for that matter!"

"Come on now, don't say things like that. You know that you are fighting a losing battle trying to stay away from me. It was fate that brought us together on your birthday. We were meant for each other. I'm cool if you only want to date me. I didn't really want to share you anyway. Really. It was just that my friends all thought that you were so hot. I didn't feel it was right to keep you all to myself."

"That is the stupidest thing that I've ever heard." I began in a quiet yell. "If you really cared about me, you wouldn't have suggested it in the first place. Just leave. I think that I am just going to go right back to school. I'll tell them I was sick to my stomach and needed to walk it off. They know that I've never done anything like this before and they'll surely let me off for thirty minutes tardy this morning."

"Well, I could tell them that I found you here and that I made you come back. Then what will you do?"

"Rob, if you did that, you would be giving yourself away too!"

"That's ok, I do this kind of thing all the time. I was tardy five times in the last three weeks. I don't care."

"Whatever! Let's just get out of here. I don't want to cause a scene."

"Sure, but first, let me buy this drink I just opened." He held out a bottle of root beer that he must have gotten while I wasn't looking.

"See ya later, Rob!"

I darted out of the store and never stopped until I got home. My dad was sitting in the living room wondering what in the world I was doing home.

"I just have some issues that I couldn't deal with today, Dad. You know that when things happen, I just can't be held in."

"Liz, you are going to have to quit running from everything. You have to face the demons that you have, look them in the face, and tell them that they have no power over you."

"Yeah, right. Demons. Rob. That was a demon alright."

"Now, I'm going to call your school and let them know that you had an appointment this morning, but that you will be there by 10:00. Do you understand me?"

"Yes, Dad, I'm sorry."

Sure enough, he drove me back to school before he went to work. It would make him late and he was already in hot water because of all of our personal issues, not including Andrew. I felt so guilty for keeping him away. No one was outside, and I knew that I was safe for the time being.

It was a long day even though I hadn't begun my school day until 10:00. I tried to stay civil to Amelia when I saw her. I decided not to tell her about the convenience store incident, or that I ran home like a coward. I did apologize. I told her that I had a chance to talk to him again and that I really let him have it that time. He knew for sure that it was over between us. She seemed like she was ok with it after all. She knew I was trying. How could she not know that before? All I had been doing for the last week was trying to get away from Rob. I shuddered when I thought of his name. I was really hoping that he decided to ditch the whole day when he thought that I wasn't going to be here.

I was wrong again. He was moving between classes, and I saw him exactly where I saw him every day. It was just in passing, but again he was there, just giving that big smile again. I almost got nauseous. I turned really quickly and ran into Tommy. *Of all the people to run into.* I was hoping that Amelia hadn't told him what kind of coward I was. I was the worst kind. I bit the hand that was feeding me when I let Rob kiss me earlier. I knew that and didn't have the guts to look him right in the face.

"So, Liz, any more boy troubles?"

I knew then that she hadn't told him anything.

"I'd rather not talk about it right now if it's ok with you." I was still looking down. Like there was a small invisible hand holding my head toward the floor. I would have to struggle against it if I were to look at him directly.

"Elizabeth, look at me. It's ok. I'm not going to hurt you. I'm not here for that. Please look up."

I looked up and saw the kindest eyes that I had ever seen. They were just like Amelia's. They were the only ones that could calm me right now.

"Thanks, Tommy, but I'm ok. I know that you would never hurt me. I promise. It's just that something happened earlier, and I think that I handled it, but I just don't know."

"What happened, Elizabeth? Tell me."

"Tommy, don't worry about it. It isn't worth it. Like I said, I think that I handled it all by myself. Do you see him around here anywhere? No. That is because I told him that this was all over, and I believe that he finally sees that I mean it."

"What did he do exactly?"

"Nothing, really. He just told me what he could to try and get me to stay with him."

"I warned him about this, you know. I told him that if I heard that he was harassing you that we would be the ones with the problem."

"It's ok, I think he got the message. I'm sure that when he kissed me this morning, it was the last."

"Kissed you? Oh, now I have had enough of that!"

It seemed like fate when Rob happened to be leaving his classroom and came into the hall that very moment.

"Hey Rob, dude, how're you doing today? Did you forget that little conversation we just had yesterday? Oh, I know, you were too high to remember anything from one day till the next."

"This isn't between you and me, dude. I was just letting her know that she had options."

"It doesn't matter what kind of options you thought she should have. She made it really clear to me that she is done being your 'friend.'"

"We weren't being friends, and she knew that. She will be back because you can't just start something like that and not finish it."

"I told you that she was finished."

Wham! Before I even knew what was happening, Tommy slammed his fist into Rob's face. He spun back and caught himself in the lockers.

"Man, this isn't your fight. This is not between us. Well, it is if you are crushing on her or something."

"You know that I am just trying to keep promises that her brother wanted us to keep. I know that just because you guys hung around and partied together, that never made you 'friends' with him either. I'm telling you! This won't stop until I see that you are leaving her alone! She made her choice!"

I turned around and couldn't believe what kind of display had just happened at my expense. Now there wasn't any hiding our relationship. If there was ever any question, it was answered loud and clear by everyone who was just hanging around their lockers. I couldn't believe that I was in the middle of all of this. I tried so hard to be invisible. Now, I was like a sculpture on a pedestal. People just kept walking around looking at me from all sides. I really didn't want it to go this way.

I ran as fast as I could to the bathroom. My tears were falling so hard that it almost blinded me. I didn't want to go out to face anyone in this school ever again. I did something completely stupid and now everyone was suffering for it. I was so confused. Would Rob really keep close enough that if for some reason I ever changed my mind, he could swoop in and resume what we had started? He said that we weren't friends. That was so low. What did he really think of me? Did he really like me or not?

Then there was Tommy. He was so protective. What if what Rob said was true? What if he was just doing all of this so that I would just fall for him? I liked the fact that he was there to help me out in this situation, but I didn't need another boyfriend, I needed an older brother. I just hoped that was all he was thinking about me when he decided to help me out.

I was just happy because no one dared to bother me while I

was having my 'moment.' No one really knew me well enough to be able to start a conversation anyway, not even to try and help.

"Elizabeth."

Ok, maybe there was one girl.

"Amelia, just go away. I already know how you feel. You let me know that you thought I was just leading him on and that it was my fault that this was happening. If your brother gets in trouble because of what just happened, I'll go to the principal and make things right. I promise."

"No, I'm not going away. No, you don't know how I feel, and no, no one is getting into trouble. It just so happened Coach Lucas was the only one to see what happened. He asked them if they need a time out in the principal's office. They both told him that everything was fine now. He left it at that. He knows that boys will be boys. As far as how I feel, I just feel sorry for you right now. I thought you were exaggerating about him coming on so strong. I think anyone would have a tough time hiding from someone who is chasing you around like that. Liz, I swear I'm sorry for ever doubting you. I'm just glad that Tommy was around when he was. The thing that creeps me out about it is that he still said he was waiting for you. What does that even mean?"

"I don't know." I sniffled. "I'm glad that I finally had someone witness what he has been doing to me other than his friends. He's been acting like he was irresistible to me or something. You can't imagine that he would have some kind of pull on me, but I can't seem to tell him no when we are alone together."

"Don't worry, from here on out, we'll be here to make sure that he isn't anywhere around you. Your feelings will pass, and then when you do see him, you won't think twice about him. It will be like he was just some old movie you watched too many times that it almost seemed real, but it wasn't."

"He is real, Amelia. *Very real.* I appreciate what you guys are doing for me, but I will have to try my best to stay away from him too."

My tears started drying up and I was able to take everything in context. I realized that I was at school, that Rob wasn't in any of my classes, and that I shouldn't see him for the rest of the day. I suddenly got very calm and brave. I opened the stall.

"Let's go to class, Amelia. I'm done being afraid."

We left the bathroom. No one was in the hall. Class must have begun already. I didn't even care that I would be going into a class late. I didn't care if everyone noticed me. The fear was now going to end. I was going to make it.

That was the end of it alright. He really did let me go. He didn't bother me anymore. I didn't know if it was Tommy's warning or if he just got tired of waiting. Things had changed. He never saw me except in passing every once in a while. I would just turn the other way and pretend not to see him. Three months had passed, and school was about to let out for the summer. I was finally safe.

I made it through another year at this horrible high school. If I were lucky enough, my parents would both be able to save enough money to buy another house. Then we could move from here. As much as I hated moving in the first place, it would not hurt my feelings one bit if I never had to step foot here again.

CHAPTER 5

Friends

It wasn't all just Amelia and Tommy that did the trick to keep Rob away from me. My parents got a call from someone at the school the very day that Tommy hit Rob. They just warned my parents that they knew that I was always well behaved, the one that never got into any trouble, and that the company I was keeping might not be the best.

I was surprised by the call. I never knew the school to interfere in the lives of the students. Except when DHS intervened. I just kept it in my head that it must have been Amelia's mom or dad calling my parents pretending to be the school.

My parents had confronted me that same night. They wondered who I was hanging out with. I was just so afraid that they might believe that Amelia was the one I shouldn't be around. They knew that I kept mostly to myself. Except for what happened in the mall, I would have never thought either of my parents was capable of thinking that I had some secret life. I thought back to that day and laughed. If my mother only knew the kind of person that she'd handed me away to that night.

The only bad thing that remained in my house after the *Rob thing* came out was that my parents became super overprotective. They didn't even know half of the facts about what really happened to me. All they knew was that he was trying to be too affectionate, and I didn't feel the same way. As soon as they realized that I really didn't want to see him anymore, I knew that he would get an earful if he ever tried to call again. Sometimes I wished that he would come over just so I could see him squirm with fear when my dad answered the door. When my mother wasn't demeaning him, my dad was actually a force to be reckoned with.

In the end, Amelia was the only friend that was allowed in the apartment. I stayed to myself as much as possible. I went places with Amelia and sometimes her brother, but that was it. Tommy really did just care about me like a brother. He was there with Amelia through the crying spells and withdrawals that I had as a result of never seeing Rob again.

As much as I didn't like him, I did miss him for some unhealthy reason. We even talked about that in class one day. It was a syndrome where people who were getting hurt felt sorry for the one who was doing it to them. I believe Stockholm Syndrome was the term. Thank God for Amelia and Tommy! They definitely kept my head on straight.

My parents were another story. Their sole purpose was worry and disbelief. They began to have endless conversations about what to do with me.

"What are we going to do with her this summer, Ed? We can't leave her on her own. You know she's been afraid to stay here by herself."

"Yeah, I wonder why. What did you actually think when you just left her at the mall on her birthday? Didn't she tell you that she didn't even know the guy?"

"Oh, I guess it's just another bad judgment call on my end, huh. You know everything that ever happens is my fault. I'm surprised that you don't blame Andrew's death on me. I did give birth to him."

"We both messed everything up so badly when Andy was here. What I wouldn't do just to tell him that he couldn't go anywhere. I could have that argument all day long if it meant that he would still be here."

They forgot that I could hear every single word that they ever said in this apartment. I heard my dad crying.

"You have to let this go, Ed. We did what we could. If he wanted to ruin his life, then he died doing what he wanted to."

I couldn't stand to hear how this conversation was leading. I just wanted them to stop arguing. I was tired of everyone being in pain. I wished so badly that I wasn't so stupid for falling for Rob in the first place. I should have known better. Especially when every real date we ever had included sex. It doesn't take a rocket scientist to understand that. I just backed up, went to my bed, put on my earphones, and covered my head with my pillows. I scuffled to bed pretty loudly and shut off my light with emphasis. I was hoping that my parents would get the hint and stop yelling for a while.

The last thing I heard were my sobs. I couldn't help but want to keep them going. They always drowned out every-thing that I so acutely heard in our small apartment.

The next morning, I made my way to the kitchen. I wasn't sure if I ever wanted to leave the security of the bedroom. I kept making the mistake of getting out of bed. I began to think that my mother had the right idea when she stayed in her bed. It was ultimate comfort. Yet, here I was venturing out into the unknown. The unknown was of course my parents having another heated discussion about me. Round two.

"Nancy, she's got to. We have no other option. You know that I just got transferred to this job and if I ever want to have anything for this family again, we will all have to make sacrifices. Why can't we just call Ryan and Rebecca Wallus? We know them pretty well. They are her best friends' parents. They probably know what our daughter is up to better than we do. They probably wouldn't mind having one more kid at their house this summer. Maybe we can just tell her to call them in case of an emergency."

"No one would be close enough in case of an emergency. Maybe we can make them aware of our situation but let them know that we have a neighbor to watch her. You know, the Domingos next door are really nice. They were one of the first ones to come here when Andy died. Maybe they wouldn't mind being part-time guardians when we are away."

"Mother! I can't believe what I am hearing! You don't know anything about anything!" I shouted.

"Well, Elizabeth, why don't you make things clearer?"

I really didn't want to get into an argument the first thing in the morning, but what else was there to do? I couldn't take them discussing me like I was a two-year-old. What they didn't know is that I was becoming a street-smart young woman, partially because of Amelia, partially because of Rob. Both of them taught me things about life that I was kept from as I grew up.

"First, I am not afraid. I heard what you guys were discussing about last night. I don't think that you understand me at all! I just didn't want to be here by myself for a while because I thought for sure that Rob would try to come and see me. If you guys never leave me alone, he will never have his chance. Now that he doesn't seem to be bothering me at all anymore, I'm not at all apprehensive to stay here by myself. You can ask the Domingos if you want, but that's really not necessary. I probably will spend time with Amelia a lot, so you can call her parents if you need to. The bottom line is, don't waste your time worrying about me and what I am going to do without you. I'll be just fine."

"Well, whether you like it or not, we have to make sure that you are safe. Even if you think that you will be just fine, we want to take some safety measures. I'm sure that you will eventually want to start dating again. When you do, we are going to set up better guidelines. There will be no more silly age-based split decisions. That was on me. From now on, you will have to be asked out first and plan a date before we will approve. That is all that there is to it. I'm glad that we could be of service to you to keep Rob away, but really, Liz, it's up to you to let people know that you aren't interested. If you noticed, he did leave you alone after he knew that you really didn't want to be friends with him anymore."

"He was *not* and *never will be* my friend, Mother—let me make that *clear*."

"Well, if you are never going to talk about what really happened between the two of you, then you can't expect me to know what to call him."

"Really, Elizabeth, I wish that you would let us in just a little. I know that we haven't had the best relationship lately, but you are important to us. We want to be there for you."

"Just leave her alone. You don't know anything at all about girls. She won't ever tell us what is going on with her. You had a son and he never let you know what he was doing. You know that we just stink at this whole parenting thing, don't you?"

"Speak for yourself. If you wouldn't be so selfish all the time we wouldn't even be here. Did you ever tell Elizabeth the real reason that you left her at the mall on her birthday? Didn't you tell her that you saw it as a way out to go see someone before you were expected home? Did you ever explain that you tried to lay a guilt trip on her because you were the guilty one?"

I didn't know what they were talking about. The conversation stopped being about me and it turned into all of the bad things that my mother did throughout the years that hurt our family. He was just bombarding her with the "what" and "what for."

"Stop it now! Never mind, you can argue all you want to, I'm going to Amelia's."

I was barely dressed to be seen by the world, but I didn't care. I thought that I would go to her house and could get cleaned up there. I stormed out of the apartment and never wanted to look back. I knew next year I would graduate and then I would just go as far from this place as I possibly could.

As I was walking down the street, I passed the convenience store that I had my conversation with Rob in. That was the very last day that we had any kind of relationship. I wondered why I was thinking about him so much. I tried to keep bad memories at bay.

"Speak of the Devil." I quietly spoke to myself as I was turning the corner. There he was, about to go into the same store that I just passed. I just put my face down and kept on walking. I was hoping that he would never notice me.

"Well, Lizzy, if it isn't my Lizzy."

I almost didn't reply, except that I was feeling all of a sudden very brave and I was tired of worrying about him all of the time. Like I told my parents earlier, I wasn't afraid of staying by myself and I wasn't afraid of Rob.

"Sorry, Rob, don't have time to talk. Go away."

I kept walking and didn't look back. I guess that he got the message because when I went about a hundred feet ahead, I looked back, and he was nowhere to be found. I looked ahead once more, concentrating on getting to Amelia's and telling her what I was so upset about this time.

"Elizabeth!"

It was still Rob. Where had he come from? I just looked back, and he wasn't anywhere. I guess it's just like I suspected that he was some demon out to harass me and make my life miserable.

"Rob, you really shouldn't try to meet me like this. You know, just one more block and I will be at Tommy's house. What 'cha gonna do there?"

"Tommy, eh. Yep, just as I suspected. He was keeping you

all to himself. I should'a known."

"Actually, dork head, he is seeing Melissa. How can you *not* know that? I mean, they walk around at school together hand in hand."

"So, calling names, are we? Yeah, well I could find a few for you. How about heart-breaking witch?"

I turned around, astonished with what I was hearing. I had actually hurt him? I mean, he was using me! So what if he really had cared? Or if the party thing was just a test or something. These thoughts had long passed, and I really didn't want to bring them back up.

"What are you even talking about? You know what you said, you just wanted a party girl and nothing more. No strings, remember? What happened to that? I mean, what would it matter to you if I decided to be with you longer or not. I know that you didn't care for *me*, you just wanted what I had for your own good time."

"Liz, I just wished you knew how I felt about it really. The guys had put me up to asking you that. I didn't know what else to do. It was either let them watch you and ask if I could share you or I would look lame to them. You know, I don't even know what the point is of even telling you this. It wasn't like you were really into me anyway. I guess that I could tell that and that's why I just treated you that way. I guess I was ready for you to go. Better to have you leave than keep you longer and eventually have my heart broken."

"I wasn't out to break anyone's heart. I wasn't even looking for anything except clothes the day that you approached me at the mall. I had never been out on a date! Everything that you do, like Andy did, was never in my life. Andy never told me anything about life. He protected me from it, and it just blew me away like a whirlwind with what you had me doing. Truth be told, I was scared of what I was when I was with you. I don't want to die early like Andrew. I didn't understand why it was so important to you to live like that either. Do you have a death wish or something?"

"Death? No. I just wanted to be free. I mean, I'll graduate this year and I have to go off to college. My parents are actually kicking me out as soon as I turn 18. Are your parents ever kicking you out? You just seemed to be exactly what I needed, and you just disappeared on me. I know that I must have scared you, especially at the party, but I really did care about you. You were my baby. I had feelings for you."

"Yeah, lust. I know what that feeling is now, thanks to you." I actually smiled a little bit when I said that. I didn't know why I had a feeling of sympathy for him. I mean, he put me through hell, or so it seemed. Just a few minutes ago I thought he must be a demon. Now, he just seemed like a lost cause that needed a friend.

"Ya wanna hang out, Rob?"

I actually couldn't believe my own words. Why on earth was I inviting danger into my life again? With all the dysfunctionality that was happening at home, I guess this was fitting.

"Really."

He said that matter-of-factly. I almost thought it sounded as if it was a smug response to his smooth talking. I forgot about that. Why had I forgotten about that?

"Look, Rob, if you're just playing more games, then never mind. My parents think that I am going to Amelia's house and will probably call there in a little while to check up on me. So, I can just go. I just thought that you needed to talk or something."

"NO!"

Now that was more of a desperate sound. It was a complete 360-degree turnaround.

"Ok, I'll bite, where do you want to go?" His smile was ear to ear. Before I could get out an answer, he instructed. "First, call Amelia, tell her that you were on your way, but you decided to just walk around for a while. You'll check in later. Tell her to tell your parents that if they call."

"Why is it that you always have an answer for everything?"

He just smiled that big smile. I forgot that I used to like it a few months ago.

I did what he told me to though. I mean, he was right, if we wanted to have any time to ourselves, then we would definitely have to lie to everyone. There would be so many people who wouldn't understand, me being one of them. I just wanted to give him the benefit of the doubt. I wanted to have a friendship with him. We missed out on that before.

He did something that I hadn't expected; he held my hand and swung it like we were kids. I just wondered if this was really him, or if there was someone around that he was displaying me to. With Rob, you never knew.

"So, the park is just a couple of streets over. You wanna go over there? It will be out in the open and I bet there will be a bunch of kids there, so you don't have to worry."

"I actually appreciate that."

I smiled back at him and hand in hand we made our way to the park. I couldn't believe our luck. It was midmorning, and no one was out there yet. I was kinda happy though. We got to sit on the swings and just hang out. He told me more about himself and his family. He opened up to me.

He finally quit treating me like an object. He made me laugh so many times. He went down the kiddy slide backwards and had me sitting on his lap going down the twisty slide. Tears were flowing when we got off and gave each other shocks from the friction of the plastic slide. Our hair was in all directions because of the static. I felt young for the first time in a long time.

Why couldn't I stop thinking about that promise of never-ending fun when we moved from our farmhouse? It always came to mind when things happened that made me happy. It always brought me down. My mind was my worst enemy. We were lying on the two-person kiddie slide. I was just looking up toward the bright sky.

"Liz, where'd you go? You look sad—did I say something? I thought everything was cool."

I got into the conversation about the move from the farm-house again. He just sat there and listened.

"You know, one of the first things I liked about you was that you truly seemed interested in my old house. Do you remember that conversation?"

"Yes, actually I do. You just made it a little more real for me with what you just said, but yeah, I really thought we could go there someday. You know, you're not the only person on the face of the earth that doesn't want to be stuck here. What do you think when I go and visit my cousin? Our parents both started out the same. My old man just decided that drinking was more important."

"Then why have you been out doing what we have? Aren't you afraid that you'll end up like that?"

"Liz, I'm sorry about that, but I didn't really drink with you. I just got you drunk. I know that was wrong, but I was just so nervous that you wouldn't like me. I just needed something to take my edge off. I knew alcohol couldn't be it for me."

"So, you just used me. You knew what you were doing, and you just used me. You know that is really cold, don't you? I shouldn't even be here giving you a second chance."

I got up I started to walk away. He came up to me and swung me around. I was in his arms so quickly. He just held me. He wasn't being rude or perverted.

"Please, just don't go." He looked down and continued to explain. "I know how that must have sounded; it was just that the particular day that we met up for the first time at the mall. I really had been ditched by my *buddies*. They didn't want to hang around me because I didn't want to party anymore. You don't think that what happened to Andy did anything to me? Well, it did. I told them that I wanted to play golf, and they told me that I was lame and left to go out drinking. I really needed someone who was willing to party for me to be around them. It's like they didn't like me otherwise. I just didn't think about the fact that you would be one of my casualties while I was one of theirs. I am so sorry."

I pulled away. I had tears in my eyes. He really meant everything that he had said. He was just as messed up as I was.

"Friends?"

This was one thing that I never thought I would ever say to him.

"Friends."

He pulled me to him one more time. We both knew that we were able to give something different to each other than to anyone else, friendship with a sorted past. It wasn't like my relationship with Amelia. We were friends. Tommy and I were friends. Rob and I almost lost the chance to become what we should have been before we started in the physical relationship that we had.

As we left the park, swarms of kids showed up for a birthday party. They were so loud with laughing and playing. They didn't have the kinds of problems that we did. They were lucky. We were lucky too though. We had time to be together as people who were still also young, doing young things and just getting to know one another. We came into the park with no expectations and left with hope.

Rob had to go to work. Even though he had expressed that he was bummed about being kicked out when he was 18, he did say that he was saving for college. He was going to do what it took to get out of town. We got to say goodbye on good terms. I even told him that it was ok to call me sometime. We were going to be friends after all. I was almost skipping all the way to Amelia's. I didn't know what it was that I was going to tell her when I got there. I had given everybody so much grief about Rob, I think that they would just have a cow if I told them that I had forgiven him and wanted to be friends.

I just hoped that she wasn't going to be like his old friends. Even if I wasn't what she thought I should be, she could see past it and accept me anyway. I think that was all I needed after all, just acceptance, friendship, and understanding. If it was from her and her brother, then great; if it was from Rob, then I was just getting more support so I could endure what was happening at home.

I still had to think it over about what my dad had said about what my mother had done at the mall those weeks ago. I didn't want to know. I always assumed it was all about her out of control spending. If it was something more, then she really was more of a catalyst of the downfall that was our family than even I expected. I just wanted my parents to be friends again. To have the feeling of that day, he told her all of her dreams would come true. That would definitely be my wish if I had one to be granted. If Rob and I could reconcile, so could they.

I got to Amelia's and let her know everything. I wanted her to really understand me. I wasn't going to ever hide how I felt from her. She was exactly what I needed once again. She was supportive. She explained it to Tommy and let him know that we had no relationship, and he wasn't going to hurt me anymore.

"Whatever," Tommy moaned. He seemed to buy it. That was a relief. I did something I never thought that I could, I gained a friend and kept the other two I had.

I eventually left the splendid confines of happy with Amelia and wandered slowly home. The whole way, I could only think of their perspective. How easy it must be to be accepting with a family like theirs. I always envied what Amelia's family had. They were safe and secure. Her family didn't seem to ever have arguments. They'd lived in their house since she was little, and it was always a little piece of heaven when I went into their home.

That was what it seemed I missed the most. A place that could actually be called home. This apartment was like a jail sentence that we all hoped we could get out of with good behavior.

I knew that it would be dark soon, and as at ease as I was

about Rob, it didn't make me any less afraid of strangers lurking around town.

If there was one thing that I learned since we moved to the complex, people were here for a reason. It isn't because they wanted to be. It is out of necessity. That can make people really unhappy. Sometimes they need a stranger to harass to make themselves feel better about their situation. I wasn't going to be anyone's source of unappreciated enjoyment. Rob was my personal teacher about that subject.

Just as I was letting go of that thought, I walked through the door. My mother was there, but my dad was still gone to work.

"So, how'd your day go with Amelia? You guys just hang out at her house all day?"

"Kinda."

"About this morning. Liz, your dad and I are having problems right now. I'm not saying that anything bad is going on, but we haven't been happy since we had to move here. With your brother gone, we just don't feel very close anymore."

"Yeah, I heard what Dad was saying this morning. You got someone else that you like better than us?" I didn't know where that was coming from. I didn't even know for sure if that was what my dad was talking about, but it was what he implied, and I just ran with it. I knew that this was harsh, but she was telling me that my family had all but dissolved. I was so tired of her mistakes.

She was the one who made all of the mistakes! The spending mistakes that all but made us move. The life-ending mistakes like the one that sided with Andrew all of the time and said that boys will be boys up until the day he died. She was the one that now was bringing our family no hope of recovery because she didn't like it.

"Elizabeth, it isn't like that at all. First of all, you know that your dad and I have had some issues these past years. You know that we haven't been happy for a very long time."

"Oh, you mean since you had to leave the lap of luxury, *everything is perfect* house? I completely understand. You thought it was more important than all of us. You wanted it more than you wanted us. Since it's gone away, I guess that we should all just disappear too!"

"You know, I just don't need this right now." She grabbed her keys off the hook by the door and turned to leave. "Look, your dad'll be home in just an hour or so. Just lock the door and wait for him, ok? I need to go somewhere."

"Mother! Wait, I'm sorry, I didn't mean it! Wait!"

She just kept on walking. She never even turned back around. I knew that I shouldn't have told her how I felt. I knew better than to think that we could even have an argument. She had so many with Dad lately that I guess she decided that she didn't need one from me too. I made her want to leave. She left because of me.

I knew what she said about staying at home. It was dark and any transportation I had would have to be on foot, unless I knew someone with a car. Split decisions never were my best suit, as I had learned the hard way and now, I usually had to deliberate over things before I could get a good answer to a question. I began to pace back and forth. I felt more trapped than ever. I picked up the phone and dialed the number. I couldn't believe that I still remembered it.

"Rob? Hey, this is Elizabeth. Can you come over and get me? I need to get out of here."

"Uh, sure. I just got home from work, but yeah, I'll be right there."

I hoped the whole time that he was coming that I did the right thing by calling him. I just knew that I needed out too. I also was still afraid to go out after dark here. As his car pulled up, I decided to write a note to my dad saying that I was out and that Mother had left. At least he wouldn't have to wonder too hard as to what happened to us.

I ran to get into the car.

"What's wrong?"

He could tell something was up. He also knew that even though we just decided to be friends, I would have needed a good reason to just call him up and ask him to get me.

"Got anything with you?" I confidently inquired.

"What do you mean?"

"I need something to make me forget what is going on. Do you have anything with you?"

"No. Well, I mean, I've got a little pot in my console, but it's old and it isn't mine. I don't even know why I kept it. They just left it in here the last time we went out and I never bothered to give it back. But hey, whatever I can do for you."

"Great. Can we go somewhere? I mean, do you know of anywhere we can go?"

"Liz, if you haven't noticed, anywhere is pretty much fine around here. Do you think that the police will be out looking for teen pot? With the gang activity and hard-core drug problems and things around here, I figure they think that we have it coming."

"I guess you have a point. Anyway, just to be safe, do you know anywhere?"

"Look, Liz, don't take this wrong when I mention this, but no one is at my house tonight. We really could just go there. I don't want to bring up bad memories or anything with us, but you did ask."

"You're right. I did. I think that it would be just fine. We're keeping boundaries though. You know already that I won't be levelheaded, so just promise that you won't take advantage."

"I can live with that. I'm just glad that you forgave me."

"I did forgive you, but it doesn't mean that I'll forget. Besides, that first night wasn't really that bad."

"Liz, don't talk about it, ok. Do you want me to keep my side of the bargain or not?"

"Sorry."

I zipped my mouth shut with my fingers and preceded to

lay my head back in my seat. I was so happy that I was free. We were at his house in no time.

"Look, my parents aren't here, and I know that you've had *beer* with me before, so do you just want some of that? I mean, you don't have to smoke-the joint. I really don't know what's in it."

"I really don't think that I care what's in it at this point."

I got teary-eyed from the sound of his sincerity. I just wasn't expecting that much compassion from him, plus he was being protective.

"Wait a minute, where is Rob? What did you do to him?"

"I'm right here, baby."

He put his arm around me and pulled me to his chest. I began to cry. He actually said it like he meant it. I was something to him and he wanted me to know that everything was going to be alright. We just sat in his driveway. My tears were getting us both so wet. I had too much to think about all day. Good, bad; bad, good. I couldn't take the drama of it all. He wiped my face with the bottom of his shirt. My tears began to slow, and I looked up at him. He kissed me on the forehead.

"Come on. Let's get out of here."

"Oh, ok." I leaned back to my door and started to open it.

"No, not here. This is not good for either of us. You're here alone with me. We have stuff to make us forget our good judgment, and you're not in a good frame of mind right now. Just sit back and I'll let you know when we get there."

That had to be the most considerate thing that anyone had ever said to me in a good long while. As I was wondering where we were going, we pulled up outside the mall. It was 7:30 and we only had about an hour and a half before it closed.

"Golf, anyone?"

CHAPTER 6

The Beginning of the End

A sincere smile came across his face. It was no longer the predatory one that preceded it. He really wanted to make me happy on his own and not from needless inebriation. He got out of his car and ran to the other side to get my door. He pulled me out and held my hand the whole time we were walking in. It was just like our first date all over again, except that he was honestly bringing me here for fun. We were swinging our arms, just as we had in the park.

I felt so young again and oddly enough, happy. Where had this Rob been all along? It was nothing I had expected when I called him earlier. I thought he would be back to his old self and supply me with all the drugs and alcohol that I wanted. I could finally believe that he was telling me the truth this morning about everything. If he cared about me, getting me drunk or high would be the last thing that he would want for me, especially because of his dad.

We went in the Putt-Putt Golf Store, and he pulled out some cash.

"I'm so sorry. I didn't know that we were going to do this. I didn't bring any money."

"Not to worry. I work a lot now. I can afford it. Besides, we have just about an hour. We can't even play more than one game in that time."

"True, but thanks all the same."

"Just no more tears, ok? I can't take any more of that."

"That's a deal."

As he paid for our one round of golf, the manager offered us a two-for-one deal because they had less than an hour and a half left before closing. We couldn't believe our luck. We laughed and laughed. He won one, and then I won the other. We decided that if we had a tie, we'd never do tie breakers. We decided we both needed to win. It was so surreal that he would be my shoulder to cry on in my time of need.

He had been through disasters in his own family because of his dad. I was going through them because of my mother. Both of our lives were unfair. It really was a perfect match for friendship. I suddenly felt a little guilty for not seeing that he was hurting when all of our past was going on. Though to be fair to myself, I didn't go around hurting others just because I was hurting.

We left the mall the same way we came in. We were hand in hand.

"Rob, I'm sorry that I just dumped you before I gave you a chance to really know you. I really didn't realize what you were going through at the time."

"Don't apologize, Liz. I don't blame you a bit. You don't know how sorry I felt when I knew that I messed up the one thing that was making me happy. Especially when it was all over trying to be cool with so-called friends. I really messed up. I am just so lucky that you heard me out today. I have been trying to find a way for a long time to explain things to you. I just figured that I had no right to talk to you. That was what I deserved anyway."

"Why don't we just say that we are both lucky to have someone right now."

He pulled up to my apartment building. It was five minutes till ten. How fitting that he brought me home safe and sound, on time, even when I was half running away. I turned to kiss him goodbye. I decided that he deserved that. I got out of the car quickly and ran up the stairs, not knowing what I would find once I got there. I was so happy for the most part.

"Hey, Dad, how's it going?"

"Elizabeth, you scared me to death! First, I get home and no one is here, but the lights were left on. Then, I saw your note! I didn't know if you were safe or anything! What happened?"

"Dad, Mother left, and it's all my fault. We had a fight because she just kept telling me that she hated everything here and that things aren't good. I was so tired of hearing her! I guess I may have said some hurtful things. I don't care though! She deserved them!"

"Your mother is having a tough time right now."

"DON'T YOU DARE DEFEND HER!"

"Liz, I know that it is hard to understand adult things, but sometimes life doesn't go your way."

"No, I don't want to hear you defending her. She was wrong. She is wrong. She shouldn't have left. You have done everything for her. You have lost everything for her. She doesn't deserve someone as good as you, Dad!"

"Liz, it isn't all her fault. Listen, do you know where she went?"

"No. She just told me to stay here by myself and that you'd be home later."

"Where did you go, Elizabeth? Who were you with? I called Amelia's house, and she hadn't even heard from you this evening!"

"I was with Rob."

"Rob?" The look on his face reminded me why I wasn't always upfront and honest with him.

"Dad, I know what you want to say, but just don't say anything. He has changed! He really has!"

He stopped me. "I'm sorry, Liz, but this just can't happen. You can't sit here and tell me that for all this time you have been afraid that he would come here and do God knows what. I mean, you were really afraid. Think about how this looks, Liz!"

"I mean, we got to talk a little this morning and we kinda worked things out. We aren't dating or anything, we're just hanging out." I continued to explain. "I know. I was just as surprised as you. But when she left me without turning back, I just couldn't handle it anymore and you weren't here! I just couldn't stay here after that. I needed out too! I knew better than to just walk around, so I called him. He understands what I am going through. He has just as many problems at his house! I just needed some support. That's it; we are just going to support each other as friends. I promise."

"Liz, I just don't know. It just doesn't make sense."

"You have to trust me, Dad. Why was it so easy to trust Andy and never me? What have I ever done, anyway?"

"Nothing, Lizzy, nothing. I just don't want anything to happen to you. I love you."

"I love you too, Dad."

"So, did you eat any dinner yet?" He abruptly changed the subject.

"You know, I guess I forgot all about it. It's nine o'clock now. I guess it's almost too late to eat."

"Na, why don't we do our old cooking lesson out of the refrigerator? You know, we used to have so much fun just rounding up ingredients from the pantry and making Redbird gourmet meals out of them!"

"I remember! Mother and Andy would always just watch.

Do you think that we ever made anything that they didn't like? I mean, it seemed to me that they sure liked our concoctions!"

"Yeah, they were something else!"

We began to pilfer through the refrigerator and the cabinets. The luxury of a stocked pantry left with the last house. Even with almost bare cabinets, it wasn't too long before we had a meal fit for a king cooking up in our little kitchen. We set the table super fancy, like they did in the restaurants that we now couldn't afford. It was like it was when I was about ten, when we did this all the time.

"You know," Dad began in a reminiscent tone, "I do really wish that this would have been enough for your mother. She always needed more. She wanted to experience the meals in fancy restaurants. She wanted to be served as if she were a celebrity. She's not here now, because she couldn't stand this any longer."

I looked into his semi-defeated eyes as he continued. "She's actually been out trying to find better work lately. She says that she just can't get a better paying job if she is working in this part of town. She always says that you need to live well to keep the jobs that make you able to live better. She's proven herself right by that in one way, and wrong in another. If I could have just told her no. That what we had was sufficient and when she got that first job after we moved to the new house, that the money should have been saved and not just wasted on more unnecessary spending. She always seemed so much happier when she stayed at home with you two. But, the more she had, the more she never saw the good in small things in life. It is true though, when we moved here, I guess I gave up hope for a little while. I know that didn't help us at all, with me working crazy hours for so long. I just didn't know how to go forward. I just lost everything that made her happy. I just wished that we were enough to do that."

He kept rambling on about what he should or shouldn't have done all the way through dinner. I didn't want to stop him. He was usually more of a sulker like me. It was usually bottled up, with nothing more than an unhappy, fake smile on his face. He was a man of few words, so if he needed to let some of them out, I figured that I had better listen up.

We ate our magnificent dinner on our fancy plates, with napkins in our laps. It seemed appropriate that we didn't share any other conversation during or after dinner. All that needed to be said between us was, and the rest was said in the food we shared. It was as loving as a moment as was available in the present circumstance. It was ten o'clock and time for bed. Another school day was just in the morning.

"Good night, Dad. It was good talking to you. I hope everything with you and Mother works out."

I went to bed wondering where my mother had gone. I prayed for my dad to find a little peace. I normally didn't do a whole bunch of praying. I was raised to believe in God, but we didn't do much in the way of actually going to any services. We hadn't been since Christmas, the year before Andy died. Now, it was nonexistent, even on holidays.

I thanked God for leading me to friendship with someone I thought was going to be an enemy. My life was so full of chaos, yet it was so calming to know that I now had a support system outside of my own family. Maybe that would be enough to keep me sane and to help them through.

My mother never came back that night. I assumed that she stayed wherever it was that my dad said that she once went. I didn't know where, and he never seemed to make me privy to that information. She did show up one day while I was in school. I came home and noticed that her things were pilfered through and there were many things missing. She evidently left a Dear John letter to my dad.

That was the second time in the last year and a half that someone in my little family wouldn't be coming back. I shivered at the memory when she told me the same thing about my brother. At least I knew that she was still out there some-where. She wasn't dead at least, even if she wanted to be dead to us.

The only knowledge I had about what the letter said, other than that she wasn't coming back, was that she was going to contact us when she felt up to it. What did that even mean? She had to gain courage to talk to her own family? I began to feel guilty. I was the last person that she talked to before she stormed out. Had I really given her such a bad time that she didn't even want me in her life anymore?

No, I think it was that she loved Andrew more, and I wasn't a close enough substitute. I knew that I was never a close second, but I loved her just the same, even through her bad moods and incoherent realities. I didn't hate her when she insisted that we moved from the house we loved so well, but she must have hated us when she had to leave her eutopia to live here. We just tied her to the ground here. She wanted to fly, and I guess that's exactly what she did. She flew the coop, so to speak. She was free from now on. Free to run off to be with her new young dentist friend in New Hampshire. He happened to be that person she went to see when she ditched me with Rob in the mall. Clothes evidently weren't the only new item in her life. "Dorky Dan the dentist," as I now unlov-ingly call him, was a graduate student at the University of Iowa College of Dentistry and was promised a wonderful job in New Hampshire, even though I was sure that jobs for dentists could have been anywhere. I knew from the moment that we were told where they would be moving that the pretentious name of the state alone would be enough to draw her away from her family.

Mother made it clear that we weren't even a part of her new life, and that they moved for a reason. I may have received two birthday cards in the ten years after she left. The careful, doting mother she once was never returned. She became the beautifully adorned pheasant, and I was abandoned in the nest, barely concealed and open to the atrocities that awaited.

Amelia, Rob, Tommy, and I became best friends before the summer was over that fateful year. Rob and I partied together as friends only. We became the new designated drivers for all of our wasted buddies. Suddenly, we were BFFs with most of the upperclassmen. I would like to say that I gave Rob the confidence he needed to leave town and find his own way in life. Unfortunately, that left me without a big brother once again.

As my defenders disappeared, the more unyielding I became. When I went back to school that fall, it was like I had some new popularity. The more popular everyone began to think I was, the more wrong people always seemed to gravitate to me. I always let in the kind that you shouldn't touch with a ten-foot pole. It became so hard to defend my own honor when there wasn't anyone around to defend it for me. Honestly, I was tired of worrying about my honor.

Basically, my senior year was one big party. I wasn't proud of what I was doing, or whom I was doing it with, but like I said, no defender left me defenseless. My dad sure wasn't around to check after me. When he got remarried to a woman with small children, my care stopped. Things with us were never perfect, but what father-daughter relationship is?

He just gave up on trying to figure me out. It was as if he was starting over with other people's children because he knew he'd failed his own. His time was consumed with them and less and less with me. He may as well have left when my mother did. It would have been no different.

Dad and "Kim the joy killer," as I now called her, knew that I was about to graduate from high school and that there was no reason that they had to cater to me anymore. I wanted to leave earlier. I wanted my mother to say, "Come on, things will be better in New Hampshire." Those words were never in her vocabulary. I know that now. I would never forgive her for that either. It was the last and final bit of dysfunction that I could take. I was a lost soul that was wide open for the world to see.

I had plans to run away, as far and as fast as I possibly could. I would ditch all of those who ditched me. To be perfectly honest, I didn't plan to look back. They had been waiting to see what colleges I got into. They were ready for me to disappear out of their lives; after all, I was the one teenager who lived. It was always hard to know that they wished it had been me instead of Andy. They honestly thought that if he had lived, then everything would have worked out.

It was bad enough that I had to learn a big lesson with the beginning of my relationship with Rob. I began to smarten up when it came to people in general. That's why Amelia remained such a special friend. She had been the one person who didn't see me as someone to use. She even helped keep the others at bay, kind of. She was the one to remind me that I would have better than what they had to offer. She always knew that there was a future for me, even if I could never seem to see it.

Just as I was beginning to give up on everything, one piece of good luck came our way.

"You know now that this was meant to be!"

This was all Amelia kept saying over and over again.

"It is fate that we can both study what we want without having to be apart."

Now, I didn't believe in fate. In fact, I was rather mad at the thought of fate. What had I ever done to deserve this? What I did realize is that I had the ability, for the first time in my life, to get as far away from my family problems as I had ever been able to.

"Yeah, Amelia," I replied as cheerfully as I could muster, *"it isn't every day that someone hands you a first-class ticket out of misery! Well, my misery anyway."*

"Oh, come on, Liz! This is going to be perfect. Don't make me remind you that I can follow your mood swings quicker than you can. I just know if you would think about it in the right way, you would know that our lives are about to change for the better!"

Man, she always had a way of saying things that either made you happy or guilt you into feeling the way she saw them. I guess this was one of those times. The mere mention of my life and perfect in the same sentence gave me immediate hope. I took a deep breath, and she knew right away that she had done her job. She had calmed the raging monster within me one more time. I always wondered why my parents lacked that ability with me. I guessed I'd never know. I was never coming back.

I was just so lucky that Amelia decided to join me in my disappearance. I hated to bask in my lack of self-worth all alone. I always needed her to lift me out of it, or I knew that I would not make it through life. Amelia, Tommy, and Rob were those friends to me. When Rob left, she was still there to pick up the pieces. She was happy-go-lucky and gave pure joy to all that graced her presence.

Amelia and I both got accepted into Contra Costa College. We were going to go on our first real adventure. We were headed for sunny San Pablo, California. I would start in the Culinary of the Arts Department. Amelia would start in Film School.

CALIFORNIA
BOUND

CHAPTER 7

Dreams

It was long ago when I came to *this place*. Almost a decade had passed. I was so young when I left. Only seventeen. I guessed that things never changed. I was still someone who ran from things. People who have come to know me would never guess that it is exactly how I really was inside. I have to say even gutless. I was shaken to my core so many times in my life that running was my only way out of a bad situation. The events of my childhood were enough to break anyone. It broke my mother and made me more broken by her absence.

Food, on the other hand, was one thing that always was able to sustain me during my endless glum. It was my goal to make a living out of doing something that could make me happy for a change. I guess that I would have to give a little credit to my dad for this. Even though we never cooked together again after the night my mother left, it was still a stupid precious memory to me. My thoughts about my infamous sixteenth birthday gave me inspiration. I could remember how happy I was to be served those dainty waffles. It was with this memory that I knew I would eventually work my way into a specialty of pastry and elegant desserts, not just cooking in general.

I would have loved to have the opportunity to go overseas to explore 'worldly' cookery techniques of exotic hometowns. I didn't want to be taught by those who just teach by being taught here themselves. I thought that it had to take away from the authenticity. Plus, I couldn't help but fantasize about the Europe that I read about in travel magazines. It seemed like you could become anything you wanted if you could just travel.

Anyway, it just wasn't in the cards for me to do so. Our money tree didn't shake off money, just pollen and dead leaves. I was lucky I even had a golden ticket out of town to begin with. Amelia and I both had small scholarships. It was enough to get us to California, put a down payment on an apartment, and pay for the first semester's tuition.

I had to work my way through tuitions by doing catering. Other than small scholarships, I had no other help. I became financially independent when I was barely eighteen.

Catering to the wealthy had its advantages. They would love my creations—so much so, that I was almost overworked. I was even a personal shopper for some of my wealthier clients. Truth be told, they all seemed wealthy to me. If they weren't living in our apartment complex, I knew they had to have some money. Especially those who lived in the Napa Valley or San Francisco areas.

My client base was growing, and really, even if I didn't get any new customers, my more established ones could have kept me financially secure enough to live the dreams that my mother had for herself. I actually thought about sticking with it after my formal education, but there was something about working with the really rich that left a bad taste in my mouth.

It was like seeing everything that my mother had wanted, all those years, and I was working with living proof that some people really made it with their families intact. I had opportunities, but something was telling me to keep going. A little money wasn't all that I wanted. It never was.

During my first year of college, my dreams were really put in a different direction. In the spring semester, I took a short film class. It was just as a fun elective.

"We came all the way to California!" Amelia persuaded. "I'll tell you what, try this class. If you don't like it, don't ever take another one. I'm just telling you that you don't know what you are missing. It is *so* much fun."

Generally, I always gravitated to anything that Amelia was led to do. At that particular time, it seemed reasonable to explore all the possibilities that life had to offer. I didn't know that the film bug would bite me. I took one more class during the summer and that caught me up. I was ready to take the class that would put me as a real show host. I would try out at KCCC-TV, the college TV station, to do a thirty-minute cooking show.

The class professor seemed full of gratitude when we decided on the idea of a cooking show. Well, or any show that they could get someone to watch for free. For the duration of the class, I learned a lot about filmmaking. I actually kept with it for four seasons—two years or two fall and two spring semesters. Amelia was already working for her own 'show' on real TV by then. I was glad when she got to work on her dream as I was finding mine.

It was never hard to do anything with her support. What I quickly realized was that I didn't just want to cook meals for people, or work in a bakery as a pastry chef. I wanted to be behind the camera.

It was amazing to think that something my best friend had a passion for, was what I was passionate for also. I wanted to tell other people what to do to make it look good on camera.

I realized that being exposed on TV was not my way of happiness. The further away from the camera and the more in control of everyone I was, the happier I was.

It was finding the meat and bones of a show and getting it to work in a way you could watch even if it wasn't free TV. I found the longer I was doing that, the longer that I could be happy. So, even though my education continued, if my abroad trips would finally be realized, it was time to find real employment.

I had to find my real place in the world. I had to get rid of the feeling of being less of a person. I knew I was worth something. Because of the KCCC-TV exposure, it wasn't long before I was able to apply to a real job at KPIX-TV, the local CBS Broadcasting station. It was this that brought me closer to the independence that I wanted so badly.

I worked on a noon TV show. It was a show of local flavors. I went to many restaurants for the program as the primary host. This wasn't what I wanted to be. I wanted to travel, I wanted to be involved with the television show process, and I really didn't want the public exposure.

It did seem to get me noticed from time to time though. Even though my studies were the reason that we came to California, Amelia liked to go out to get-togethers on and off campus. My social life would have been nil if it weren't for her encouragement not to give up. I kept mainly to myself. High school taught me that being with others can get you into trouble. I wanted to leave that behind, so I hid as long as I could.

I hid in my coursework and baggy sweats and glasses. Amelia just shined the way she always did. Her approach to life was that of abandon. She was unafraid of what was to come. I was always ready for the next big catastrophe. They always came at home. Why wouldn't they follow me here?

My love relationships were the same way. Never too close, always guarded, always broken. After Rob, there were only a couple of guys I really tried to date. I knew to keep romance away from the groups that wanted me to party with them. I think I knew that with all the brokenness that was in my own family, love wasn't anything I was actually looking for— besides, it was my goal not to get stuck in a relationship that wouldn't allow me to leave our horrible little town.

It was Amelia's dream that drew me into what would make me the most confident in the long term. I had a chance to turn my one true love, cooking, into a self-sustaining way of life.

Although I had a nonexistent love life, I couldn't help but have hope for a future relationship. Nothing ever happened though. That would definitely be because I couldn't seem to find time for love, or at least that was my excuse. I always wondered how normal people did it. How did they go on with life and actually find time for love? How did they hold on to it when they did find time?

Even Amelia had found her someone. Of course, who wouldn't love Amelia? His name was Adam deClair. He was nice enough, and he really liked the same things that she did. I guessed that is what made them so compatible. It was as if they were two bright lights molded together, and with that they formed the sun.

For me, everyone I ran into liked my show, but for some reason, didn't like me in that fashion. Or, at least if they did, they sure didn't tell me. It was more frustrating than anything.

But truth be told, there was nobody that held my attention either. So, other than a few dates, and very short-term rela- tionships, there wasn't anything to it.

In the end, I was still that same girl with trust issues. From all my past experience, my radar only attracted losers. I knew that loser wasn't going to be in my adult vocabulary.

I somehow found myself wanting a way out of local TV. I did get to travel to many somewhat exotic local destinations. I went all around the Napa Valley's wine country. I even got to go to Vegas, but that was just not where I wanted to be.

I knew that it would take a broader station with a more

specialized audience that would approve of that kind of travel for food. It was the opening of a new television station that finally got me out of the public eye.

The Culinary Shopper's Network had just started and needed a professional cook with broadcasting experience. I became the Producer for the Dessert Food Division for the entire network. It was my Culinary Arts Degree in Pastries and Confections and my six years of television experience that got me the job of my dreams. It also didn't hurt that it was a fact that if it was sweet, I could bake it.

CHAPTER 8

Sundae, Sundae

The normalcy of the morning was overwhelming. Some kids were showing how easy it was to make ice cream sundaes with special kits that they had for sale. They had multicolored and chocolate sprinkles, as well as whipped cream in a can, and the fudge was in a squeeze-as-you-go decorating decanter. They were called Dream Sundaes. The kids who represented the company said that they literally dreamed them up. They were really incredible.

Our production room was large. A little warm from all the lights, like normal, and I was sitting in the back of the open room as we were shooting the live feed. Ned, my production manager, was just entering the room quietly. I was showing him what had happened while he was gone. I realized that even with looking at the sweet goodness of a sundae, it didn't look as good as his lips. He was sitting about two people's length away from me.

"They look good, don't they?"

That was his reply to my inadvertently licking my lips when he looked into my eyes. That was my wake-up call. That is why my production manager didn't have a clue. No one could see any more to my moistening of my lips than having dry lips or being hungry.

People didn't see me that way. While working at the Culinary Shopper's Network for two years, all the sweets that I had made and taste tested for the sake of good programming caught up with me.

You never realize how you look till your picture is made. Unfortunately, as well as increasingly, we had young kids on the set that were all too sentimental. They got out their new little cell phones, iPads, and other handheld devices and asked to have a picture with literally everyone there. It would be fine for me to just have the picture made and know I may never see the kids or the pictures again.

They never ceased to amaze me with how conscientious they were, sending thank you cards with printed photos, or sending follow-up e-mails, texts, or posting pictures on our Instagram and Facebook fan pages. They knew that we would all just enjoy memories of them.

Well, it seemed that every single one had me in the background, the foreground, and everywhere in between. I was in constant horror, picture after picture. Whose body did they put my head on? I couldn't believe it! I could always have a lot of things said about my character, but my body had remained constant.

I knew girls that had to force salad down just to keep from weighing three hundred and fifty pounds. That wasn't me. All the years were catching up. My stress of everyday life was less, so I guess my body decided that I could hold on to some of what I ate.

I was a twenty-seven-year-old never been married, half

grandma look-alike. You could hug me if you had a problem, and I would be soft enough that it would be comforting to those around me. A twenty-seven-year-old grandma—ugh!

"Yeah, I guess those sundaes really do." That was my only way to reply. It was a good thing that he couldn't read my thoughts, or he would have known the real meaning of the fiasco.

"So, you want to go and get some? There is definitely some left. Like always." He was tempting me more than he knew. That was another verification that I must be lonely.

"No, you just go ahead and enjoy yourself. I think for my own personal growth, I'll stay away from five hundred empty calories."

"Since when did you care about calories, or personal growth for that matter?" With this, he firmly held his rather pudgy stomach and shook it a little. I guess it never occurred to me that he of all people couldn't have seen me in any other way than what we were every day. It was me who changed. We had been working so many hours together. And we were single. It wasn't so far-fetched. Or so I thought.

"You know that I'll never catch a husband if I go around looking like a grandma!"

To this he laughed, a little too much for me and my already wounded ego.

"Grandma? Huh! Now that's a new one. Since when were young, extremely successful professionals the same as grandmas? I mean, I know in this recession more and more older people are coming out of retirement, but I wasn't under the impression that it included twenty-five and above! That's gonna be great info for my mom!" He wouldn't stop laughing. "And, since when did *you* want a relationship?"

"Another thing... You know, that is what is wrong with *this* relationship that we have going on here. You have stopped seeing what has been happening to the both of us! I mean, when is the last time you had a date, anyway?"

I knew that this was hitting below the belt, even for me. I mean, all the guy did was show up when I was in a 'mood.' I felt guilty in the instant that I was saying it. I was just too stubborn to admit that I was stupid and in the wrong to bring it out so harshly, even if it was the truth.

"Funny you should say that! I just so happen to have tickets to the Lakers game. You know, basketball?" He said this condescendingly.

"Yes, I know what the Lakers are!" I retorted.

"Well, I've got front row seats and I was going to ask you to be my guest. You know, I heard that if you go to these events with someone from the opposite sex, you might attract someone. It's the whole security thing. They think that if you are with someone, you must be worth being around. Besides, you're right, we could both do away with eating so much of what we broadcast, or be transferred to the lite eating division!"

I couldn't believe what I was hearing. I wasn't really interested in him; I was interested in finding someone. He was my answer. He knew most of the time when I was in one of my moods, and must have come to work prepared for just this occasion. Was I sure that friendship was really all that I wanted out of this relationship? Yeah, I guess that his wanting me to be his prop date was his answer. That is the only way he saw us. Friends.

"Where are you? Earth to Cleopatra!"

This was his response anytime I spaced out and needed to be brought back to the present. The Cleopatra thing was a pet name he had for me after we worked together on the Egyptian week in desserts. The group on set all dressed up and I came in looking normal. Long mostly straight black hair, with a smidgen of black eyeliner. I guess it was enough. Even though I wasn't dressed up, that is what he called me ever since. I think that it was the non-alikeness that he was referring to.

"I'm right here! Look, I know that I have been in a mood

today, but I think you are right. When's the game?"

I tried to look pleasant and willing to go along with his experiment.

"This Saturday night. Seven o'clock sharp at the Staples Center. Are you coming then?"

He was smiling even more now. I was even more exasperated by this because I really knew that this wasn't for me, it was for him. To find hot chicks! I was so afraid that I would end up alone!

"Yeah, I'll be there. I guess I'll meet you at about 6:45 at the stadium parking lot?"

"No way!" He said that almost too loudly.

People were starting to turn around. I guess they thought he didn't like something in the program. He did tend to overreact to things like that.

"I mean," he began again in a lower voice, "we have to go together from the beginning to the end, or nobody will buy the 'together' part."

I couldn't believe what I was hearing. It was a real pickup sort of date. This somehow was turning into what I was waiting to hear all morning, even if it wasn't.

"Hey, wait a minute, if I'm just a decoy, then what happens if you find Miss Right? Are you just going to ditch me and leave me to find my own way home?" I was confused and I hated to be left anywhere without a clear plan. That is one thing that I learned over the years: never assume anything or you will always end up regretting it.

"Come on, would I do that? I give you my gentleman's promise that I will not leave you, no matter what. Phone numbers only. If there is some good-looking lady out there with my name on her, then she can wait one day to hear from me again!"

With that, I agreed to his proposition wholeheartedly and was actually a little nervous about the possibility of *me* finding love. Was I supposed to be looking at the players as possibilities? I was somewhat of a celebrity in my own way. I couldn't even imagine.

The stint with the Dream Sundaes finally ended, and we went to the next set. They were selling cookies that you could also decorate yourself as the morning show came to a close. I yawned, and realized that for once, I hadn't touched anything we were filming so far. That had promise. That is what I needed. Promise of something better to come. I always worked on my dreams, and they had always come true. It was up to me to dream for something better.

CHAPTER 9

What a Date!

It didn't take long for the weekend to arrive. I wandered around my house aimlessly looking for something to wear. I never was into sports much, and really the only tee shirt I had was from Contra Costa. I'd ditched the sweats and tee shirt look after college. I was trying too hard to hide my age and look professional at all times. Wearing sweats and a tee would never do.

I reluctantly put it on, hoping that it wasn't so noticeable. Contra Costa was upper state, and the schools around here were their rivals. I sure didn't want to go out and get attacked. I slid into my shoes and waited patiently for Ned to arrive.

It was so warm and there was a nice, subtle breeze coming to the door when I opened it. The palm and eucalyptus trees were swaying in the breeze along the street. I felt like I was in tune with the rhythm of the earth. I no longer felt bound by anything. It was so freeing to know that I wasn't really on a date. I didn't put too much thought about us going there to pick people up either. I figured that my chances for finding anyone were slim to none, so I wasn't nervous at all.

He came up the steps with some flowers and greeted me with a peck on the cheek. I was instantly red and wondering what he was up to.

"Ned, what are you doing? I thought that this wasn't a real date!"

"Well, you know, if the whole 'go by yourself' thing doesn't work out, then we have a backup plan, right? Besides, if I do find Ms. Right out there, she might be impressed that I am a gentleman."

"Ned, in these two years we have worked side by side, I can honestly say that you have been nothing but a gentleman." With that, I smiled, glanced at the swaying trees once again, and led the way to his convertible.

"So, what's our game plan?"

"Ok, first we will take our seats and from time to time throughout the game we will take turns going to get concessions, taking bathroom breaks, etc. It will give us time to look around at the crowd and scope out perspectives. Then, if they see you going to the concession stands, they may follow you."

"Yeah, I can see it now. I will gaze across the court, I will take a sip of drink, I'll realize that it's out. I will get up to get my refill, but just as I start walking, some great looking guy will sweep me off my feet. Great, what a plan."

"Hey, it's better than just sitting there hoping for a miracle. That's what we are going to be doing for the team."

We finally arrived at the stadium. It was so packed; it reminded me of why I never cared much for going to these things. It was putting myself out there and that was usually what persuaded me to stay home. We made our way to our seats. I felt like we were in a huge fishbowl because we were so close to the court and everyone was looking down at us, even if they weren't really looking at us. I almost started to chicken out when the game began.

It went exactly how we planned, except that I was so nervous that I couldn't look around to see if the man of my dreams was even around. I did get up several times to get refills and use the bathroom. So much for feeling brave.

"Would you stay put for just a few minutes, please? People are going to wonder if we have some kind of incontinence disorder. Either that, or they'll think we are alcoholics. Either way, sit down and stay for just a few more minutes, please, Liz."

About five minutes later, I sprang up out of my seat and made my way to the bathroom/concessions area. I was going through the hallway that led to the concessions. I realized that I hadn't stopped for a long time. Something told me to look up.

This man was so tall. Not completely basketball player tall, but over six foot two for sure. He was long and lanky, but muscularly built, all at the same time. He had the most beautiful eyes and matching hair. They were almost the same shade of shimmery brown. He looked down toward me. A vision of him and me just came like a movie in my head. We were married and sitting in front of our guests at the reception. We were at the head of the table. I almost tripped over my feet. As I stumbled, he grabbed my arm. Oh no.

"Whoa there. You looked like you were about to fall. Did you have too much to drink already? It isn't even halftime." Ned was right, and I realized that it must have looked that way if someone had been watching me. Ned and I did what we set out to do and sitting idly and watching ball was not it. It probably appeared that I had at least five drinks by now, especially to someone who had been watching.

"Uh, no. Thanks for catching me, but it's not too much drinking, it's just the crowds, I guess. I mean, I'm here with a business associate. This is hardly what we normally do from day to day. I guess I've been a little nervous sitting at the bottom of the court. I'm not a front and center kind of gal, if you know what I mean." I didn't know why I was spilling my guts to this fantastic looking total stranger. Was I trying to scare him off or what?

"Ah, now I understand. Well, you could just hang out back here with me if you'd like. I kinda know this place inside and out. It beats drinking yourself senseless. I can't stand to see young beautiful women in danger around so many willing men."

Willing men? What in the world did that mean? I hadn't been able to will anyone to do anything most of my life. Besides, didn't I just get through telling him that I wasn't drinking all that much yet anyway?

"Uh, thanks, I guess, but I'm not drunk, and I seriously doubt that there are so many men waiting to take me on as prey."

"Well, you are wrong. Before we go any further with this conversation, let me introduce myself. I'm Scott Baker. It's a pleasure to meet you face to face. It's Elizabeth Redbird, right?"

This whole conversation was going too quickly. The man that I saw myself married to was suddenly telling me that he knew who I was already!

"Yes, actually, it *is* Elizabeth. How did you know?"

"I guess that's where you are better not knowing, seeing that you are already self-conscious sitting where you are."

I stood there waiting with my hand on my hip.

"Go on, I can take it."

He continued. "Honestly, those who have ever watched the noon show in San Francisco would know who you are right away. I sure hated it when you left. Where did you go, anyway?"

I didn't know what to do with all of this free talking, especially about myself. How could this great-looking man know anything about me anyway, or care for that matter?

"Listen, as much as I would like to tell you about my last couple of years after the noon show, I really feel like this isn't really the time."

"Wait," he interrupted, "before you go off into the night of the basketball game and leave me here in this hall alone, you have to take my card and promise me a date sometime soon. I would love to take you out and hear all about it."

He gently took my hand and placed a card in it. Then he raised my hands to his mouth and lightly kissed them. A semi-permanent blush came over my face.

"Thank you," I said so meekly that I didn't know if he heard it or not.

"Now, was I stopping you from going to the ladies' room or the concession stands?"

"Neither. I think that I will be just fine." I turned and started going back the way I came. I felt like running and getting high fives from the audience. I was really going to owe Ned a lot for what I'd just accomplished.

"Whoa there, Liz, what's going on?" Ned asked. "I thought that you were going for another drink. What happened? Why are you smiling?"

"You were right, Ned. You were right about everything!" I replied enthusiastically.

I sank into the seat and began to tell the tale of how my prince had finally come. He was here and he was going to call me later.

"Did you give him your number?" he inquired.

"No. He just handed me this." I slid the card into Ned's hand.

He rolled his eyes.

I was suddenly sober. I realized at that moment that I forgot to tell him how to get a hold of me. I wouldn't even tell him where I was working now! I really was an idiot! I started looking around. I was in a panic. How could I let this happen?

"Calm down, Liz. It's just *Scott Baker*. I'll just call him really quickly. I'll let him know that I am your business associate you told him about and tell him your number. It's *really* no big deal."

"It's *just* Scott Baker, huh? Really no big deal?" I looked at him questioningly. "I don't even want to know what you mean by that. If you think he's worth calling back, then..."

"Shh, I'm trying to call here."

"Oh, sorry."

"Ok, it's done. I told him how to get ahold of you and he thanked me and told me how lucky I was to be sitting with you right now."

"He's somewhere up there watching us?"

My face turned red, and I was suddenly sinking in my seat for another reason. I hated to be the center of attention, even when it was good attention.

"Just calm down, Liz. He said that he's in one of those club seats up there. He can see everything from where he is."

"Oh, I guess you're right." The surge of panic was replaced by warmth and excitement. The man of my dreams was looking out for me. "You know, Ned, I'm glad that I gave you such a hard time the other day. This is exactly what we needed to put ourselves out there."

"You'll be putting yourself out there for sure since you'll probably be coming to these games a lot more when you two start dating."

"Why would you say that?"

"I guess some things are worth waiting for!" He snickered.

"Come on, tell me!"

"Keep your voice down, Elizabeth! You'll distract the players! He won't be happy if you distract the players!"

"Oh, whatever! You are just trying to scare me. What, am I going to find out that he owns this team or something?" I said sarcastically.

"I told you, you won't get any information from me. It's up to you to figure out what your boyfriend does for a living. Maybe you can ask him when he calls you."

"Fine."

"Fine."

The rest of the night was spent in silence. We decided to try and watch the game. He was right, if I wanted to know any more about this Scott Baker, it would be up to me.

As for Ned and me, we still had a night to finish together. I felt a profound sense of security as we left the stadium together. Alone in a crowd would never have done.

"So, here we are."

"Yep."

"Thanks so much for taking me out tonight. I may have found the man of my dreams."

"Well, at least one of us was lucky."

"What do you mean? I thought you gave your number out to at least two women! I'm sure any of them will be happy if you call them for a date!"

"You're too kind. You know I don't look like that Scott guy. Girls naturally fall all over him. He's always looked gorgeous."

"First, I don't look like a cheerleader either, *and* there were plenty of those types out there too. So, if I can attract someone like him, you can too."

"Liz, I told you, I'm looking for a girl!"

We began to laugh for a while. It was sad that we were even in this predicament. We really should have had our significant others by now, or at least relationships of some kind.

"Now, listen! I wasn't done! Secondly, you have a lot to offer any girl and you know it. We are both successful professionals. We threw the ball at the net, and I may have made the hoop thingy, but you may have blocked the pass of the other team." He started looking at me funny.

"Oh, you know what I mean. You know that I don't know those basketball terms!"

"Well, I'll help you out with them. You'll need them, seeing as you'll be with Scott and all."

That almost constant smile was back on his face.

"You know, I just know you're saying that to scare me!"

"Yeah, maybe."

"It could be that I decided that tonight was a wonderful date, and I wished that Scott guy didn't come and sweep you off your feet. It would have been convenient to be in love with the person you work with side by side every day."

"Do not start with those *I'm already giving up* words. I won't even hear them! Would it make you feel better if I told you something about work the other day that you didn't know?"

"What would I want to know? Am I getting canned or something? Wow, no date and now I have no job!"

"Quit being sarcastic! No, that is not it at all." I knew that it would sound stupid, but I really felt like his ego needed a boost. I wasn't sure if that is what you would call it, but anything to keep him from self-loathing. "I mean, you'll probably think that I was stupid or something," I continued.

"Would you just get on with it? Whatever it is, I think that I'll take it just the way you think that I will. I have faith."

"Well ok, you know when you came in the other day, and you saw me licking my lips?" I began to blush. I couldn't help it. I couldn't believe that I was going to let that cat out of the bag.

"Yeah, and..."

"And do you remember when you asked me if I wanted some of that to eat?"

"Yep, I have a small memory of that too. You said no because you were fat, right?"

"Oh, shut up! Let me finish my story."

"The court is open to you, Elizabeth." He was smiling so widely by now that I almost couldn't continue my story.

"Ok smarty pants, what I was trying to *say* is that I wasn't looking at the *sundaes* that day when I was licking my lips."

"Well, do tell, what were you looking at then?"

"Yours." I looked away immediately, as my face was the soft hue of scarlet. I didn't know why I thought that would be something appropriate to tell my coworker at that minute. I maintained the thought that he might just need someone to lift him up a little.

"Oh." He paused. "Liz, what does that mean?"

"It means that you are not a loser. It means that if you had noticed the good things that are around you and how you make people feel, then you wouldn't be here with me having this conversation. You wouldn't be alone. Do you understand what I mean?"

He got closer to me than before, as soon as that came out of my mouth. He was looking at me straight in the eyes. I started to look away. I was suddenly embarrassed by what I'd just shared.

"Don't."

"I'm sorry, I shouldn't have said anything, Ned."

"Don't."

"I just thought that if you knew how special you were you could perk up a little. Have a little hope."

"Please, Liz, you don't know what you are saying. We both know that you ramble when you get nervous."

He picked up his hand and placed it on my neck and slowly caressed it to the nape of my neck.

"You have been everything to me these past two years, you know. You have been my best friend." He paused. "Someone who makes it able for me to get through the day. Every time I see your smiling face it makes me so happy. I don't know why I didn't see it before."

"Don't."

"So, you're taking my lines now?"

"Ha, ha, no, I am not. These are my own."

"Ok, well if these are yours, then what else do you want to say?"

I couldn't help what was happening. I was being so reckless by what I was doing right there. I couldn't see anything but my everlasting loneliness. Even with the thought of someone like Scott that could be in my future. I couldn't see past the here. I couldn't see past the now. I leaned in closer to Ned, lost in the moment. He held my neck and gently grabbed my arm as he pulled me into his embrace. The kiss lasted so long it seemed. It was so gentle and loving and I wondered right away why we weren't looking to do this earlier. Like two years or so.

"This could be so easy, Liz, you know?"

"Yeah."

I leaned against his chest, and we sat together and waited for what we were going to decide to do. But nothing ever came from either of us. We sat in silence. I was too scared to say anything. He wasn't trying to seduce me, get me drunk, or steal anything I had. No wonder it took so long for us to come together. He wasn't a loser or a monster. He was the exact opposite of every guy that I was ever attracted to.

I wasn't even really attracted to him the other day, even though that was what I was leading him to believe. No, it wasn't about that kind of attraction. He was my friend. He was who took over when Amelia went off, got married, and moved away.

He was the only true friend that I had at the moment in this whole big city. I knew everyone else at work, and I liked them well enough, but there were never real friendships like the one that Ned and I shared.

"Ned, I just wanted you to understand that whatever happens for us, you are like my best friend in the world right now."

"Ok, is this your kind way of letting me down easy?"

"Look, I started this conversation, didn't I?"

"Yeah, but I bet that you never thought it would end in a kiss like it has."

"Well, no, not really, but it was nice. Ned, you are nice. That is what I am saying. I really think that we should put ourselves out there and find our true loves."

"One date, and she breaks up with me already!"

"No, Ned. It's not like that and you know it. We weren't even on a date tonight and you have at least two girls to call back tomorrow. I just know that you and I both may have found the one."

"Like I said earlier, I know that I am no Scott Baker, so please, do me a favor and quit trying to cheer me up while you tell me that we have no future."

"Look, we have a future. We are always going to be friends. What do you think would happen if we started dating for real? Just say that we start to get into petty fights. Where would that take us at work? You know that they frown on workplace romance anyway."

"Ok then. You've made your point, and it is well taken. Listen, I better head home."

I reached over and grabbed his arm. I knew that I was giving him mixed signals, but I still didn't care. I reached up to his face. I grabbed his chin and brought it to mine. I began to aggressively say that I was sorry using no words. Why, oh why, couldn't I have just let this go. What was wrong with me? Here he was, he had the message loud and clear. Now, I was just erasing everything that I had just explained. He pulled away, took my hand, and kissed it for the second time that night. Just now it was by the man who I wasn't supposed to be on a date with.

"Elizabeth, thank you, but pity sex with a coworker is definitely not what we need right now!"

He began to smile once again.

"Shut up, Ned."

We began to laugh. It was the perfect ending to the fiasco that we nearly created. I watched him get in his car all the while hoping that I hadn't done the wrong thing by stopping him. The realization that all my future love life was riding on some handsome stranger that I only met once was so frightening. I turned and went inside, took a hot bath, and went straight to bed. There had been enough excitement for one night.

"Ugh, fake dates."

That was the last thing that trailed out of my lips before I drifted off to sleep.

CHAPTER 10

The Future is Now

I had been waiting my whole life for it to begin the right way. How many times had I started over in my life just to be lacking in the one thing that would get me through it? I needed love. I needed that close relationship that I had lost so long ago with my family.

It always brought me back to the fact that my parents found time for love. No, it wasn't with them together and it definitely wasn't shared with me. What was wrong with me? Why was my love so unobtainable?

I needed more than what Ned could have given me. Yes, he was my best friend, but that was all that I could see him as. He just wasn't my *it*. It had been almost a week from that fateful *date* with Ned and I still had yet to hear from Scott. I glanced at his card from time to time, wondering if I should be bolder and just pick up my phone and call him.

"Look, Liz, if you really could see a future with him, I say go for it. You know, maybe he lost your number the other day."

"Ned, you know good and well that if you called him on his cell phone then he would have a record of your call at the very least. He could have called you back and asked for my number again."

"Well, maybe he's shy. I mean, after all, just because he's a multi-millionaire playboy, that doesn't mean that he has courage in dating. Aren't you the one that told me that he was a fan of yours at one point in your career? Maybe he's embarrassed now."

"*Yeah right.* Oh, another thing, would you please stop talking about him that way? You're starting to freak me out. Is he really rich, or are you just being totally full of it?"

"I told you, it was for you to figure out. Did you try to check out his name on the web yet?"

"No, and I'm not going to. I will find out about him face-to-face."

"Suit yourself."

"Quit with that smirk or I'll have to come over there and wipe it off myself."

"Oooo, what are you going to do, come and kiss me again?"

"Would you please be quiet? We are around other people, you know. I really doubt that we want what happened to go around the set. Did you want people talking?"

"Oh, alright then, I'll lay off of the personal stuff here. Well, or at least while there are others around us. You better hope you never get caught alone with me."

"Yeah, well then *maybe* I'll call Scott. *Maybe* I can get him to make *you* be quiet."

"Liz, I didn't say anything about him being a hit man. I really don't think that is how he gained all of that wealth."

I went to slug him on the shoulder for that one. I unfortunately had to stop. Our next item was up for sale. It was a set of seemingly normal springform pans, but these were made from some new material. It was dessert alright. It smelt wonderful. I leaned back in my chair and took in the aroma that surrounded the set. This was going to be hard to resist the rest of my life. I quickly wondered if this was even the job that I should be in. No, it was without saying that this was the job that I was meant to do. I loved it, even if it was tough not to pig out on desserts all day.

"Why don't you give me that card. I can call him for you. I'll ask if he's still interested. I'll let him know that you have other guys lined up for you and he'd better hurry or the rest of us might just try to sweep you off of your feet."

"No, you won't, and shh, the program is starting."

"Ok." He winked at me and turned to look over at the set.

The rest of the day had been very uneventful. We had anything from a five-minute show to a thirty-minute one and by the time 11:00 o'clock came we were really ready for our day to be over.

"So, what did you decide? Are you calling him or what?"

"Wait right there." I pulled out my phone and began to make the fateful call. It went right to voicemail.

"Listen!" I handed him my phone. "Ok. See? I tried. He's not available for some reason right now. I'll just text him, if that makes you happy."

I began texting Scott. *Scott, hey there! This is Elizabeth Redbird. Just thought I'd see if you were busy this weekend. Call me.*

"There, that's finished. He will either call me, or he already forgot about me."

"If he knew who you were, he didn't forget about you, I can promise. I bet that he's just really busy working. I don't see how he'd have time for anything, really."

"Don't gloat, Ned. Just because you know him doesn't mean you know his schedule. Besides, just because you say he's rich and I say that he's handsome doesn't mean that he is worth my time. He'll have to prove that!"

"Well, good for you. We all know how picky you are with guys. I mean, look at me. If I wasn't enough, then how does that poor guy have a chance?"

I really felt that I needed to stop that conversation. I wasn't going to bring him down. That was not why I told him what I did yesterday. It was to boost his confidence, not to tear it to pieces.

"Ya wanna go for some coffee?" I asked.

"I told you that I'm not dating you. I've had enough of that mistreatment," he teased.

"What? Kissing you was mistreatment?"

"No, stopping. That was mistreatment." He smiled crookedly.

Again, I didn't want this kind of conversation.

"Do you want to get some coffee with me or not?"

I was beginning to get agitated.

"Ok, ok, you don't have to get all riled up. I was kidding, just kidding."

"Yeah, well, keep it up and we'll see if I ever invite you out again."

We went to the coffee bar down the street. Since it was so early, lunch was just starting, which meant that the nooners hadn't come out yet. We had the place almost to ourselves.

"Do you know that I really do hope he calls you? At least then we will be on an even playing field."

"What are you talking about?"

"Well, you know, if he comes a calling and turns out to be a rich prick that treats you badly, then I'll have my chance."

"Wait a minute. I thought the whole reason for us going out was for you and me both to find someone. Where are the girls that you got numbers from? What if they are like me and wondering if they were just unmemorable?" "I doubt that, but ok then. It just so happens that I have their numbers right here in my wallet. Maybe I will just start the calling spree."

"I wish you would. This whole fixation on me thing is beginning to get old."

"Are you sure that you won't be jealous?"

"Just call."

"Ok, but it's your loss when they fall head over heels for me and you lost out on your chance."

"I'll make a deal with you. Let me just talk to Scott and if nothing happens, then we will see about us. I have to at least give him a shot. I pictured us married the moment I saw him. I mean, wouldn't that be like giving up on true love if I didn't follow through?"

"I guess. I know that none of those feelings happened when I met Jessica and Maria. They were really good looking, but I know that our front court tickets were what impressed them. So, they are both probably gold diggers. I guess I'll see."

He took his phone out of his pocket and began to dial.

"Yes, this is Ned Deblin. I talked to you the other night at the basketball game. Yes, I gave you a number.

"What happened, do you think that this kind of beauty will just wait around for someone that doesn't appreciate it?

"Yes, I am.

"Yes, she is.

"Nope, not now. She seems to be hung up on you."

At this very moment I began to cringe. He wasn't talking to Jessica or Maria. He was talking to Scott Baker!

"Stop, Ned! Why did you call him?"

I guess I shouldn't have said anything because he abruptly handed the phone to me.

"Hello?

"Yes, it's Elizabeth.

"Yes, I guess I have kind of hoped to hear from you.

"No, I'm not involved with Ned.

"Yes, I would like to see you sometime.

"Right now? What do you mean?"

I slowly turned around and there he stood. He was still as tall and as handsome as ever. His dark hair just seemed to flow with the air that was around us. He was beautiful. I started to breathe hard. I didn't understand what was going on. How did he know where I was? Did he know or was it a coincidence?

"Ms. Redbird, I presume."

He took my hand and gently brought it to his lips. I began to shake.

"Mr. Baker, where on earth did you come from?"

"Come and sit down and I'll tell you all about it."

He pulled the seat out for me, and we sat at the same table I was just sitting at with Ned. Ned, where was Ned?

"Where is Ned? What is going on?"

"He just wanted to set up a time for us to meet for the first time, and he is giving us space. "

"I don't understand."

"The other day after the game, Ned called me and told me how special you were to him. He told me that if I didn't contact you soon that he was going to do everything in his power to keep you for himself. I guess that it was kind of a warning."

"He's been talking to you?"

"Yes, for the last couple of days."

"Then, why didn't you call me?"

I couldn't believe that I was talking to him like this. He owed me no explanation.

"I really don't know. I guess the fact that you are beautiful and successful and that Ned really seemed to like you. I just felt that I was imposing on your life. I mean, you guys were on a date the other night, right?"

"Look, I don't know what Ned told you, but I thought I made it clear the other day that I was there with a business associate. Didn't I make that clear?"

"Actually, yes you did. I guess it was Ned's reaction to me that made me a little confused. I know that there are work-place relationships all of the time. Why should your life be so different?"

"Maybe because I have been waiting for someone special. I mean, don't get me wrong, Ned is wonderful, but we have been working together for years now. Why would I just decide now that this was our time? He is like a best friend to me, but not compatible as a love partner."

"So, you are looking for a love partner and you think I'm special?"

He began to smile and took my hand across the table. I looked him straight in the eyes.

"If there is someone special out there worthy of my love."

"Whoa, now don't be so cold yet. Don't we at least have to date before you can throw me low blows?"

"Sorry, I have been on my own way too long, I guess. I don't know how to speak other than very frankly."

"I'll forgive you. I have to say that I am the same way."

The order just came up when we made our truce. At least food would get in the way of saying anything else to scare him away. He continually gazed directly at me with his large russet eyes. I began to smile unwillingly. How could this be happening? I was captivated and he knew it. We both could feel it.

"So, Liz, you work for the Culinary Shopper's Network?"

"Yes, I do, and I love it."

"It's good to find a job that you like so well. I wished I could say that about myself all of the time."

"Ok, I have a question for you then."

"Shoot."

"Who are you, Mr. Baker? It seems you know a lot about me, and I am at a definite disadvantage."

"Well, I am many things. I am one of the only people out there that didn't invest badly, so you could say that I am an investor. I invest in things that either I enjoy or that I know will make me money."

"Ok, that still doesn't tell me who you work for."

"Oh, I guess you could say that I'm self-employed then."

"As an investor."

"You catch on very quickly." There was a kind smile in his voice.

"Anything I have heard of?"

"Maybe."

"Did Ned put you up to this? He knew that I had no idea of who you were, and he wouldn't tell me a thing. He just kept calling you rich."

"Ned is funny. I really like that guy."

"Well great, I'll tell him and maybe the two of you can go out sometime."

The sarcastic tone was back in my voice.

"Sorry, but I have a feeling that I'll be busy with the love of my life."

What did he just say? Did I hear that right? Was it possible for two people to think of each other exactly in the same way?

"Well, I'd better go then. I don't want you to keep her waiting."

I just couldn't help but throw that in. I was getting giddy at this point and needed something to release the tension I was feeling. I began to laugh. He began to smile.

"You know it took a lot to say that just now, don't you?"

"I know. I guess that you are just braver than I am. If I told you how I felt about you the first time I saw you, then you probably wouldn't be here right now."

"I am here, Elizabeth, because of how I felt the first time we met."

"Oh. I guess you have a point. I just never imagined in a million years that you would have seen me the same way that I saw you."

"How would that be exactly?"

I was looking so intensely into his eyes that it seemed as if we were alone. Everyone else seemed to be gone. We were on our own planet. We flew to Venus, and we were suddenly sitting in a room of pure love.

"If I tell you, please don't laugh or put too much into it."

"Promise."

Just then, his phone began to ring. How could this be happening?

"Keep going. I'll call them back."

"Ok, I looked in your eyes and I could see a future. I saw us on our wedding day. We were so happy and so in love. I almost didn't want to leave you that night. I would have, would have..."

His phone began to vibrate again.

"Go on, they can take care of things without me during one lunch!"

"Just tell me you want to see me again or not. I need to know. I want to begin my future now, if you know what I mean."

"I know exactly what you mean. Look, I guess I'd better go. These people don't know their way out of a paper bag!"

"Ok."

I looked down. I was suddenly wrought with sadness. How is it possible to feel like you don't want to let go of a stranger?

"Come with me today. You are done with work now, aren't you? Come with me and I can show you what I do. It's much more fun than just hearing about it, I guarantee."

My mood cheered up at once. It was like he could read my mind.

"I would really like that."

He paid for our lunch and left a sizable tip, even though I never remembered a host, and grabbed my hand as we headed for the door.

It was beginning to rain as we left the coffeehouse. I reached above my head in response. We ran toward his car. It was a Tesla. He clicked for the doors to automatically open and we jumped in. I asked him what I should do about my car. He said that we could always go back and get it later. I was worried about getting a ticket for it being there too long. He didn't seem concerned.

"Really, I think that it might be best for me to meet you where you are going. I really don't need to be breaking the law by leaving my car there longer than I need to."

"I know that we don't know each other too much yet, but take my word for it, it will be ok. I'll explain when we get to my work."

We pulled up to a large building in the Upper Downtown district of Los Angeles.

"Here we are. This would be where I work."

I was a bit confused. We were at Bakersfield Towers.

"Um, is it just me, or does your name somehow resemble the name of this building?"

"Yeah, you could say that. My grandfather built this from the ground up. He named it Bakersfield Towers because this land was once our family farm field. It was literally the Bakers' family field."

"That's cool. FYI, I was actually raised on a farm for half of my adolescence."

"Well, well, we have things in common already. The rest of the family land is still farmland. It's a little east from here."

"Let me guess, you own the vast land of the rolling poppy fields?"

I said that kind of sarcastically. I knew that there was no way they owned that too.

"It's like you're picking my brain and reading my mind. That is exactly where our land is!"

I couldn't believe it. I was just kidding. I was in awe of such a lucky estate. I realized that not only did he have the looks and we had this wonderful raw connection, but he was brought up with the same family values that I began my life with.

We entered the doors of Bakersfield Towers.

"Hello there, Mr. Baker!"

"Hello, Conrad!"

"Who's this lovely lady you have with you today?"

"This is Elizabeth Redbird. She is here as my guest today. She unfortunately left her car in town at the coffeehouse. What do you say to rounding it up and bringing it to her house?

She will give you her address along with her keys. We would appreciate it all so much, Conrad."

"As you wish, Sir. I will contact you when the car has arrived at its destination."

"Thank you, Conrad, you are the best."

I stood there stunned by what was happening. I handed the keys right to Conrad and told him my address. I knew that Ned was talking about how wealthy that Scott was, but I never could have imagined that it was like this. I was in awe once again. It was so interesting to feel that way about someone. It took so much to impress me and usually no amount of money could warrant my respect, but this was different. He was different. I was different.

"Uh, Scott, you didn't have to go so far as to interrupt his day for that."

"Silly Beth, please know that with Conrad, whatever I need for him to do is exactly what he is supposed to do at that very moment. You could call him my assistant if you want."

Nicknames already? No one ever called me Beth before. I suppose that was better than Lizzy. I wouldn't ever be able to handle anyone calling me that again. Not with all the bad memories that the old name brought back to me. Actually, the only person left in my life that was allowed that name was Amelia.

I suddenly wondered if this was how she felt when she first met Adam. I had always thought of them as some kind of bright sun. Now, I couldn't help feeling like I might just be glowing myself.

Without even a single hesitation more, I reached to place his beautiful face in my hands. I somehow didn't care if his colleagues were around, or if anyone at all was watching. I leaned in and lightly kissed his lips.

"Thank you, Mr. Baker."

There was such a warmth coming from both of us then.

"Elizabeth, you *really* need to come to my office. Hopefully, there won't be anyone in the area right now waiting for me. If there is, I promise that I will take care of it immediately. I don't want this place to ruin what kind of magic we are experiencing right now. You may want to stay in reception with my secretary while I take care of business. It might get a little rough, especially after they ruined my lunch with you."

I never knew of any man willing to fight the masses just because we were interrupted. I'd been on tons of dates in the past that ended early due to friends overtaking our time. Very rarely did I even hear a sorry, let alone a real brawl in the boardroom. Not over me.

"Hey, if you are asking me if it's ok for you to get people off your back so you can spend time with me, then I say do what you have to. I'll miss you while you are in there."

He reached for my hand and gently squeezed it and placed it to his lips. Kissing hands must be a proper gentleman thing. Never in my life had I been treated so much like a queen—yet it wasn't with Ned, even though he'd associated me with the great Cleopatra. Scott really was my Mark Antony.

CHAPTER 11

History

We were suddenly caught in another time in the fields of the Bakers. He kept my hand in his as he led the way to the elevators. As we were traveling up to the fifteenth floor, the elevator became suddenly crowded.

We were pushed somehow to the rear corner. He was wedged in the corner and I in front of him. We were so close, I could feel his breath on the back of my hair. I wanted nothing more than to turn around and show him that even though we were almost total strangers, I wanted him more than any man I had ever wanted in my life. Nothing even compared to the raw feelings that I had for this cornered lion who was ready to defend his lioness in just three more floors.

The doors opened to the fifteenth floor, and nothing less than a mass of people suddenly surrounded us. They were grabbing at Scott. They were grabbing him and showing him papers and became somewhat aggressive towards him. They wanted his time as much as I did. He took it in complete stride, kept my hand, and explained to everyone that I was a very important guest and he needed to seat me before any business could take place.

As he took off his suit coat, I suddenly noticed the sheer quality of the plain white shirt that he was wearing. It was professionally pressed, and he was the sexiest man that I had ever seen. I was blindly guided to my seat in a very intimate seating arrangement. His secretary, Lucy, offered me something to drink, which I declined. I didn't plan on waiting long enough to finish a beverage of any size.

In five minutes, Scott returned to me. He had a large smile on his face. It was the closest to going home as the old farmhouse would have been, earlier in my life.

"We'd better go. I think that I left them stunned. They are very unaccustomed to me not staying on task with what they have for me at every moment. Like I said before, they cannot think for themselves. They worry me constantly with such trivial things."

"You do not have to tell me twice! Where are we going next?" I replied in excitement.

"Well, I would like to take you to my office. It is just around this other corner. As you can tell, it is kind of hidden. You would have to have been in my office in the past to even know that it existed. My grandfather designed it with security in mind. It was a rougher time back then and I think that he wanted a place of refuge if something were to go badly. Luckily, it never did, and now I have the most secluded office anywhere in LA and it is right under everyone's noses."

"Your stories of your family are so fascinating! I would love to meet them someday!"

"Oh, Elizabeth, it is so rare that I encounter someone who knows so little about me. It is refreshing. Thank you for the goodwill towards my family, but they are all but gone. Heart disease runs so badly in my family. I lost both my grandfather and my father to the horrible disease. I always assumed that I would probably have the same fate that they had. I want to turn it around for my grandchildren to have someone to look up to, like I did my grandfather. I'm not as young as they were when they started their families, so I need to live longer just to see future generations grow."

I'm not sure how it happened, but as we were making our way to the entrance to his hidden office space, I think he was implying that he was ready to start a family with me. This must be the oddest of all conversations that any two almost strangers ever spoke.

"Well, I'm sorry to hear that, but also happy to hear that you plan to live a long and healthy life."

We entered what could only be described as the most ornate space that existed in this city. I never knew that such beauty existed anymore. Most of the old buildings had fallen throughout the years due to earthquakes, fires, and disrepair. The thought that there would be one place left restored was like going back in time. From the fixtures to the hand-carved wood panels along the wall. It was grand enough for some king, just a bit smaller than that of a room in a palace.

"Oh, this is the most beautiful room I believe I have ever seen in my life. I can't believe it is even here! It's just as hard to imagine that I am here with you. If this is a dream, don't wake me up."

He took me by the hand and sat me down on a leaning bench. One that has no back, except for on the side. It was one that two could sit on or one could lie on. He seemed to be fascinated by how I fit just right to its specifications.

"This was once my grandmother's bench, a chaise lounge, actually. My grandfather made it so that when she came to visit, she would be in nothing but pure comfort. It was said they were first built for Egyptian royalty. I know it's old and probably doesn't feel as good as it did seventy years ago, yet look how well it supports you. I hope you aren't taken aback by my comparison with you and my grandmother."

Did I hear him correctly? Egyptian royalty, really? How is this happening to me yet again?"

"Actually, the way you describe them, it would be an honor even to carry out any of the heritage that you have left of them. To tell you the truth, it *is* very comfortable. Even comfortable enough for a queen!"

"Good. You are a queen indeed."

He leaned down and began to kneel in front of me. I almost didn't want him to do anything that would damage the suit that he was wearing, unless I was doing harm to it while unclothing him.

His face became so close to mine I could no longer tell whose breath was whose.

"It's a tradition in my family to sit in front of this bench and look into the eyes of the woman that you feel you could spend the rest of your life with. It is supposed to make things clearer. The world outside can't touch us here."

I was a bit weary at the thought that what I did at this very moment would decide some fate that I was never a part of. I reached down and touched his soft, thick hair. I leaned down to kiss it like he was a child and I was saying goodbye before school. It was as if our family had already started. This place was waiting for me my whole life and in my wildest dreams I could have never found such a perfect place or man to go along with it.

"Is there something that I should be doing?"

"Yes, actually."

Before I could get *what* out of my mouth, he leaned up, caught me by the waist, and pulled me to the floor. I suddenly felt disheveled. I was unprepared for this level of passion. It was all of the passion that I wished for all of these years out of relationships I had tried but was so unsuccessful with. There were many times that I wished that this guy or that were the one. It never occurred to me that it really existed. The one, he was *the* one.

It wasn't long before we were regaining our composure, having just experienced the best moment *I hoped* that *either* of us had in our lives. Pure elation wouldn't be able to describe what had just occurred. We were completely clothed, and it astonished me how a kiss could give you that same feeling as making love.

It was like the first date I never had. I would have given anything to erase the past at that moment. I wanted to forget all of the lessons that I learned the hard way. He respected me too much to take full advantage of me in this foreign place. I knew at that moment that he was in it for the long haul. He wasn't looking for a girl of instant gratification, even though that is what he just gave to me.

"Well, Scott, thank you so much for the most enjoyable tour of your historic office. I do hope that I didn't get lipstick on you. I don't want anyone on the outside of this office to get the wrong idea."

"Elizabeth, I don't care what idea they have. Let them think what they want. You will be the one that I will share my life with. This room confirmed everything that I was ever told."

"What exactly were you told?"

I was beginning to worry. Was this going to turn into some predestination stuff? Was I going to find out that he was a little off in the head?

"It's nothing, really. It's an old wives' tale in my family. Like I said before, it had to do with the seat you were on. It was how you reacted to what we were doing. Elizabeth, I have never taken another woman in this room in my life. My own grandmother and mother were the only women allowed in this office. Very few men are allowed in here, for that matter. We usually do everything out of the boardroom that you saw as I was meeting with my colleagues."

"Look, not to say that I didn't just enjoy that immensely,

but you are kind of creeping me out. I mean, oh, I'm sorry, I should just learn to keep my opinions to myself."

I looked down in fear of looking into his eyes. Was he disappointed or mad? I slightly raised my head and peeked through my eyelashes.

"No, don't worry. I don't blame you in the least bit. We don't even know each other properly yet and I am already talking about this future that I am sure we are going to have. I just hope that I'm not scaring you off."

"I doubt that I could ever be frightened by you. I guess I'm just not sure how to comprehend what you are saying. I've never had a future with anyone. I definitely have not had anyone that lays claim to me after just a lunch date. You are a rare individual, Scott Baker. I'll give you that."

"Thank you for the kindness and understanding. Look, why don't we get out of here. I would like to show you something."

I didn't know whether to be afraid of this or not. It wasn't like anyone to be so blatantly enthusiastic about me. It almost reminded me of the horror show you'd see when the guy turns into a ghost and then disappears into a graveyard, or when some girl goes onto some country road and then breaks down and gets hacked up. Either way, it wasn't the kind of outcome I wanted out of my day.

"Scott, I am grateful for the time you've given to me, but unfortunately, I have to go back to work for a while. We're done taping, but I have some paperwork that is still waiting on me. There is also prep for tomorrow's segments that needs my attention. I don't generally take the day off after the show. That is why they like me so much. I have no life, normally. As your associates are used to your every attention to their needs, so are mine."

I looked him straight in the face when I said this. I wanted to make sure that he got it loud and clear that as fun an afternoon as we were having, it was going to end.

"Elizabeth, I do understand. What do you think that I was doing the whole time I was in the room with all the suits? I told them that even though I was there like an overworked mule, I wasn't interested in carrying any of them the rest of the day. I gave up everything just to be with you today."

"Oh Scott, I'm sorry. Please don't be angry. I guess my work can wait for a day too."

I had such a hard time saying that. I just hoped that he didn't know me enough to know I didn't mean a word of it. I just wanted to get out of there. I didn't care how it happened, I wanted to find a place away from him. I guess that he was coming on too strong and I wasn't prepared.

"Beth, why on earth would I be angry with you? If you need to go back to work, then you just go back. I promise I will be completely quiet while we are at your office. As soon as you finish up, we can go where I want to go. I can be patient, I promise."

For some reason, the thought of him coming with me to work eased my tension a little bit. If he would so wholeheartedly accept that I needed to do something rather than be with him, then maybe he wasn't such a creep.

"Thank you so much, Scott! Thanks for understanding about my job!"

"I understand completely. We can't *all* own the companies where we work, now can we?"

He stood with a weird smirk on his face. I turned from him and headed out the door. I went straight for the elevator. I never even looked back. How in the world could we have gone from complete bliss to being freaked out and scared? It didn't make sense. I must be putting more into things than they are. *So what* if he compared us to his family? *So what* if he wanted us to be together forever?

Maybe this was all moving just a little too fast for me. I wasn't so used to letting people in. I wasn't used to having people let me in the way that he just had. I wasn't used to people liking me for no good reason. It's one thing to tease myself about my body beginning to look grandmotherly, but the last thing that I wanted was for someone to like me for it. That was creepy.

"Elizabeth, wait!"

I guess that I was walking at a jog instead of the brisk pace I thought I was keeping.

"Scott, really, I think that this is just going a little too quickly for me. I'm so sorry, but I really just have to go."

What comes around goes around. My same old habits of retreat were still engrained in me as they had ever been. He caught me before the elevator closed. It was an awkward trip down the fifteen floors we had come up earlier. I said nothing, and neither did he. I began to see that he finally realized that he had said too much.

He was too enthusiastic about someone he'd just met. Of course, he didn't know how to take things in stride. He was usually in control of every situation and people bent over backwards to give him what he wanted. I was just not a bender.

"Get the town car now, Conrad. She has to return to work at this instant!"

I wasn't sure if he was mad about my rejection, or if he was just trying to show how helpful he could be in my time of crisis.

"Elizabeth, you will return to work without me, and I promise you that I will keep my distance if that is what you wish. Perhaps one day we will meet again. Until then, I do suppose that my colleagues would appreciate my presence." He had such a look of anguish in his eyes.

"Scott, that is not what I meant at all. I don't want to keep my distance. You have just left my head spinning to the clouds and I am so used to being grounded that I must have become afraid of heights. I'm so sorry. I was being silly. Please, let us continue this afternoon together. Take me where you wanted to. I would love to come."

I wasn't sure why I was all of a sudden so willing to spend the rest of the afternoon with someone that had potential red flags. At that moment, I wished that I had time to text Amelia to just let her know what was happening and to see her point of view on the subject. Was I being too eager to please because I so desperately craved the love that he was promising? Could I wholeheartedly trust my feelings that told me he was my love at first sight?

"Elizabeth, I can see with my own eyes when things are and aren't right with people. You don't have to lie to spare my feelings. I can see now that our feelings were not at all the same."

"Scott, you couldn't be farther from the truth. Please let me spend the day making it up to you."

I took a deep breath as I contemplated my decision not to run for the first time in my life. Conrad brought the car around and had a solemn look on his face. It was as if he knew the temper that his boss could possess and knew when to be friendly and when to be quiet and do as he was told.

"That will be all. I will drive her myself. Thank you very much, Conrad."

"Yes Sir, Mr. Baker."

"If that is really what you would like to do, then I will be eternally grateful for the second chance that you are giving me."

We got to his Tesla, and he reached for the door before I could get a chance at it.

"Ladies first."

At that moment, I remembered that he made me feel like Cleopatra from the beginning. My Mark Antony was still being respectful despite my apprehensive attitude. That seemed to be all it took, and we were both on the same playing field once again. I turned before I entered the car. I placed one hand on his cheek, pulled myself towards him, and brushed his lips with mine.

"I am so sorry for acting so strange a minute ago. I don't know what came over me."

He looked at me with the eyes I had instantly begun to adore, grabbed me by the shoulders, and kissed me rather fervently. He forgave me as I had forgiven his behavior from before. We both weren't going to let this newly budding love just vanish without a fight.

CHAPTER 12

Mystery

Gone without so much as another word, we headed for the country. I knew almost right away where he was taking me. The traffic in the city was horrendous. It seemed to take almost an hour just to get to Route 55. I sat with the anticipation of a child about to open a present at Christmas. The further we drove into the country, the more we were heading for the mountains. I was giddy with expectation of the sight and then they appeared. They were just what I had read about hills and valleys of beautiful orange poppies. I began to smile unconsciously.

Scott drove to a post and then began to turn off of the road onto a small, unpaved drive with seemingly no end. It was leading up the mountainside itself. There were bright blooms cascading wildly around us. We turned a corner and out of nowhere was a small village of cabin houses. It, like his office, reminded me of a different time. Other than the farmhouse when I was little, I was never exposed to any kind of country setting.

"Well, what do you think?"

"It's beautiful!"

"You're beautiful."

His handsome smile was back where it belonged. Everything *was* beautiful. It was so surreal.

"We'd better get inside pretty soon. I think that the rain front is following us."

I looked back, and he was right. It was looming just over the first hills we passed on the way out. By the way the wind was blowing, it would reach us in about ten minutes or less.

"Oh, Scott, can we just go look at the poppies for a little bit? I heard of these hills when I first moved to LA, but I never found the time to go and find them on my own. The view here is spectacular."

"I have to say, they are probably much more impressive to you than they are to me, since I grew up in these fields."

"Well, tell me something about them that only *you* would know."

"Did you know that these fields are at least a hundred years old? The flowers reseed themselves year after year. I hear it began with just a small garden, and one day the winds came and blew on the little flowers so hard that every seed from the poppies spread far and wide and each seed produced a new flower by the next spring. The hills have been left pristine ever since just because of the sheer beauty. Only this side of the hill belongs to me, up to that fence." He pointed to a fence many yards away. "Our family donated the rest as a nature preserve to keep anyone from trying to purchase and develop the land."

"You have been very blessed, haven't you?"

"Oh, let's not go to that conversation. Everyone is blessed if you are alive and willing to fight for what you want in life."

"If that is true, then why was it that when we were leaving

Bakersfield Towers you were so ready to let me go? Why didn't you fight for me?"

"You remind me of the seeds, Elizabeth. You are wild and untamed. You go where you want, and you do what you want. We are both very similar in that aspect. I also know how I feel when I have been made to accept people that I may find not so entertaining. I never wanted you to feel that way about me."

"Scott, I don't think that anyone could call you unentertaining."

Our hands found each other's as the breeze picked up. The rain was getting closer all the time. I had somehow allowed us to wander out into the fields about a quarter of a mile. I began to turn around to try to make it back to the car before the storm. As we were approaching the vehicle, large drops of rain fell down on us.

"Oh my gosh, we'd better hurry, or we'll be drenched in a matter of seconds!"

"Where are you going, Elizabeth? We are not going back to the car. We are headed for that cabin over there!"

Just down the path a bit was a rustic yet fairly large log cabin. Hand in hand we ran, drenched with the rain he told me would come. I should have listened to him earlier. I shouldn't have led him so far out into the field.

We ducked for cover under the large porch. He led me to a porch swing that was just to the right-hand side.

"If you would like, you can sit out here and watch the rain come and go over the fields. I will just go inside for a few seconds and start some coffee and bring out a towel."

"I can go inside with you if you'd like. I mean, this is just fine, thank you."

"Quit being so polite. You are not a guest here. I'll be right back."

What could he mean that I wasn't a guest here? Of course, I was. I had no rights to this beautiful countryside more than poor Conrad back at the office. I leaned back on the swing and noticed a beautiful mural painted on the ceiling of the porch.

It looked like the old west. There were buggies and steam trains and women in long dresses. It was of a sunset very similar to the one that was approaching us this very moment. I was suddenly aware of how long it had taken to get here. It was nowhere near sunset when we left LA.

I heard the creaking of the door and looked up to a huge towel and a platter filled with a coffee setting. There was a small cut log on its end in front of us. He set the platter there and brought me the towel.

"Are you cold?"

"A little. If it weren't so windy, I think that it might actually feel nice."

"Well, please let me wrap this around you and get some warm liquid in you."

"Thank you."

I sat there being waited on hand and foot. I wasn't sure where this was going. He obviously didn't want me to go inside. He'd brought me out here for some reason, yet he seemed apprehensive of showing me the final piece to this puzzle of the afternoon.

He finally joined me on the swing and began to share my towel without hesitation. Any closer, and I would have been sitting on his lap. My head was leaning against his shoulder as he rocked us back and forth. The sound of the rain and the warmth of the towel, body heat, and coffee were too much for my consciousness to handle. I was drifting off to sleep and there was nothing I could do about it.

I began to dream. I was in an old Western town, and I had a beautiful, very large dress on. There was a man with a poppy in his hand. It was Scott, but he was dressed like me, in old formal wear. We were out in the streets, and he was coming towards me. I was smiling because I knew that he was my beau. He held the flower that was in his hand as if he were passing it to me. It wasn't long before I heard a loud bang. Scott fell to the ground. The flower got picked up by the wind and blew away. It was as if the flower was somehow his soul and it had left. It scattered in the breeze. Complete sadness came over me and I began to weep in my sleep.

"Beth, wake up. What's wrong? You must have been having a bad dream."

I lifted my head, realizing that I may have not been sitting particularly ladylike, hoping that I was still upright. I looked in his eyes and was swept up in the moment. It was a dream. He was not dead. The love of my life was still here. He had not gone away. Tears were still streaming down my face.

"I love you."

The words came out of my lips before I could stop them. It was like some force was surrounding us. Like we were the people in the picture on the ceiling. He sat his cup down and began once again to pick up where we left off in his office. Awake or sleeping, I had only one conclusion. This was the man I was supposed to live the rest of my life with. My cries began to back off the more my true consciousness took me into reality. We sat back in the swing for a moment as he dried my tears on the large towel.

"Not that I am not enjoying this enthusiasm from you, but may I ask what prompted the crying?"

"I had a dream that you died right in front of me. We were standing in an old town, and we were wearing clothes that looked much like those"—I pointed up to the painting on the ceiling. "You were coming to me with a large orange poppy and as you reached out to give it to me, you were shot in the back and fell to my feet. As I awoke, I was never so happy to see someone in my whole life."

"Well, that would justify the enthusiasm. You do realize though that I am just fine, and we are sitting here, right?"

"Of course, I do. I am perfectly awake. I know that there is nothing that is going to take you away from me right at this second. I know that it was just a silly dream."

"Look, I don't want to freak you out again, but what would

you say if I told you something very similar happened around the 1890s?"

"Is this again coincidental to your family history?"

"*Maybe.*"

He gave me the smirk that he had given me earlier at the office. This time I took it for what it was. He wasn't trying to be creepy; he was just expressing his pleasure that our lives were supposed to coexist for some reason.

"Well, we all know that we can't change the past. I also know that I am part of the future, not just some rerun of a past event. I just know that at the moment of my dream, I had a strong connection to you. I won't ever be able to let you go. Why do you think that is? Please tell me this story of your family."

"Believe it or not, you just dreamt it. My great-grandparents came here to build a home. They went into town one day and my great-grandfather, who was the town banker, was gunned down by no other than a stranger. He had seen my great-grandmother and wanted her for himself. The sheriff came out right away and arrested the man. He was hung the next day. My great-grandfather was buried right out in the field. The poppies that you see now actually started on his grave site. Like I said, a gust of wind took all the seeds and spread them. Every spring they spread to more areas and my great-grandmother's broken heart was healed a little every year. She would say to my grandparents that it was like he was bringing more flowers the older that she got. Our family will always see them as a flower of perfect love."

"Is that what the mural above us is?"

"Yes, basically it is the story of their lives. Throughout the years, we have seen some disrepair come to the porch, but out of respect for the story, we leave it so it can be told again."

"Wow."

That was all that I could think to say at that very moment. I wasn't sure what that meant for us. Our future was surely not the same in any way. There was no Wild West, there were already poppies covering every square inch of the fields. I knew that the story of our lives would be dramatically different. No past event had any bearings to the real life of today. I just wished I could get that sinking feeling out of my stomach.

I looked over to him once again and stared in his eyes. Maybe what was going on was a bit mystical. Either way, we both expressed earlier how we would both live till we were old and gray. It didn't seem like that couple ever had that chance. I almost felt like crying again. I had a flashback of the dream and could picture him dead once again. A chill came through me. It wasn't the wind, but just a cold, dark chill.

I knew immediately where that feeling came from. I had experienced it long ago when Andrew died. It was in my dream then, when I had seen him die. I had been unable to stop the tragedy from happening. I was once again reminded by the flowers they possessed. Andy had my wild rose and Scott had a beautiful field of poppies.

He could sense my continued uncomfortableness. "Would you like another cup of coffee?"

"Do you mind if we just go inside?"

The look on his face told me the answer right away. It was a look of disapproval. The same one he gave when he all but told me to leave him and never come back at his office.

"Uh, maybe another day. It looks like the rain has passed. Let me just go and put up this coffee mess and turn off the lamps. We need to head back to civilization. No cell phone reception."

He seemed to try and play it off to his inability to check in with work. I had no right to argue with him. He was sharing all that he felt comfortable with. I wasn't exactly an open book either. I was just lucky enough to live very far from my home place. I don't know if I would want him to see the farmhouse that seemed special to me as a child. Maybe he felt the same way. Maybe I was beginning to go too fast for him.

I watched as he disappeared into the cabin. As the lamps were turned off in the house, it became pitch black on the porch. I wished that he would hurry up and come out. It evidently didn't take much to spook me all day today.

As he returned to me on the porch swing, he took my hand and guided me to the car. There was a pleasant after-rain country scent in the air. I took a deep breath and began. "The poppies won't even say goodbye?"

"Nope, they close their blooms every night. I guess it's their polite way of saying it's time to go."

"Goodbye, sweet poppies," I whispered as we drove away. He drove me through the city to the other side of town where I lived. He pulled up right in front of my house. My house. The one he had never been to before. He seemed to be reading my mind.

"Well, here we are, Miss. Just in case you're wondering, I cheated. When Conrad brought your car home today, he entered your house in the GPS system. It was just following the routes that he set earlier. In fact, if you look in the glove compartment, you will find your keys safe and sound."

"I guess you just think of everything, don't you?"

I gave him an approving smile. I also appreciated the explanation that he'd given. I had enough weird for one day. It really would have been too much to think that after meeting him once at a ball game, he'd found out where I lived and even driven by or something. I mean, I liked him, but that was going way too fast. Although, at this point, what was the point of worrying about *too fast*?

"I'll never take the directions out of the GPS. I'll know that from now on, wherever I go, I'll always be able to find my way back to you."

"Well, Mr. Baker, I do believe that is the sweetest thing anyone has ever said to me."

I felt like we were from another time, and he was bringing me home in his carriage. He would have all but proposed marriage to me at this point if that's what life really was like.

He began to laugh. "Sweet, yeah, that's what all the people say that I am. Just a sweetheart. In fact, I'm sure that all day today the men at the office were just telling each other about the sweetheart that they thought that I was."

"That's different, and you know it."

"I don't know. Some of the women I've dated may not say that about me either. I mean, don't get the wrong idea. I am almost thirty and I have had my share of relationships. I even almost asked someone to marry me once, but I never let her in my office. I knew if I didn't want to share the history of my family with her, then I really didn't want to make history with her."

"So, you're a bit of a playboy then, huh?"

I was laughing by now. It was so nice that the day had ended on a lighter note. I was so glad that I didn't let myself get scared off. I was controlling my need to retreat when things got too heavy. I was proud of myself.

"Uh, yeah. I'm not going to lie. There are women at those games all of the time that know all about me. They wait around for the right moment and seem to have their sights on me. I was so happy when I ran into you. All night I just told those gold diggers that I had someone and they were just too late. Well actually, Conrad told them. He is always there to assist. You should have seen their faces!"

"That also makes sense. I always thought I had seen Conrad somewhere before. I just couldn't put my finger on it. As far as the gold diggers though, yeah, great. I didn't actually want to picture you as a playboy like I was saying, but thanks for being honest, I guess."

"Oh, come on now. You can't be jealous already. For all you know, those girls could have looked like they belonged on the street."

"Yeah, that's pretty much how I imagined. Pretty women of the night," I teased.

I was amazed that I could keep my humor at this point. At least he seemed sincere about me being his forever.

"Don't be silly. They were mostly cheerleaders! *Women of the night* know that I'll find them when I want them!"

I smacked him on the arm for saying such a thing. He gave me a wildly playful look and began once again to laugh.

"Well, Mr. Baker, would you like to see my recent history in progress? I would love it if you would come in for a while. I know that it's getting late, but could you stay?"

"That sounds very reasonable. You aren't going to take advantage of me, are you?"

I raised my hand once again—this time to gesture that I was swearing to tell the truth. I didn't feel it was appropriate to continue beating his arm every time he said something unconscionable.

As I led him through my door, he took my arm and swung my legs out from under me. In one swoop, I was in his arms. He gazed down at me while his hair hung in his face. I took my hand and brushed it away so I could fully appreciate him.

"I am blinded by your beauty."

"I think that is called hair, but thank you for the compliment."

With that, he pulled me closer to his face. He reached for my neck with his lips, then trailed up to mine. The hair that was once between my fingers for styling purposes was now intertwined in my hands. He did not know how my house was laid out, but the first moment he found something to set me on, he did.

We somehow ended up in the kitchen. I was on the cold granite island top. For some reason I didn't feel as cold as I thought I should have. He pulled back and began to stare at me.

"So, just to make this clear, I am not here to take advantage of you. As much as I want you at this very moment, I want us to wait. We may have a lifetime of impromptu love making, but not today. Not yet."

This really was the polar opposite from any date I'd had in the past. Usually, I had to pry the guys off. I was usually the one sending them home without a how do you do. In fact, I know that half of my relationships ended because of the men not wanting to wait for instant gratification and not understanding why anyone would want to wait for even a second date before we got it on.

"So, you're here with me and you don't want to control yourself, but you will because of what?"

"Because I love you too."

I almost forgot that I told him I loved him earlier. I was just waking from a nightmare, and I was just so happy to see him that the words slipped out. I never imagined that he might feel the same way, especially in a normal setting. There was no magic in my newer housing development. There was no history, no stories to tell yet. I supposed that this was one that was being made right now. It would be ours.

"Elizabeth, as much as I never want this evening to end, I really do need some sleep. I'm sure that they will be calling me by five in the morning just to make up for my taking the day off today. I wish you could have seen more of what I do. I think you could fully understand that way."

"No, don't apologize. How is it your fault that you are a successful man who happens to have a life of work? Wouldn't the opposite make you a bum or something? Besides, I am almost as ambitious, and I have worked very hard to get to the job that I now have. I promise that I understand your predicament."

"And this is why we are a match."

He graced me with another soft but seductive kiss and turned to leave. I followed him to the door all the while screaming *don't go* inside my head. This day was too good to be true. We had some really crazy mystical connection, and I was so afraid that if he left, it would disappear.

"Don't go."

I whispered the words, half hoping that he wouldn't hear. He turned around immediately and embraced me as if we would never see each other again.

"Beth, I promise that this day is ending, but we are not. You know where you can find me. If at any time you need me, just call. I will be busy for the rest of the week; luckily, tomorrow is Friday. I'm sure we can work a coffee in here and there. Maybe even a dinner or two by the time the weekend is over."

I felt odd acting like this. I had never cared if I had anyone in my life. I must not have been ready to be swept off of my feet.

"I know, I am just being silly. It seems like I have spent my whole day with you like that. I swear that I don't generally act this way. I am actually a little embarrassed."

"Don't be. I completely understand. I am just so glad you gave me another chance. Especially after what happened earlier at my office. I'll finish explaining it to you someday, I promise. We might even go back to the mountain cabin. That's why this is so wonderful. We can plan to do anything we like. We have the rest of our lives, right?"

"Right. Please be careful going home. I don't want anything to happen to you. Not now."

"You do the same tomorrow."

He bent down and kissed me on the forehead.

"Goodbye, Beth."

"Bye."

CHAPTER 13

Reality

I went back in the house wondering if this whole day was just a dream. It couldn't have been real. Even though I actually had a dream while we were together, it still made more sense that I was dreaming than that I found my soul mate.

I continued to look out my window. The breeze had stilled, and I found myself just waiting for him to come back. I knew that he would not, yet all I could think of was that I had an uncontrollable need to never let him go.

The alarm clock started blaring. I set it for a quarter to five. He wasn't the only one that had a busy life. My workday always started by six and I knew that there would be no time to sleep in, especially after taking half a day off.

I made my way to work the way I always did, but I couldn't help looking out of the corner of my eye for Scott. I heard what he said last night. He would get together with me for coffee, or dinner, or whatever.

Now that I knew he knew everywhere that I ever was, he might just go and try to find me, or so I hoped. Suddenly all the hard work that I had given my job didn't matter. My career was now second place in my life. Scott had been pushed to the top of my list.

As I entered the studio, I thought about Ned. Oh my gosh. I had opened up a complete can of beans with him only two days ago. I led him to believe that we may have some future. Why, oh why did I have to go and tell him about that day with the Dream Sundaes?

How do you explain to your best friend that you will remain just friends forever and that there is no hope for anything else ever? Should I even explain about the true love that Scott and I had found? Would that be rude after almost giving myself to him?

"Elizabeth, Elizabeth, Elizabeth. Where have you been? You could have called after lunch was over, to tell me that you weren't coming back, to help me edit for the final online presentation!"

"Look, Ned, I know that sorry doesn't cover it, but I was just busy yesterday."

"Let me guess: your Casanova flew you to Hawaii or something?"

"Hardly. We actually went to his offices and then out to the mountains to look at the flowers."

"So, did you decide you know what he does? What did he say that his business was?"

"Investments, I guess. He never did say specifically."

"Didn't think that he would."

"You aren't going to start on the *I know something you don't* thing again, are you?"

"Hey, if you want to go into this blindly, then that is your own bad judgement. I am really just trying to help."

"Well, I know that his family built Bakersfield Towers

themselves. He also told me about his grandparents."

"Look, I would love to talk about Mr. Tall, Dark, and Handsome, but I think that we have some work to do. The first client will be here in just ten minutes, and we still haven't got the final draft for the host prompter!"

"Good point. Look, I'm sorry I brought him up. I promise that I won't do that anymore today."

"I guess I started it. No harm, no foul. Let's just get our work done. We don't want to start the day so unorganized. You know we never regain stability once that happens."

He was referring to a time that we had an earthquake. It wasn't a large one, but we were on edge the whole morning. We barely got any preliminary work done, and it was like watching an impromptu comedy series. The hosts had to wing everything, and the clients barely sold a thing. That was the only time that I knew of that the Network gave money back to the clients for not doing well enough for their products.

It wasn't long before our shift was over. Though we usually didn't have time to sit around and gossip, we did normally talk a little more than we did today. I wondered how much of what he had said to me lately was how he really felt. Was he really waiting in the wings, hoping that things didn't work out with Scott? It was so hard to tell with him.

The silence that he was giving me was a definite clue that at least *something* was wrong. I didn't know whether I wanted to ask him or not. I didn't really want to know the answer, especially if it had to do with love and me and Ned in the same sentence. I knew that at the end of the day, you could say that I did lead him on the other night.

I was just so lonely that any male companionship would have done. What did he expect? I wasn't perfect and never claimed to be. However, Ned was my very best friend right now and I would be so disappointed in myself if I did anything to compromise that.

"So, I guess you have lunch plans, Liz?"

"How did you know?"

"Oh, let me try and guess: *Oh Elizabeth, I love you so much, we can never be apart. I will have to buy your network if you work any longer than you do. You must take off every day and eat every meal with me.* Is that about right?"

I had to say, I deserved the sarcasm that was so clearly directed at this new relationship that he'd hoped would never happen.

"No, actually, nut head. I was talking about lunch with you. You do understand that even when you are in love, you still have separate lives, don't you? I mean, just say if you found a hot chick the other night, would you just drop your livelihood and spend every waking moment with her? I don't think so. I was planning on working late tonight to make up for the time I took off yesterday. I was sorry for leaving you in such a lurch. However, you were the one that helped set the date up in the first place."

"Are you done? I mean, you have never been able to explain your way out of a paper bag. You have too big of a conscious for that and you know it!"

"I am officially ending this conversation, if that is ok with you. So, where would you like to go to lunch today, Ned?"

"I have this awful craving for a burger and fries. We can go to the more upscale sit-down restaurant, or the burger joint would do just fine. I mean, it won't be diet food. You sure that you still want to go with me?"

"If this is some kind of standoff you can forget it, Ned! I won't play these weird games with you. You happen to still be my best friend and unless you want that to change for the worse, then you will let the sarcasm go."

"Whoa, *sorry*! I forgot what kind of temper you can have when people throw you off. I guess that I've never been on the receiving end of this situation before. I've only heard your stories of Iowa, but that was with your old bestie Amelia. Let's go to Burger Rama and I'll buy, to make it up to you. You can text her and explain how your new best friend doesn't know how to treat you! How does that sound?"

"Sounds wonderful. Thank you very much."

It wasn't at all that I wanted junk food for myself today, but I felt that maybe that's what he needed. It would be comfort food. Our relationship was weird enough lately and anytime I heard him spurt out Amelia's name, I knew he thought I'd rather hear from my *actual* best friend.

If I just went with him, he'd know that I was here for him and that we were still best friends. I sure hated these games, but what could I do. On our way there, Ned received a phone call.

"Hey, this is Ned."

"Yep."

"Nope."

"Whatever. I'll see you later."

He wasn't very happy with who he was talking to. I couldn't imagine who on earth it would have been on the other line. I literally knew everyone that was in his life and unless it was his mother or something, I couldn't imagine.

"Your mom?"

"No, Liz, not my mom."

"You gonna tell me who it was?"

"You know what? No. I don't think that I am. It would really be none of your business now, would it?"

"Someone upsetting the best friend I have here would definitely be my business."

One thing through the years I realized about myself is that I might run from my own problems, but I couldn't stand to see my friends in pain. Just like it was with Amelia and her brother Tommy, when I was in pain, they helped with my situation. I learned something from that. I was now that same kind of person for those I loved.

"Yeah, Liz. Thanks, but no thanks. There is no one that is upsetting me. You know everybody I know. I promise that it's no biggie. Just let it go."

"Whatever you say, Ned. Whatever you say."

We arrived at Burger Rama, and it was packed.

"Are you sure that this is where you want to go? It's spring break now and the kids are all inside. We both know how you feel about kids."

Ned had some kind of problem dealing with kids. He never fully told me why, but he tried to avoid anyone ten and under at any cost.

"You know, I think you have a point. I guess it's to the upscale burger and chicken joint down the street now."

"I knew you'd change your mind."

We finally arrived at the Steak and the Sea Restaurant. It was busy, but at least we knew that the mature clientele would not disrupt our conversation by crying and screaming.

"Do me a favor, Liz, go inside and get us a table—I have a call I need to make."

"Oh *kaye*, if that's what you want, then I'll be happy to oblige."

What was going on? First, he gets a phone call you could clearly see that he didn't want to receive. Now, he had to make one that seemed to give him that same amount of pain.

I went inside the restaurant and got us on the waiting list for a table. I decided to just sit at the bar and wait. The only thing about going to fancier restaurants for lunch is that it is never in and out. The fact that there is limited seating and you are even on a list takes up at least a quarter of your lunch.

It was good that we had a flexible schedule. There would never be anyone to tell us what time we had to be back. With our job, as long as it is done by a certain time, they didn't care how long you were there to do it. There was also quality control, so if we didn't spend enough time on it, they would be the first to let us know.

As Ned was entering the door, they called my name to be seated.

155

"Just in time, you lucky boy. I've had to sit at the bar all by myself while I was waiting. Did you have a better conversation with whomever this time?"

"Oh yeah, better. Look, let's drop the subject about who I was talking to, please. We came here to eat, not for you to pry."

"Hey, if you don't want to talk about some new stalker girlfriend, then that is entirely up to you!" I couldn't help the laugh that was coming from my mouth, or the intense smile that I was giving him. It just wasn't like him to be so upset about anything.

"Yeah, girlfriend troubles, ha, ha."

The waiter seated us in a larger booth than was needed for the two of us.

"Sir, isn't there a smaller booth that we can go to? I mean, it is the two of us, as you can see."

The waiter began to smile and swiftly declined my request. He asked for our drink order and left rather abruptly.

"What on earth was that all about? Ok, Ned, what is going on?"

"Nothing that you won't appreciate later. Just trust me."

I sank into my seat with a confused look on my face. I couldn't imagine what on earth he was up to. It just wasn't like Ned to have a surprise waiting for me.

In all the years I've gotten to know him, he always was on the up and up. There was never a time when I had to wonder what he was thinking, or doing, for that matter. It concerned me in more than one way that I simply couldn't figure him out at this moment.

I began to look around like a paranoid mess. I just couldn't relate this to any occurrence that had happened to me in the past. The only surprises that I had always seemed to turn out badly.

Suddenly, a hand touched my shoulder from behind.

"Ma'am, would you like to order?"

I tried to turn around to look at the waiter, but he seemed

to keep from my direct view.

"Go ahead, Ned, you order first. I'm not sure yet."

"Oh no, Madame, you must order first. It would be rude to allow such a thing in this restaurant, especially on one so beautiful!"

At this point, I was turning in my seat, trying to just get a glimpse of this waiter. Ned had an unpleasant smile on his face. It was one of those smiles that you used when you were completely unhappy in the situation, but someone expects you to be happy.

"Well, in that case, I guess I'll just have the grilled chicken salad with house dressing on the side, please. Ned, how about you?"

"Oh, ok, Elizabeth, just turn around all the way, for heaven's sake. I just can't take any more of this." He said that in a small yet agitated voice, as if to leave the waiter out of our conversation.

I turned in my seat. Low and behold, Scott was standing over us, acting like a waiter. I was so thrilled to see him.

"Scott! What a wonderful surprise! Come and sit down! Ned, did you help arrange this? I just can't believe that you pulled it off!"

"Yeah, me either!" He had such a sarcastic sound to his voice that I was immediately confused to whether he planned this or not. But, either way, I had my best friend and my *new someone* sitting with me. What could be better?

"Well, I guess that's my cue." Ned stood up and turned to leave.

"Oh no, you don't! I think that this is a perfect time for you two to get to know one another. I want the two most important people to me to be friends too! Now, sit down, I'm not telling you again."

I wondered if that was too bossy, especially with Scott there, but really, this was the perfect time for them to see how they both could be so important to me.

"You know, Ned, if the lady tells you to do something, I think that I would do it, if I were you!" Scott was smiling ear to ear. He evidently found my behavior funny and charming. Whew!

"Yeah, yeah. Believe me, Scott, you are only beginning to see what you will have to deal with if you spend any time together in the future."

"Well then, I can't wait. I love someone who can speak her mind. There is nothing worse than someone who just does as they are told constantly and sulks!"

Uh oh. Well, funny and charming, better be able to get rid of the sulking and hiding that will eventually show itself in my nature. My only hope I had in that matter is that I usually only hide and sulk when times are extremely bad. Maybe, just maybe, the bad parts of my life were over now, and I wouldn't have to display that part of myself.

I remained sitting happily at what I had brought about. *My* two people sitting together with me. This was the way that Ned was letting me know that he was ok with my choice for love and that he was happily out of the running.

CHAPTER 14

Competition

I sure hoped I was right. To think that I was hurting him in any way made me sad. There were going to only be happy times from here on out. I had decided that.

"So, why don't we start about where we all came from?"

"Elizabeth, I think that we all know everything about where you came from. It only took the first week to get you to open up about your life. I hate to say it, but you're like an open book."

"Ha, ha. That is simply not the least bit true. There are many things that you don't know anything about."

"Ok, name one."

"Alright, I'll start."

I smiled. I knew with Ned if I got a challenge out of him, he would let the talking begin.

"First, you know that I came from Contra Costa College,

that I worked for the network out of San Francisco, about all the catering jobs, but what do you know about where I grew up? I'm pretty sure that I never said anything about that!"

"Oh, I know, I know!" I turned to look at Scott, half imagining him with his hand in the air like an elementary student.

"You grew up on a farm!"

He was smiling ear to ear, proud about knowing something that my best friend/ business associate did not know about me.

"Yes, you are right, of course."

He smugly leaned over to grace my cheek with a kiss.

"Look, Liz, how could I possibly know that, when you never bothered to tell me."

Ned started mumbling something else about not fair, two years friendship, then whatever. Please don't tell me that he was actually mad that I told my history to Scott first.

"What? Don't look at me like you just lost your best friend! I am here with *you both*. And you are *both* equally important to me, in different ways, thank you very much!"

"Well, I can help you out really quickly with that one! I'm suddenly not in the mood to eat this type of food anymore!"

Before I could say anything else, he was up from his seat and halfway to the outer door. I started to reach for him at first, but Scott told me to let him go.

"Look, I know you have to spend the rest of the day with him, so don't fuel the fire he's trying to set."

"What do you mean?"

I sat down immediately, waiting for an answer. I generally never have other men to tell me what another man was thinking. This was opening up a whole new world. The only world I previously knew was back in Iowa. It brought me back to Rob and Andrew and how they had educated me previously. I cringed, yet began to listen intently.

"Look, I didn't want to say anything to you, but from the get-go, Ned made it clear that he was your best friend and that he would do anything for you. I believe he may have said something about if I mess up that he would be there for you. I think that he is technically waiting for you."

"Oh."

I slumped in my seat, not believing what I was hearing. How could Ned be feeling this way about me? I thought for sure that the other night was an ending for us in the romantic sense. How could he still want me? Nothing, absolutely nothing for all these years, and now boom. At the exact same time as I find the true love of my life.

"I'll just have to talk with him at work. Yeah, that's what I'll have to do. I'm so sorry. I just really wanted you two to get to know each other."

Scott began to smile.

"We already do, Elizabeth, we already do."

"What on earth do you mean? You guys just met the other day at the game, right?"

"No, Liz, that's not true at all. Didn't you think that it was funny how he knew so much about me when we first met?"

There was a look of confusion on my face.

"Liz, didn't he tell you anything at all about me?"

"No, actually. Other than leading statements and hints about your possible wealth, he never told me a thing. Believe it or not, what I know about you today is from what *you* told me and what I'd heard about your family from the news."

"Ugh, no wonder he was mad. He wasn't on the same playing field. I told you everything about myself, so he didn't have to. He probably thought that I owe him something."

"Or maybe he didn't want to start something."

"I really doubt that Ned cares whether things are started between us or not. It's always been the same old, same old with him and me."

"Scott, you are just saying one confusing thing after another. First, you meet me here while I am supposed to be having a casual work lunch with Ned, and then we offend him with my stupid line of questioning. So, just tell me what your connection with Ned is, anyway?"

"Would you believe that he's family?"

"At this point, sure, why not?"

"Well, we are actually first cousins on my mother's side. In other words, his dad is my mom's brother."

"I thought you had said before that you didn't have any family anymore!"

"Yes, and I told you correctly. My parents and grandparents are both gone. I never said anything about extended family!"

"Well then, why would Ned have any problem with you?"

"My mom married my dad and with that, married into a lot of money. Her family was normal, middle-class, hard workers. There was nothing wrong with them. I knew my grandparents on that side too. They loved me just the same as my rich ones. I guess if it really came to pinpointing what tore us apart, it would be when my mother died."

He gazed sadly into space as he spoke.

"She had a really hard time when Dad died. I couldn't stand to see how it tore her apart, but she just reacted the same as my grandmother did when my grandfather died. She was still pretty young and even though my dad was the very love of her life, she actually began to fall in love with someone new. I had no problem with it, but my grandfather put in his will that if ever a woman were to leave the family either by divorce or death, then they could have only an allowance."

"That's tough!" I exclaimed. And gestured for him to look deeper into my eyes for comfort.

"Yea, but here's the kicker. In the end, the family fortune would belong to me, or the next rightful blood heir."

"So you had to take your own mother's money away from her?"

"She was ok with this. She just wanted me to be taken care of anyway. No matter what allowance she was given, she knew that she would never have to worry the rest of her life with money. She would have nothing to give to any heirs that she may have other than me, but at least she was taken care of."

I sat amazed by what I was hearing. What kind of family was this really? It was so intriguing.

"Wow! So, Ned's dad was pissed at your grandfather because he didn't want his fortune to leave the family? I have to say, I don't blame your grandfather!"

"Now, don't go venturing a guess at what really happened, although I have to say, you're really close."

"Sorry." I sat with my head in my hands. My elbows were on the table supporting them.

"Ok, first, can you take hearing the rest of the story? I have to say, you look like you are on the edge right now."

We began to laugh, and I gestured him to continue.

"Ok, ok. So, my mom left our family home to be with her new guy. She was actually on her way in our car when a tragedy happened. Somehow, the car was blindsided at an intersection. The other person had just gotten off work on the graveyard shift. He fell asleep at the wheel. He died a few days later in the hospital. It was tragic for all sides involved. No one was to blame."

I grabbed his hand and mouthed *I'm sorry*.

Flashbacks from my own family demise gave me a chill.

"The controversy started when her estate was settled," he continued. "She had always been very giving to her side of the family. She bailed them out more than once in financial difficulties."

He paused as if he were going to say something then stopped. He was being particularly careful with how he told the story. I again associated myself with what they were going through, not believing the similarities. Although I would have liked to stop him and share, I knew this was not the time. My head was once again in my hands.

"When she died, I guess they thought some inheritance should have gone to them. She hadn't told him about my grandfather's will. They had no idea that none of her family would get anything just because she left our family home to be with someone else. I agreed at first that it was unfair and unfortunate for her siblings and parents not to have any more financial support just because of some rule my grandfather thought up to protect an old fortune that no longer belonged to him."

"I knew that you could never just leave anyone high and dry. Especially if they were in need."

I looked sweetly into his eyes and smiled.

"Not so fast. It's not as a happy ending as you would imagine. Basically, I gave her immediate heirs about twenty-five thousand each. With her having only one brother and a mother, it equaled fifty thousand dollars. That's not a lot, sure, but I let them know that if they needed any more financial help, all they needed to do was call. It wasn't long before the first of the money was spent and their money troubles started again. Ned's dad begged me to invest in some fly-by-night get rich scheme. I knew it wouldn't work in the real world. I told him that he would have to pay me back as soon as he had made money. Of course, when it didn't, he blamed me. Even though I never came to collect, he's basically owed me a hundred grand, and he embarrassed his whole family. All Ned can see is that I am some rich cousin who looked down on his family."

"But that's untrue, right? You could never look down on Ned for what his dad did!"

"You know, you're right. I never acted like I was better than he was. Even when he called me for you at the game, I half wished he'd just invited me down with you guys. I'm part owner, you know. I can get floor seats too!"

He sat with an annoyed half smile on his face. I realized very quickly that I was in the middle of something I never wanted to get into. I was the one at the beginning of lunch that wanted them to know each other better.

Now, I could only wish they never had met. It just wasn't in my plan for my boyfriend and my best friend to be enemies. At least it sounded like Scott didn't bear any bad will toward

Ned. I knew from this point that the person I had to work on was Ned.

"Listen, Scott, I know I just barely finished eating lunch, but I feel like I should get back to work and get this straightened out. I have to try."

"Elizabeth, as much as that sounds fine and good, I don't think that confronting him about this will help. He'd just get more upset with me for telling the story."

"Trust me, Scott, if anyone on earth knows Ned at all, I do. What is the worst that could happen? He will resent you?"

"No, actually, he'll be resentful of *you*. You two have been good friends for some time now. I wouldn't hear of doing anything to hurt that relationship you've built. It's you that will have to work with him every day."

"I refuse to argue with you about Ned. It sounds like his family has done enough unrightfully to you. I promise to be tactful when I bring it up."

I leaned over to kiss him and headed out the door. It wasn't long before I had to turn right around and ask Scott to bring me back to work. Luckily, he just laughed, paid for our meals, and courteously led me to his car.

"Oh, Conrad, it's so good to see you again!"

"Thank you, Ms. Redbird. The feeling is mutual."

He held the car door open. Scott and I got in and before we knew it, we were back at my work. It was now my destination for promoting peace.

There was nothing more that I wanted than to make some understanding between the two men I so adored. I slowly made my way to the production room.

"Hey, Ned. Nice to see you made it back safe and sound. Did you ever get a chance to eat?"

"Yeah, you know me. Food finds me even when I'm not looking. It just so happened that as soon as I got back, they told me about a new item in the Lilly's Lunches Show. She was selling pre-made lunch packs that were similar to those in the fancy diet centers. Anyway, I got to be one of the first to try it. They actually were good—I even called in when I was done and ordered a month's supply of them."

"Oh, starting our diet without me, eh?"

"You don't need me for diet support, Liz. I think Scott could do that."

I so hoped that his upbeat demeanor about what he had eaten meant that nothing big was actually happening. His last response, on the other hand, confirmed what I feared. It would be a strain on us whether we wanted it or not.

Family trouble is family trouble. I would be the last person on earth to not be understanding of what that was like. You just couldn't fix your family. It's like that saying, *You can pick your friends, but you can't pick your relatives.*

"Look, Ned. Look at me. I do not care about your past, your family, or some crazy feelings of inadequacy that you bring out at the very minute you even hear about Scott Baker. Get over it may not be the words that you want to hear, but as your best friend in the whole world, I am begging you to please let this go."

"Oh, now I see. Mr. Scott Baker decided to tell you everything, did he? I always thought private matters should be kept private, but I always knew he wouldn't play fair."

"No, that's not true!"

"Oh, so he didn't give you some sob story of my dad and his gambling addiction? Oh, or he didn't tell you about the loan sharks that came to collect?"

"Ned, wait, please don't tell me anymore!"

"Why? Do you think that it is so sad that you can't bear to talk about it anymore?"

"Actually, no! I don't know why each of you thinks that the other one would talk bad about each other, but you are both stupidly mistaken!"

"Oh, let me guess. He asked you if I told you all about his family, right?"

"Well, yes, but..."

"But what? He just thinks because he would sink so low, that I would!"

"Would you please shut up! First of all, you just told me all about your dad and family. He didn't! In fact, he just lied for you! He told me that your dad was borrowing money for an investment for a business. You know, you are both the same! Why do you have such a hard time seeing that?"

"Oh yeah, we're twins alright! Tall, dark and rich, to pasty white, barely six feet, and well, you know my financial status!"

"Yes, I happen to know exactly what you make, and as far as it's concerned, you make a good living for an average family, and you are single."

"Yeah, I am! Do you have to remind me of that all of the time?"

"Look, Scott may not be the man of your dreams, but I really like him a lot."

"Oh, I know how *charming* he is. I've sat all my life watching as he makes his way through tons and tons of women!"

"Stop talking like he is so much better than you! I told you, you are both on the same playing field as far as I am concerned!"

Suddenly he stopped. I didn't know if it was the heat of the moment or what, but very abruptly, his lips were on mine. There was almost nothing that I could do. It was probably the guilt for leading him on in the first place, but I let his kiss linger about ten seconds longer than I should have.

"Ned, please, don't take this wrong, but please be happy for me. You know that you and I will always be friends, best friends, but nothing more!"

Ned turned around and turned back to face me once more. He touched my cheek with his warm, soft hand.

"I love you, Elizabeth. I can't help it. I don't want to. I don't want to compete with someone like Scott Baker, but I want you in my life. Not like it is now, but more. I want you to be with me when the sun comes up in the morning and when the moon is shining with the stars, through the darkest of the night. Isn't there any way that you could feel the same way?"

"Ned, you know how I feel. You know that after the other night happened, I realized that we weren't meant to be together!"

"Why not?"

"I promise, if I thought for one second for all these years that we were supposed to be more than friends, we would have made it happen. We were both lonely. I can find someone for you, I promise!"

He made a sound that sounded like *ugh*, turned, and left the room. I could hear him calling me down the corridor to the sound studio.

"Come on, Elizabeth, time to finish our editing for tomorrow's show!"

I did the only thing that I could've done. I too went down the corridor to the sound studio. The look on his face was as if none of this had ever happened. I wasn't sure what was going on, but it was like I was looking at someone besides the one that I was just in the supply closet with.

The rest of the day went on exactly the same. Nothing more was brought up about this apparent love triangle that I had accidentally created. When it was time to go home, he just got up and left. I didn't know if he just didn't want to talk about Scott anymore, or if he just came to realize that he and I were never going to be anything.

"Ned, wait! Don't you want to finish our conversation?"

"Nope. What you told me will do just fine. Look, Liz, I'm just a little tired today. I think that I'm ready to go home. Besides, tonight I have a date. I want to be refreshed for that. You could say that before was just a test. If I thought for any moment at all that we might have had a future, then I promised that I would go for it full force. I just know that when a lady says no, she means no. That's ok. You know how I feel. If you ever change your mind, let me know. Maybe, just maybe I won't already be married off myself!"

I had so many strong mixed emotions suddenly. I was so happy that he was going to let this go. Scott and I would finally get to progress the way I wanted us to, and I was going to keep Ned as a normal friend. I found myself relieved and sad all at the same time. This I didn't understand. Why would I be sad if Ned was letting me off the hook? Wasn't that what I had wanted ever since that fateful night?

"Well, bye..."

CHAPTER 15

Date Night

He was out of there like he was running from fire. I never got to talk to him about his relationship with Scott or anything. I didn't blame him for wanting away from that conversation. He must have had the forethought to know what conversation was coming next.

The day had been long, and I really was ready to go home and get some rest myself. I walked or should I say moped to my car. What did I have to be sad about? There was a note attached to my windshield. I thought for a moment that it was from some flyer for a bar opening or something, but on closer inspection, it had the Bakersfield Towers logo on it.

I carefully opened it up. It was a little damp from a light shower that had just fallen an hour ago. The sun was out and basically dried it, but it was still compromised in the strength department.

Elizabeth my love,

I am blindly going through my day. My body and soul are with you always. I must see you tonight. I will send the car to pick you up for dinner around 7:30pm.

With all my heart,

Scott Baker, esq.

I wished at that very moment that I hadn't accidentally torn the corner of this wonderful little note. This was one of those you could see in some scrapbook that you would show your grandkids someday. This was literally the first thing that Scott had ever written me. It was in his own wonderful handwriting. I held it to my heart as I somehow made it into my car.

Happy would not be enough of a word to describe how I felt. Ecstatic, exuberant, wonderful. Maybe those would suffice. The true word never came to me. The whole way home, the only thing I could think of was warm. I felt warm. It was like I was cold for all of my life and Scott Baker had thawed me out and I was glowing like a warm fire was consuming my soul.

As the night progressed towards the fateful 7:30, I desperately searched for the perfect clothes to wear. I tried calling him to ask what I should wear. Instead, I kept getting Conrad on the phone. He was like his personal answering service of the evening, as well as his driver.

"Mr. Baker has instructed me to keep the evening a complete surprise."

"But Conrad, I have to know at least if it is something I should dress up for or dress casual for."

"Mr. Baker has instructed me to tell you that whatever you wear will be just fine."

"Well, tell Mr. Baker that I can always just go in footed pajamas with my hair in pigtails if he really doesn't want to let me in on this at all."

"Very well, Ms. Redbird." There was a long pause, and then

I heard the most wonderful robust laugh in the background. "Ms. Redbird, Mr. Baker has instructed me to say that if that is really what you would like to wear, then that will be just fine with him."

"Conrad, you tell him that I don't even have footed pajamas, nor do I have rubber bands to tie my hair up, but I am waiting patiently for his arrival."

"Thank you, Ms. Redbird, please wait for our arrival outside your home. We will be there shortly. Goodbye."

"Goodbye."

Honestly, what he was thinking, I didn't have the least bit of an idea. That would be the same amount of idea that I had about what we were doing tonight. I hated to, but I just put on a pair of jeans and a long-sleeved half-dressy tee shirt. I figured that he was either going to take me somewhere that was extremely casual, or to a place where we would be totally alone. Either choice was fine with me.

I knew all of the head chefs in all of the restaurants in town, as well as the surrounding towns. I knew that there were several quaint casual places that had exceptional food, as well as those that were outlandishly expensive that didn't. I hoped that if ever given the opportunity, he would at least know to value my extensive knowledge on the subject.

The time had come and gone. I was almost a bit nervous when 7:35 hit and still no Scott. I didn't think that it was appropriate to be late for a date. That would have been a deal breaker with other men in the past. I always said that if you weren't punctual, then you really didn't care. I was hoping that I could let this one slide, and that my opinion would remain unvoiced.

I sat nervously awaiting him on the front steps to my home. The night reminded me suddenly of the one with Ned after the game. It was windy and the warmth seemed to be picking up as the night was fast approaching. I wondered if the long tee shirt was a bad idea. Now, not only was I waiting impatiently for Scott, but I was also beginning to perspire.

That also brought me back to the night with Ned. I wished so badly that Scott would just hurry up so that my night wouldn't be consumed with thoughts of the wrong man.

Wrong man, yeah, that is what I call him now, I guess. Best friend, yes, but also wrong. The wind through the trees brought a faint scent of the last flowers that had bloomed. It was now becoming unpleasant to smell the stale breeze. The smog had been heavy today. Tonight was no better.

I stood, stretched, and began my ascent up the small staircase to my front door. I was not going to wait out here a moment longer. I barely touched the handle when I turned toward the road. There were lights coming quickly down the street and to my house. *About time.* I decided to mark my post and stay on the steps until he properly came to visit me. If he could see that I was unhappy, then maybe he would try harder to be somewhere when he said he would in the future.

As Scott made his way to me on the steps, I noticed he was dressed in a tux, and carrying a bouquet of different types of roses. I was astonished as I looked up into his eyes and saw that despite his lateness, I had forgiven him completely, as it had never been an issue. In fact, I had melted into a puddle right before his feet.

"Words cannot express how sorry I am for keeping such a beautiful woman waiting out in the night. These are for you."

After handing the roses to me, we turned to go back into my house so I could put them in water. I opened the door and switched on the light. What was right before me I couldn't believe. Somehow, he had managed to come into my house, set my table for dinner, and fill my home with many vases of flowers.

"How did you do this? I was just outside. I...I..."

"We were very quiet. I was watching you as you sat. I knew that if you gave up on me and started going back into the house, I would have to call you to stop you. Basically, I got lucky, really lucky. Please come with me."

Even though it was my house, he led me through it to the dining room. The smell was overwhelming. He had a full course dinner waiting on us. Conrad was there with an older woman that I didn't know. I guessed that she was the server.

"Please, may I seat you, ma'am?"

I had never been good in situations like this.

"If you would like for her to join us, I suppose that would be alright."

I let out a nervous laugh. I think that they got my joke but didn't find it as humorous as I would have liked. I did let Conrad seat me and I noticed that Scott had seated himself across the table from me.

The candles that they had placed in the middle of the table were lit. They dimmed my lights and all of a sudden, it was like we were in some upscale swanky restaurant, except a lot more private. I glanced over to Scott. I was wondering if he was as nervous about any of this as I seemed to be.

I wasn't even sure why I was. It was my house, and my dining room. I wasn't, however, used to having strangers in my home. Well, or anyone that I hadn't invited. In fact, I had never invited anyone into my home to eat in the two years I had lived in this apartment. Looking at the fancy table, I dimly pictured the last time Dad and I shared a Redbird Gourmet meal. I looked down in unexpected sadness.

"Elizabeth, if you would like for us to go somewhere, just say the word and we'll be out of here in a second. I didn't mean to impose. I just thought that this would be nice and quiet is all."

"No, Scott! That's not necessary at all. I was just caught off guard. It doesn't happen very often, but when it does, it takes me a bit to find my bearings."

"If it helps," he began whispering, "I asked them to serve us our first course, then leave until I call for them later in the evening. I just wanted to be alone with you more than you could believe."

My heart continued to melt as I was hearing everything I could ever ask to hear from my first real love. My memories vanished and my mind was taken by the experience he so wholeheartedly set before me.

"Well, sounds like a perfect plan to me. But, please keep in mind that if you ever want to visit with me here in the future, just let me know. I would be more than happy to cook for you. I *am* a chef, you know."

"Wow, do you realize that I never thought of that? I always think of you as a television producer. I almost forget that you can really cook! You'll have to fill me in on the whole career choice thing. We all make different choices along the way that we never expected. Well, I hope that you will like what I brought us for dinner."

It was funny, but now I could hear the nervousness in his voice also. He too was caught off guard. The lady they called only by Miss came out to serve. I think that he was happy for the interruption. She and Conrad did what they were supposed to do, and then they left, just as Scott had promised.

It was nearing the eight o'clock hour as we took the first bite of the lobster tails with seasoned rice and steamed vegetables. As we were eating, my mind was racing with all kinds of thoughts. I wondered why he decided to bring dinner here instead of taking me to his place. I wondered what he had in store for us.

My mind started veering to my earlier thoughts of Ned. I wished that Scott would just start a conversation already, as I couldn't stand the silence anymore!

"So, Scott, what brings you here tonight?" I decided that if he wouldn't start the small talk, then I would have to.

"You know, I had it in my mind completely differently. I'm not sure why, but it's like we are missing something here."

"It could be the background music. You know there is always background music in restaurants. Why don't you wait here, and I'll be back in just a minute or two? The dinner is lovely, by the way. You've made a very good choice."

"Uh, ok." He seemed to be distracted by his own thoughts at the moment.

I left the table and quickly found my way into my bedroom. I decided that I didn't have long before he would wonder where I'd gone, so I quickly scanned my wardrobe. There I found the perfect black dress for this very occasion.

It wasn't only the lack of background music that made it awkward, it was the fact that I was completely underdressed. I slid the silky gown over my head, pulled my hair up into a makeshift French twist, and doused myself sufficiently in perfume. I found my highest set of black sparkling heels that I owned and left my room knowing that even though I was quick, I was also looking pretty darn good. As I passed through the living room, I took the remote control to my stereo and turned it on to a soft music playlist.

I returned to the dining room with a confidence that was not often in my life.

"Hello, Scott, I am so sorry to keep you waiting. How is the dinner?"

"Uh, good. Good."

He continued to look down at his meal. I wasn't sure exactly what it was that kept him in such deep thought, but I was bound and determined to get him out of it. I went to his side of the table, moved his meal out of his way, and placed myself ever so carefully in the exact place. It was at this point that he had to look up and notice what I was doing.

"Oh my gosh! Elizabeth, you changed! You look stunning!"

"Thank you, thank you. I'm glad you could take your time to notice. If you can also listen, we now have intimate background music."

"Yes, I can. I am so sorry. I don't know why I let my thoughts get the better of me when there is so much more here in the present to divert my attention."

"That's me, your very own attention diverter!"

I looked into his troubled eyes and kissed them carefully. I decided that even though dinner was wonderful, it was nothing compared to the feelings that I had for him at that very minute. I moved my lips down to his and gently caressed them with my own. I lowered myself from the table into his lap.

We began to kiss much more fervently and before I knew it, he lifted me into his arms, and we were leaving the table to go onto the nearby couch. Just as before, he had such beautiful clothes on that I hated to be the cause of any wrinkling.

"C-can I get your coat? I will just take a minute and it won't wrinkle or anything."

I could barely get the words out between the passionate kisses that I was giving as well as receiving.

"This is what I think about this coat, Elizabeth." With that, he took it off and threw it to the floor. He didn't even flinch as he removed it, his tie, and his shirt. He became progressively close to me with every moment. I felt like I was in excruciating pain as I thought about waiting for one single second more for us to be together.

Just as fast as he had removed his upper clothing, he undid my hair and began to remove the silky dress from around me. A sudden flash about a moment a couple of weeks ago that Ned and I shared prompted me to stop him.

"Um, Scott." I couldn't seem to get any words out from the continual kissing. "Sweetie, do you mind if we don't do this here? The bedroom is just down that little hall." Again, he proceeded to pick me up and carry me down the hall. He kicked the door open to the bedroom.

"I'll fix the damage later if there is any." I didn't want him to apologize, so I overturned my lamp.

"I'm even. So, you can't worry about it if I don't."

We began a muffled laugh as we fell to the bed. I guessed that I was right about my choice of clothing. It had done the trick to break his concentration. This wasn't exactly what I was looking to do when the night began, but this moment seemed to be written in the stars.

He was being so gentle and loving. He caressed my body with his mouth. The pleasure was continual. This was the first time in a long time that I felt like I was doing the complete right thing. There was no hesitation into the night. There was no second-guessing. I belonged in his arms long before I knew who he was. I was destined for this. He was destined for me.

As we began to make magical love for the first time, it felt like something that I had waited my whole life for. The night was slowly progressing into a dream that I had never dared to dream. I hoped I would never wake up. As the pleasure passed, we cuddled among the sweaty sheets, half-exhausted.

"I wasn't planning for all this!" I wanted him to know that I didn't dress up like that just to get him in bed with me.

"Believe me, neither was I. Never for a moment while I made plans for this evening did I think that *this* was in those plans. I really did just want to be here with you to get to know you better."

"Well, I do believe that you may have a better understanding of me than you had previously guessed."

We began to laugh, and I fell into his arms to rest.

"What about Conrad and the lady? When do you need to call them?"

"At this point, I could just call and let them know not to pick me up until the morning, if that would be alright with you."

He had such a sincere smile. It was warm and loving. It wasn't one of a predator. He didn't say that he immediately had to go. In fact, he was doing everything in his power not to just love me and leave me. I almost thought that this must have been a dream. There is no way that I could be here with this unbelievably sexy, handsome man.

"That would be nice." I got closer to his face and began to lightly kiss his lips.

"Now, none of that! I came here to get to know you better,

and that is precisely what I intend to do."

We got up and took a shower together. The urge to be impulsive and make love again lingered, yet we restrained. He got dressed in his slightly wrinkled yet elegant tux. He left off his coat and rolled up the sleeves of his shirt. He almost looked comfortable enough for a walk on the beach. I really wished that there was one nearer to where we were. I left my hair to dry on its own.

I just wore my towel-like spa robe. I figured that it didn't probably matter at this point what I was wearing. Along with the fact that my makeup was half off, maybe I wasn't too sexy for him to look at while we talked.

We went into the living room. We sat in opposite corners of the long couch. My legs were up on his lap as we sat talking about what our lives had been and how they would like to go. I tried to elaborate more about my entire family and how they were too unexpectedly taken from me at an early age, but by their own doing. I explained everything about Amelia and the choices of my career.

We skimmed the surface of everything we did for the past nine years or so. I explained the relationship that I had with Ned. I think that he may have begun to worry just a bit as the part about the game came into the explanation. I guess that I felt that if he was going to love me, then he would need to know what was going on between Ned and me also.

"You know," Scott explained, "I never felt that Ned could have anything that I needed in my life. Now I see how lucky he has been in the last two years. He really was a fool to not see what was in front of him right away. I also feel sorry for him. It seemed like my family took his family's dignity enough as it was in the past. I never intended to compete for anything that he had as long as we lived."

"You have no competition, Scott. Like I told you, what he and I shared was from the both of us being lonely. Immediately after it happened, I knew that I had made a mistake."

I just hoped that he believed that I was sincere about what I was telling him. The thought of him believing he had to compete against Ned was horrendous. Never in my life did I want this to happen. I looked deep into his eyes and gave him a reassuring smile.

"I believe that you love me, Elizabeth. I do. It's just that you have a deep friendship with Ned, and I have to say that I'd be lying if I thought for a minute that it didn't matter. It certainly began to matter to Ned. It's either that or once he saw that we had something in common like we now do, he thought that it could be his turn to get what I couldn't."

I had concluded that he wasn't buying my explanation. In fact, at that very minute I wished that I never brought it out in the open. What was he saying? What you know can't hurt you? On the other hand, with the way that Ned was talking to me about his feelings, I knew better than to rely on his silence when it came to our relationship. He would be sure to bring it out when it suited him. Or, maybe he wouldn't.

Both of them were brutally silent when it came to personal history. Neither would give the other up for anything. That alone made them more of a family than I ever wished for with my own. There was something to be said for that kind of omission.

"Well, let me explain why you are so special to *me*."

I reached over and pulled him to me. I placed my lips on his, then sat back to explain.

"How did you feel when we just kissed?"

"You don't want to know!" he mused.

"No, seriously! Ok, let me tell you how it felt to me. It was soft and warm. It felt like waking up to something warm cooking in the oven on a cold winter's morning. There is nothing that can truly compare, except that it feels like home to me. In fact, if you didn't have any weekend work to do, I could totally spend the whole time with you just like this."

"Alright, I see your point. You're sure that it wasn't anything like that with Ned?"

"Look, are you trying to fix us up or what? I told you how I felt; this has to be the end of it. I will not be in the middle of a cousin competition!"

"Elizabeth, I promise never to bring Ned up again unless you bring him up first."

"I knew that we could make progress if everything was out in the open!"

I still felt like I needed to send him a reassuring smile. He leaned over to me this time and gave me a soft, seductive kiss.

"So, what was it that you were saying about staying the weekend together?"

It was then that the talking was over and our affection for each other could be shown in ways you could only show with your body. It was as if we were in the heat of the moment of the discussion one second and in bodily bliss in the next instant.

"You know," he breathlessly mouthed, "all you have to do to get me to stay is to ask me, you know."

"Stay," I breathed in his ear.

It was everything I ever wanted. We had such long talks about the businesses he owned and how I had my own catering business a few years ago. Every nook and cranny of him was like a map I had read, and I was a happy traveler on my way home. It seemed that almost everything that I had wondered about was coming into clear view. The only thing that we both still evaded was our distant pasts. Even though I shared that I had a family who lived far away and separately, and my brother had died, and he told me so much about his family and how he grew up, neither revealed the complete circumstance of our families. That would have to come sometime later. We were so engrossed in what was already said, the subject never came up.

Sunday evening came too quickly. There are moments you can't wait for, like the beginning of the weekend, then there are these moments, when you wish that tomorrow would never come.

"I am truly hating this moment." I wrapped my arms around him, like I would never let him go. "I wish you could stay forever."

"Don't say that, Beth. Forever is such a long time. Why don't we agree that we can't live without one another more than a few hours at a time? That way we can both go to work in the morning and yet know that we will be with each other soon."

"That sounds perfect. So, are we going to lunch again tomorrow?"

"That may be where we meet again."

"Till tomorrow, then."

He reached into my robe. It seemed to be his permanent residence that weekend, after the first night. I never bothered to actually get properly dressed. He too held me as if he never wanted to let me go. He placed a kiss upon my head and pulled away to leave. As he was walking down the front porch stairs, he turned back and grabbed my hand.

"I know that we haven't been together long, but I know now that I could never love another woman in my whole lifetime more than I love you."

"That goes for me too. I love you, Scott. I think that you are my sunshine."

He would understand that because of what I told him about Adam and Amelia. He knew now how important it was for me to find my own shining light.

"I know you are mine."

He held my cheek in his hand and once again kissed me. It was the last one he would give me before the new day began.

CHAPTER 16

More Surprises

I awoke to the sound of the garbage truck outside my home.

"Oh my gosh! What time is it?" I screamed out as I saw that it was already a quarter to eight in the morning. I was never later than 6:00 a.m. since the very day that I had taken the job. It was inconceivable that this had just happened.

I noticed my robe lying on the bathroom floor. I was joyfully back to the moments that Scott and I shared over the weekend. It made getting ready in five minutes bearable. I didn't do anything to fix myself up for the day but put on eyeliner and mascara, a little lip gloss, and quickly brushed my hair.

I ran from the Culinary Network parking garage to the waiting elevator. In moments I knew that there would be no excuse that I could give anyone here about my tardiness. Our colleagues didn't know anything about Ned and me. They never allowed workplace romances. They knew what it could do with great teams of people working together.

"Hi there, everybody. You would not believe what happened to me this morning!"

"Um, yeah, I think we can."

I didn't know how to take that comment. Did they all really know what I was up to? I stood mortified at the thought of them knowing what was going on. It brought me back to that first night with Rob. I just knew that everyone at school could tell by looking at me that I'd had physical contact with him. I was wrong of course, but the feelings seemed to stay with me to this day.

"Ok, why?"

"Elizabeth, you have been overworked. You have been working far too long with us all, for us to not know when you are getting exhausted from doing too much. Why don't you just take the day off?"

I didn't know how to take this kind of compassion from my network heads. It wasn't like them to give you a 'get out of jail free' card.

"Ooh kay, well, I still need to tell Ned what is going on. I have never taken a personal day like this. Besides, I'll be alright, it's Monday. I had the weekend to become refreshed. My alarm clock just didn't go off, I guess."

"It's going to be taken care of, Ms. Redbird. There is nothing more that you need to worry about. Just rest and enjoy your day off. We will see you tomorrow."

I really didn't know what was going on. I stood confused as they all turned and left the room. I did the only thing left that I could do. I took out my cell phone and began to call Ned. I knew that there was some reason that they didn't want us together today, but he was still my best friend. It was like we were being put in time-out for something we did that was wrong. It felt like I was being treated like a preschooler. I speed dialed his number and the phone began to ring.

"Hello?" Ned asked in a muffled voice. It was as if he was

trying to hide the fact that he was talking on the phone.

"Ned, what is going on?" I began to whisper along with him.

"Liz, can't talk right now. Editing with the execs. Call you later."

Uh oh. I couldn't believe what I was hearing. Were we doing something wrong? Were they about to see what I help Ned with so they'd know what my replacement would need to do? I became a basket case in such a short period of time. I still couldn't seem to move.

"Ms. Redbird?" Ashley, the intern, began to ask.

"Yes, Ashley? What can I do for you?" It wasn't like me to be bitter with the staff. I always went out of my way to be extra nice to the new people. I just felt that everything must be accusatory at the moment. It was as if I suddenly felt a thousand eyes on me.

"Oh, nothing, Ms. Redbird, nothing." She turned and seemed to pick up a very brisk pace, walking away from me. I would have some making up to do in the morning. I turned and headed for the elevator that would lead me directly outside to the parking lot. I sulked to my car, still wishing that I knew what was going on. I just knew that the best job I ever had was in that building. I could never get over losing it.

I got in my car and headed home. I was so devastated by what was happening that I stopped at the Coffee Bar to try and calm myself with a hot latte. I couldn't seem to sit still long enough to drink it in there.

I fled once again to my car and decided to head for home. By the time I arrived at my driveway, tears began to flood my eyes. I was so happy that I had the ability to hold them back on the highway. I could have been in real trouble. I felt as if I had lead in my shoes. I just couldn't make it up my front steps to the door.

I sat down with my head in my hands and sobbed. How could this be happening now? I would have to move if I had to find a different job right now! My whole world seemed to be coming apart. What happened to my new perfect future?

I glanced up towards the street. A car was coming down my driveway. I cleared my eyes of the tears and looked again at the Tesla just feet from me. It was Scott's car. What on earth was he doing here? Did he have someone watching me without my knowledge or consent? How else could he have known that I was home?

"What are you doing here, Scott?" I forcibly voiced. It was so unlike me to be so abrasive. I wondered when this was going to stop. First it was Ashley, now it was Scott.

"A little birdie told me that you had the rare opportunity to play hooky today. I thought that I might just join you for a little while. I'm not lucky enough to be able to take the whole day off like you are. Those people sure are great!"

"What people, Scott? What are you talking about? For your information, you are right. The executives sent me home today, but I can't see how my losing my job can bring such joy to you!"

"Whoa, calm down! Nothing is wrong with your job, I promise!" He began to pull himself towards me, smiling like he'd won the lottery.

"Don't patronize me, Scott!" I pulled back. "You don't know what it's like to work your way up to your favorite job on earth and know that you are about to lose it." I began to ramble frantically.

"I mean, the first thing that they told me when I was late was that I looked tired! Do you know that I have never been late a day in my life? I can only imagine what they were thinking this morning when I didn't show up! Poor Ned was left to do this on his own. Well, not exactly. He had one of them in there doing my job!"

I was talking hysterically, and I knew it. I was so upset that new tears were forming to replace the ones that were drying on my cheeks.

Scott looked so unprepared for what he was encountering. He must have thought that I was going to be jumping for joy at the thought of having a day off. He really didn't understand the reality of a normal working person. He was looking at me with a fading smile and big puppy dog eyes.

"Elizabeth, please don't cry. Everything will be alright, I promise. I am so sorry. I had no idea how this would upset you. I guess that I wasn't thinking earlier."

He came to me with his arms wide open. My face went directly into the cleanly pressed collar of his shirt. We stood at the bottom of my stairs for at least three minutes with my tears freely flowing. The more that I stood there in his protective custody, the more I was pondering what it was that he was saying to me.

"Scott, please tell me that you didn't have anything to do with this!"

I abruptly backed up to the first step and looked at him in the face. He began to face the ground at the very same time. My question was answered without a word being said. He wasn't here to comfort me; he was here to gloat for getting me out of work for the day! I suddenly noticed the mess I'd made out of his expensive shirt, and I found that it brought me some satisfaction.

"Wait, Elizabeth, you may have a little more of an idea about this day than you thought at first."

"What do you mean?"

"First, let me explain to you that I never intended for this to upset you."

He tried to reach out, but I pulled further away, looking for his answer.

"I just found out that my old friend Collin Singleton was one of your co-executives. I knew that you really needed the sleep, but that you would never admit to it, and you would do everything in your power to act like you were indestructible. I knew for myself that it was too much to stay here that late and

I guess I just expected that you would be the same. I thought that you could use time to recuperate with me today. We could both use it."

"So, what exactly did you tell Mr. Singleton, Scott?" His name stuck on my tongue as if I were licking off peanut butter. I was almost unable to form my words, I was so mad.

"I just said that you were a friend, and I knew that you were working too hard, and asked him to do me a personal favor by letting you off today!" He was beaming as he was lifting his head to tell me this. He seemed so confident that I would be impressed by what he had done.

"UGH!" I turned around and started up the last of the steps to open my door. He grabbed me from behind and pulled me into him.

"Let me go, Scott! You don't want this fight with me right now. I am walking away because I would rather take this all in and think for a minute instead of saying something we both might regret in the near future!"

I tried to pull away, but he kept his grip as firm as ever.

"No, Elizabeth, I don't want to go. I didn't want to go from the first time I met you till last night, when I had to go home. I never wanted to let you out of my sight!"

The tears in my eyes returned, and I felt a little like a trapped wild cat. I didn't want this conversation yet. I was still so confused by what I had heard already. Could he really just think he could interrupt my life on a whim?

"Well, you are going to have to! I'll tell you what, let me go inside alone. I will call you as soon as I can calm down. I just really don't like surprises. I wish that with all you know about me already, you could realize that!"

"No, Beth, I won't let you go like that. These are things that we should work out together."

"Why should we? We barely know each other. Everything is happening way too fast, and you know it. How can you sit here and tell me that you love me when you don't even know who I really am inside?"

"The same way that you can do the same with me. I know you feel the same for me as I do for you. We have that connection to each other that we have been searching our lives for."

"Ok then, just think about that for one second then. You are telling me that we both feel the same about each other. Now, if I were to agree, then that would be a compromise. Why can't you see that my time to myself would also be just a compromise? You would still eventually get what you want, and I would also. Please, Scott, just let me go."

This was one fight that I didn't want to have. This whole conversation was so overbearing, yet I could see that he wasn't backing down.

"I know when I should and when I shouldn't compromise, Elizabeth. It isn't like I don't have to do that on a daily basis. I'm sorry that I seem too pushy for you, but if you would just hear me out, then it might help." I could see the pleading in his eyes as much as he could see the anger in mine.

"I will hear you out soon. Not right now, but soon. If you really want to compromise with me at all, you will sit on this porch and let me go. You will let me go inside because you know that is what I am begging you to do. I will go and take a shower, think things through, and let you know what I decide when I am out."

With all the frustration and madness that we were both displaying, it was no wonder what was actually happening. Scott moved toward me rapidly. I hardly had taken a breath when he was encompassing all of my space with his.

"No." His words were soft and breathless. They were not those of someone being harsh and abrasive.

It was sudden, but I gave in entirely. For the first time, someone broke past the defenses I'd built up my entire life. It was like he had a little army troop wearing me down to defeat my resistance. He had won, and he knew it.

He took the keys to my house out of my hand and quickly

opened the door. I was actually unclear how it happened so fast, but we were in the foyer by my large fern that was set on a small bamboo table. It wobbled as we brushed past it while we were crashing into the stucco-covered wall.

I literally couldn't think of anything but the sweet taste of his mouth. It was like a mixture of sweet cappuccino and heaven. I liked both, so either was perfect. It mixed with the musky smell of his cologne. As quickly as I was spun around up against the wall, he pulled away from me.

"I have something to say, Elizabeth. Please hear me out." His voice was still just above a whisper. He knew now that trying to persuade me by raising his voice was not the way to get my attention. It would scare me off. I guessed that even if he didn't give me the time that I felt like I needed, he finally grasped a little about how I was. He seemed to understand. That alone was worth the struggle.

"It's ok, Scott, really. I understand that you were just trying to be nice and get me the day off so I could spend it with you."

"Not that I don't want to get into that conversation again, but I don't want to get into *that* conversation again." He snickered.

"Then what?"

"From the very moment I met you I knew that I could never let you go. Last night was like going somewhere other than home for the first time in my life. You are my home, Elizabeth. You are. When you asked me how I felt when you kissed me, it was like it was the one pair of lips that I had waited to feel all of my life."

He got down on his knees and wrapped his arms around my waist.

"You will never know how sorry I am for causing you the uncertainty with your job. I promise that as long as I live, I will never interfere with it without your permission first."

"Scott, please get up. I can't stand to know that I am the cause of messing up any more of your beautiful clothes." I looked down and smiled at him disapprovingly.

"Well, there is one more outfit that I would like to crumple to bits with you, my sweet Beth."

He shifted from around my waist to one knee. I saw him reach into his sport coat and pull out a beautiful box. I almost leapt backwards, but the stucco wall was still in my way.

"Scott, what are you..."

He gently placed his fingers over my mouth to stop my words. He opened his to replace the negative ones that would have come from mine.

"Beth, marry me, please. Marry me today. Neither of us have any real family anymore and we both have a limited number of close friends. Please, fly with me to Vegas and marry me now. Nothing is stopping us. I don't ever want to be without you again!"

"Wait a minute!" I said concretely. "Who was it who said never say forever, just say that we can have moments together, or something like that!"

"I was wrong. I am wrong. My life without you is incomplete. I need you like I need the air that I breathe."

He was rising up from his kneeling position on the floor. I knew that the wood floors had to be uncomfortable to kneel on. As much as I would have liked to deliberate about this for a few hours, I knew that he would never give me that. It was like everything that I felt earlier—all the anger and frustration, along with all the confusion and mistrust—just melted. Tears started forming once again. I wondered if this whole day would be filled with tears.

"Elizabeth, don't cry. Please, I'm sorry, if this is too soon..."

I stopped him the same way he stopped me earlier. I placed my hand in front of his mouth. I replaced my hand with my mouth. I kissed him as if we were practicing for our moment when we were at an altar saying our vows.

"Yes, Scott. Yes, I will marry you!"

I couldn't believe that I had just made a life commitment

to someone I'd known for less than a month. It didn't seem to matter. We were in love. We were going to Vegas to vow our lives together forever.

In a matter of minutes, he had me going through my clothes like a whirlwind. How was it that we were packing for a getaway marriage on a Monday morning? As I was packing, he was on the phone. He called two people that I knew about.

First, he called Conrad. He wanted him to get everything ready in the plane. Evidently, he had packed bags before he came to see me. What did that say about his confidence? Collin Singleton was his second call. He actually told him that we were getting married and that I wouldn't be in the rest of the week. I would have surely been fired if that had happened with any other staff member at the network. Nobody, I mean nobody, dared to ever take time off for fear of ever being easily replaced.

I tried to call Amelia when I was alone in my closet, but it went right to voicemail. How could she not answer at a time like this?

"Amelia, I just know you'll never check this voicemail, but just in case you do, call me right away!"

I tried to call Ned one more time. It went straight to voicemail as well. How could neither of my best friends not answer my calls? I knew it was difficult during work hours to get ahold of Amelia and I decided that taping must still be going on, or Ned was still editing with the execs. I knew from that moment on, I would be on my own. On my own because Scott had taken care of everything.

Either way, it really was enjoyable not to have to worry for one day out of my life. Scott did use the *get out of jail free* card and they took it hook, line, and sinker. He had a somewhat daunting aura of royalty about him most of the time. It was as if he had all the world for the taking. That included me.

CHAPTER 17

Plans

As soon as I was done packing, we locked up and loaded the little car with many more belongings than I probably needed. I began to think about our honeymoon. Although Vegas was very fun when I'd gone previously for my noon show hosting job, I always knew that it could be even more fun if the right person were to come along. Also, having a little money to gamble away would bring more joy. He stood at my door as I climbed in.

"You sure you want to do this, Elizabeth?" He said this as if he were waiting for me to chicken out of something. I was just hoping that it wasn't really him that was now beginning to freak out.

"Did you just ask me to marry you or what? Whose beautiful antique three-stone engagement ring did I accept?" I smiled and as soon as he got in the driver's seat, I reached out my hand.

"Oh my gosh, Beth! It fits! It fits! I just knew for some reason that it would. I just knew that if we had to, we could go get it sized however you needed it. Oh, but *of course* it was *me* who just asked you to *marry* me!" He winked, smiled, and kissed my hand.

Before I knew it, he turned quickly out of my driveway, and we were somehow as quickly on the freeway. We were headed for the airport at elevated speeds. We wanted nothing more than to be in Vegas already and announce our love for each other to the world.

"Uh, Scott, are there going to be reporters there? I mean, if I got married on my own, nobody would probably care less, but I *am* marrying *you* after all. Is this going to be discreet?"

"Why? Is there someone that you might want to hide this from?" he teased.

"Well, I may not have mentioned much about them, but my parents still exist."

"Elizabeth, I remember you saying you had parents that you don't keep in contact with!" he laughed.

"Oh, well, I just know that we never really got into that part of our conversation about ourselves, specifically."

"I noticed." He stared intently into my eyes. He knew that it was time to listen to the past me, whether he wanted to or not.

"Yeah, well, there is something that I want to tell you about my family, then. My mother kind of disowned us when we lived in our last apartment in the city. She left us for a dentist that could give her the things that could make her happy. It was money, Scott. It was all about the money!"

I started getting teary-eyed as I was giving him this quick summary of my mother. I tried not to ever think of her. It was always better that way.

"Hey now, my sweet Elizabeth, please don't get sad again.

Today is our happy day. It is about only you and me. The other stuff we can talk about later."

"I just wanted to warn you. I haven't spoken to her in all the years that I've been in California. I'm pretty sure that she knows my success in my own field, but this would possibly make her come out of the woodwork. You are everything that she always wanted. You are everything that I was never looking for."

"I know that, Elizabeth. That is why I love you so much. Please, don't give it another thought. I am used to gold diggers. If your mother was or is one now, I know exactly how to handle her. She won't hurt you, I promise."

I snuggled up closer to him in the already cramped car. He really was my true companion, the love of my life. He was my Antony and I, his Cleopatra. This just confirmed it. I was riding to the airport with the man of my dreams, not because he had access to everything the world had to offer, but because he had the warmth of love toward me, which I had never felt before.

We arrived at the airport. I looked around and we were passing all of the check-in booths.

"Uh, Scott, isn't there some kind of check-in that we have before we can get on a plane?"

"No, sweetie, that's for commercial liners. We are taking my private jet."

I tried so hard not to be impressed. I was the one person in his life who wasn't interested in his immense wealth. I always thought that I was too good for money. I would never be like my mother.

He took my hand and led me to the plane that was awaiting us on the concourse.

"Wow, Scott! That's really incredible!" I stood there looking awestruck.

"Now don't go getting all impressed by me now. You nearly broke up with me when I used my power to get you a day off of work!"

"That, my dear, would be because you didn't consult me first. If I'd have known that my job was still secure, then it would have been an entirely different story. Don't you remember what I said about not liking surprises?"

"Actually, yes, I do. I hope to never surprise you unhappily again."

"What do you mean, unhappily? What happened to no surprises?"

He looked at me with a crooked smile.

"Beth, you will just have to know that I am a man full of surprises. Please just try to take them for what they are. Acts of love."

"Scott Baker! You don't have any more surprises in store for us today, do you?"

Even though I was possibly a little panicked, I was not mad. I would let things roll off me as a duck did to water. Nothing was going to touch me today and bring me down. He just smiled at my line of questioning and pulled me into his already running jet. We were off the ground in no time at all.

The trip was way too short. It was the first time that I had been in a private jet of that size. I was surprised how well it handled through all of the turbulence. It was so nice to be back in Vegas with a friend. It was even better to know that I was there with the one person who loved me most in the world. I couldn't believe that this was happening.

"So, where are we going to get married?"

I looked at him like a begging animal.

"Please tell me your surprise!"

He looked at me with a loving grin and I knew that he would never give himself up.

"If I told you, then it wouldn't be a surprise!"

We laughed and laughed as we got into the limo that waited for us outside the airport. How could this be my life? Just a few short weeks ago, I was bored and lonely. I had almost given up on finding love. It was beyond my comprehension that this was actually happening. The limo was so lavish. It had wraparound seating for about ten people and it was equipped with a mini bar and flat-screen TV.

"Geez, Scott, do you think that we have enough room? Or is this a way for us to be in a room that is the size of a small bedroom?"

I slyly looked at him and put my hand on this thigh.

"Now, none of that. Why is it that I am always the one to set physical boundaries in this relationship?"

"So, are you telling me that when we are married, I won't have you available twenty-four hours a day to do what I want with? I don't know, Scott, that could be a deal breaker!" I winked jovially at him.

"Oh, I think that you'll possibly have all you could want of me by the time we go home!"

"I can't imagine that being a true statement. I couldn't have enough of you in a whole lifetime!"

"I do love you, Elizabeth. I love you so much."

We sat in the oversized vehicle as if we were in a two-seater roadster. I wished that this day could last forever.

"I love you too."

We stopped along the way to the hotel. We seemed to be at a bus stop or something.

"What are we doing now, Scott?" I was wondering if this was part of the good surprise he was talking about earlier.

"Wait here."

He left the limo and went toward two people who looked like they were waiting for a bus. They turned around, and to my surprise, it was Amelia and Adam deClair. Somehow Scott must have done his homework with me and decided to find my oldest best friend. I guess that meant that Ned was not a part of the guest list. That didn't surprise me a bit. I knew right away when he said Ned was his cousin that there would be boundaries to our friendship, no matter what Scott said in the beginning.

"Amelia!" I cried.

"Amelia, come here right now!"

She was in the limo quicker than I could say peanut butter sandwich. It was so comforting to have her close to me again. She helped me through so much in my lifetime. It seemed so fitting that she would be here to help me now.

"Did you come to be my matron of honor?"

"Of course, silly Lizzy, of course. You still haven't changed a bit, have you?"

I hadn't. I really hadn't changed from what I was like the last time she saw me. It had been only about two years since she moved away. We had vowed to always keep in touch. We did so with phone calls, texts, e-mails, and social media but we hadn't seen each other since then.

"Well, I guess I must have changed a bit. I mean, I have been working in the dessert division for two years now. Can you tell that we actually taste test everything that we sell?"

"Oh, you look just fine. You were always so thin to me before. It just looks like you are more filled out, is all. More womanly!" We laughed and laughed together for the first time in years. I was so happy by his surprise.

"Wait, Amelia, how did you even know to be here today? It's a Monday, for heaven's sake! How could you both get off of work on such late notice?"

"Late notice nothing, Liz, he called me after your first day together when you went to the poppy fields! You must have mentioned something to him about me sometime during your time together. He said that he had to look me up through school records at Contra Costa College and he only had my first name to go on! He's really unbelievable, Lizzy! He said that he knew that you were the one right away, and that he was going to do everything in his power to get you to marry him today. We've been talking on and off for weeks!"

I sat there stunned for a moment, then asked, "Why today? Did he say why today?"

"No, he didn't, as a matter of fact. Why?"

"Did you ever have a feeling like you were living someone else's life? This may sound crazy, but he kept comparing me to his grandmother, and he was telling me about his whole family history. It's like he's trying to get me to fit into some kind of puzzle that he had to solve."

"Oooh, so you're the missing puzzle piece? That's cool!"

"Yeah, that's what you would call it, wouldn't you, Amelia?" I said with sarcasm.

I truly didn't know what was going on. How could he have known that I would want to spend the rest of my life with him so soon? I did, and I do, but how could he be so sure of himself? He knew that money wasn't anything I was interested in, and he never wooed me with anything extravagant, but there was something else that I couldn't quite put my finger on. To not know that he would be mine forever caused me deep harm.

Maybe I was part of some destiny that I just never knew existed for me. Maybe I *was* his missing puzzle piece, just as he was mine. We both fit together in perfect harmony. I became giddy at the very thought of it.

"Oh, Amelia, isn't this just wonderful? I finally will have a family like you and Adam! We both worked so hard for what we had." I turned to the limo bar and grabbed us both a sparkling water. "Cheers, Amelia! Who could ever say that dreams didn't come true?"

"Cheers! That's what I have been saying all along! By the way, you will never guess who I saw here when I first checked in."

"Who would that be? Donald Trump? A movie star? Who?"

"It would be no one other than Rob!"

"What Rob do you mean? Like Rob Thomas, the singer?"

"No, Liz, I mean *Rob* from *high school* Rob. He works here at this hotel as the manager. Since it's a casino and hotel, I hear it's a pretty prestigious job. He's in charge of all of it."

"Now is not the time to play with me, Amelia!"

I began to feel like I could hyperventilate. Never in a million years did I ever think that we would see each other after high school, let alone when I finally decided to get married!

We had become such good friends my junior year, but along with that were the memories from the past. The ones before we decided to be just friends. These were the memories that I didn't want to remember this weekend. These were the ones that I wanted to remain in the back of my mind on a shelf that was left untouched.

"Elizabeth! Elizabeth, calm down. He's just an old friend, nothing more. He won't interrupt any plans that the two of you have for this weekend. I even talked to him, and he sounded happy that you were so happy. You see, everything's just fine, I promise!"

She was trying to calm me down. She knew right then and there that it was almost better not to tell me, except for the fact that she knew that I would likely run into him here at one point or another. She was just trying to take away the surprise ahead of time. I was suddenly feeling grateful to her for that.

I could just see it now, Scott and I happily walking around in the hotel lobby or playing at the casino, and Rob appears out of nowhere. It seemed better to freak out and get it off of my chest now. I took a deep breath and let it out slowly.

"Whew. Ok, Amelia. I think that I will be alright now. Thanks for warning me! I think that it's just been one big surprise after another today and that was one that I didn't see coming at any point."

"I hear ya, Liz. I hear ya. So, are you excited? I know I was so excited on my wedding day!"

"Well, it isn't like I have planned this for months or anything, but you would not believe how psyched I am about the whole thing!"

"Did you realize that Scott co-owns this hotel and casino? So, I mean, technically your *then* works for your *now*."

"Amelia, I don't want to think about it. It is just too coincidental, don't you think?"

"Yeah, it is. Also, the fact that he has been key in getting this wedding going from the get-go!"

"Did he know who the wedding was for?"

"Well, if he didn't already, he does now. He didn't seem all too surprised, so maybe he did know. I mean, he supposedly had been working along with Scott the whole time."

"Do you think that Scott knows that we had a relationship in the past?"

"If he does, Rob probably told him that you two were friends, and that's it."

"Well, I'm glad you told me, but I am here to concentrate on one man."

"Speaking of which..."

We both looked toward the door of the car.

"Hey, ladies! I believe that we are now checked in and ready to go. Elizabeth, would you like to go up to the room and rest for a while, or would you like to go shopping with Amelia for your wedding dress? That is one thing that I wouldn't even try to buy for you!"

"You know, Scott, I appreciate the resting and all, but why don't we do that in a few days, after this is all a little less new? I couldn't imagine trying to rest at a time like this!"

"Well, shopping it is! Mr. Steven, please take these special ladies anywhere they would like to go for wedding dresses. I would suggest the one down the strip. They'll be close, yet they may be able to find an original."

There was such a glow about him when he was instructing the driver what to do. It was his happiest day, just as it was mine.

"Wait, Scott! What time are we getting married? I have to get my hair and face done too if I am going to set foot in a wedding dress!"

"Seven o'clock sharp. It will give you about six hours. Good luck!" With that, he gave me a quick kiss and said goodbye. He was going to stay with Adam. It was apparently not the first time that they had talked. I wondered quickly if they had prior conversations when Scott called Amelia to talk about me.

The thoughts faded quickly as we started the mad dash to hunt for the perfect wedding attire.

"You do know, Amelia, that as my matron of honor, you have to have a fancy bridesmaid dress!"

"See, Lizzy, you're already talking like someone with unlimited money! Normally, you would have told me that I would have to come up with something or ask what I brought to wear! I'm so proud of you!"

CHAPTER 18

Finishing Touches

We looked through at least four shops with wedding and bridesmaid dresses. I finally picked the perfect one for me. It was simple satin and lace with delicate beading around the bustline. It fit closely to my waist and flowed bountifully onto the ground in a simple, almost six-foot train. Amelia found a simple pale pink silk dress to wear.

We had just finished our shopping trip when I began to wonder about the cake. I suddenly wished that I could have prepared for this a little. I would have loved to have made my own cake. With all the hard work that I had put into some of my earlier catering clients, I was one of the most sought-after cake designers in mid-west California. In fact, that was one of the reasons that I had the job I did. I would help all of the people with dressing up their desserts before we put them on live TV.

We returned to the hotel after our little shopping spree. I ran into Scott's arms as soon as I caught sight of him. I couldn't wait to start my life as his wife. I let him know right away that I was going to use the beautician that was recommended by our hotel to do my hair and makeup.

"The ladies at the dress store said that this was actually one of the best places in Vegas to go."

"Well, I can't argue with that! We do have good taste here!"

"Wait a minute. Scott Baker, how did you know that I was on my way here? I mean, you actually met the car at the door!"

"I have my ways."

That was all of the convincing that I needed. I knew that he probably had the driver call on the way while we weren't paying any attention. I really didn't care. I was just so happy to be back with him.

"Well, Elizabeth, let's get a move on! We have some flowers to choose."

"Do you mean it? I thought that you would just have planned this whole thing yourself! What about the cake? Do I get to choose the design or the ingredients?" Really, this was the one biggie to me. I really didn't care much about the flowers, except for those that might be on my cake.

"Actually, I thought of a few things to help us along. First, I got through at least a dozen flower arrangements and picked three for you to finally approve. Trust me, the others would have not done our occasion justice. As far as the cake is concerned, I had to order it already, or it was sure not to be done before our ceremony was over. You of all people should know how much time and effort it takes to put together an amazing wedding cake. I just couldn't see doing that to somebody on the spur of the moment, even if they were being paid twice the amount they were used to."

I actually did understand that. I couldn't help but be disappointed about the whole thing just a little. I knew now that there were just some things that we would have to compromise on in the future. I was always up for that. He gave me a lingering kiss and sent me and Amelia off to choose the final floral arrangements and get ourselves wedding glamorized at the beauty parlor.

"I'll see you at seven sharp at the chapel."

"Which one?"

"Just call for the car and it will take you there. Surprise!"

"Scott Baker, you said no more surprises!"

You could hear him laugh as he left the lobby of the hotel. I had no idea exactly what it was that he and Adam were off to do, but I decided to blindly trust the process and know that everything would work out exactly to my wildest dreams.

We stood in the lobby a little stunned. Even Amelia was a little taken aback by what was going on.

"I told you that he had been planning this for at least a week or two." She gave me a shrug. "That's all I'm saying."

"Well, do you happen to know where it is that we are supposed to go for the flower viewing?"

"Not a clue. Why don't we go to the front desk and find out if they know anything there?"

We agreed that we needed help finding the flower arranger, the beauty shop, and our room that we had not been to yet.

I rang the bell at the front desk. It appeared that there was a missing clerk from behind the check-in counter.

"Hello? Is anyone here?"

"Just a second!"

I could hear a man's voice from behind the wall that led back to the employees' area. I looked at Amelia with a smile of suspense. That smile was short lived when I looked up.

"Hello, Mrs. Baker, I mean Ms. Redbird, or should I just call you Lizzy?"

"Cut it out, Rob! I can't believe that you are actually here! Come around here—I want to see my friend I haven't seen in almost ten years!"

"Oh, don't remind me. I'll be right around."

Even though the thought of seeing him after all of these

years was cringeworthy before, I only had feelings of peace and reconciliation when I finally saw his face. It was as if my past vanished before my eyes and standing in front of me was someone I could turn to as just an old friend. My dread dissipated into excitement.

He left the way that he came out. In a few short seconds, he appeared in front of me, grinning from ear to ear.

"Would you believe that I wondered if you would know me at all? It's been so long, and I have gotten a little older and I wear a bit fancier clothes than I had to in the mall back home!"

"Ugh, don't remind me about home, please. That is one place I wish I could just get rid of my memories of."

"All of your memories?" He moved his *happy to see you* grin to a mischievous one.

"Now, Rob, none of that! Just give me a hug and get this reunion over with!"

He came at me so quickly that I was actually scooped up and in his arms, before I could say anything. My feet were dangling at least three inches off of the ground.

"Put me down!"

"You're lucky that I didn't kiss you hello for old times' sake!"

"Look, Rob, I am happy for you to be here. I am happy that you have such a wonderful job that you love. You have to know though that any public affection you show to me will get back to Scott. Do you really want to make your boss mad?"

"Ah, already putting me in my place! Yes, Ms. Redbird. What will you require today, Ms. Redbird? How can I be of service?"

I smacked him on his shoulder, and we began to laugh.

"Really, Rob, I do need your services."

"Oh! Does that mean I'm about to get lucky?"

"Are you going to help me find my flower arranger or not? I'm sure that if I asked anyone else around, they could point me in the right direction!"

"Ooh, I almost forgot about that temper! Look at me, I was

just kidding. Do you think that I would honestly jeopardize my livelihood just to get into bed again with you?"

"That's enough, Rob!" Amelia finally intervened. She knew the amount of power that Rob had over me. She had seen it from the beginning and realized, without me knowing it, that he still must have possessed that same power even after all of these years.

"Oh, ok, take all the fun out of it for me! Come here by the desk. I have a map of our property. The florist is waiting for you in Suite 1B. It's just down this corridor."

It looked like it was pretty close to where we were. I was happy to see that. I was afraid that all this talk with Rob would set me late with the florist.

"Thank you. I think that we will get it from here!"

"I guess I do have some work to do. Just call me if you need anything more."

He handed me his card and turned to go back behind the desk.

"My Lizzy," you could hear him saying to himself as he turned the corner.

I automatically shivered. If there was one thing that I never wanted to hear again in my life, it would be the phrase *my Lizzy*. It had a creep factor for me now that I was an adult and Amelia was the only friend that I kept in contact with who knew me by that childhood name. Why did he have to go to other places when I was ready for a happy reunion? So much for that.

"Do me a favor, Amelia, don't call me Lizzy anymore. I think that Liz or Elizabeth would be just fine from now on in my adult life!"

"Not a problem, my friend, not a problem!"

We hurried down the corridor toward Suite 1B. It was the easiest thing we had done all day. Scott was right when he said that he had three floral arrangements to pick from. They were each equally as pretty as the next, yet had distinct differences.

One had multicolored flowers of every variety possible. It was a plethora of color and texture. There was one setting that was white only. They had everything from calla lilies to white roses. The final setting was all red. I found this one a bit funny. It was beautiful, of course, but it looked more like something you would have at a bachelor party. I quickly picked the white one because it would match anything.

The flowers were so elegant. The white also reminded me of the innocence that I had before my sixteenth birthday. I would have given anything to have found this kind of love so early in my life and not have gone through what I did. The white flowers were my way of letting go of the past and starting fresh and pure for my husband.

The florist treated us like we were celebrities. It was everything she could do not to curtsy and bow every time I made a slight request. The one request I had was for one pale purple rose to be added to the middle of my bouquet. I wanted more than anything to forget my family even existed, but not my brother.

This single rose was for him. I just wished that he was looking down on us right now and was happy for what I had made for myself. I couldn't help but get a little sad as I thought of him.

"Thinking about Andy?"

"Yeah, but I'm ok. Do you think that this is stupid?"

"Liz, it's whatever you need to make *you* happy today. I think that it is nobody else's business why you are doing what you are. If you want to feel close to him on an important day like today, then that is exactly what you should do!"

She smiled reassuringly and gave me a comforting hug.

As soon as we were done choosing the flowers, we were off to the salon.

"Ooh, this is fancy, isn't it?" Amelia said, impressed by what she was seeing.

"Yes, Amelia. I have to say that I have never been to a fancier ladies' salon in my life!"

"Welcome, ladies, please come right this way! We have arranged two teams to work on you both. We want you to look as lovely as you ever have in your life!" the man with the salon said with a slight accent. I wondered why it seemed that half of the men that worked in salons had an accent. Amelia and I looked at each other and smiled. We really had come full circle from where we were from, and we knew it.

"Right this way, Ms. Redbird. Coco, please take her friend in the other room and begin on her hair."

"Bye, Amelia!"

"Bye, Liz!"

With that, we were separated, and for the first time all day, I was alone with someone I didn't know.

"Allo, Ms. Redbird! I am Memphario. I will be your hairdresser today. Missy will be doing your face and nails. First, please tell me about the dress that you are wearing!"

I explained about the dipped collar and the long train. He seemed pleased by what I had picked out.

"Oh, yes, yes, that will be just lovely. This will frame your style perfectly!"

He began to put me in an elegant swept-up hairstyle with tendrils hanging from the sides. I looked into the mirror and for a moment didn't recognize myself. It was so rare for me to get my hair cut, let alone fixed professionally. It was truly the most beautiful that my hair had ever looked.

"Oh, thank you so much, Memphario! The ladies at the dress store were truly correct when they told me to come back here to get myself ready for the wedding! Now that you are done, where do I go to next?"

"Right this way!" There was a lady's voice coming from around the corner of the room divider. I stood up to go her way and as I rounded the corner, I spotted Amelia. She, too, was a wonder to look at. We both became giddy and began to giggle like schoolgirls.

"Now, now, girls! You don't want to go crazy yet. I still

have your makeup to do!"

We both said *ok* like little girls doing what their mother said and we began to sit down.

"First, I will get you ready, Ms. Redbird. As soon as your nails set, you need to go right up to your room to get dressed. I will send your friend up to help as soon as we can get her finished also. She will get dressed in her room first."

"Amelia?"

"Hey, don't look at me, I am just going with what the professionals are telling us to do!"

Missy started on my face as a nail prep tech was soaking my hands to get them prepared for my manicure. It wasn't long at all before she was done with the magic. I looked into the mirror, and once again, had a hard time recognizing who was staring at me. She looked too pretty to be me. They lightly colored my lips and nails with a soft lilac. The flower scheme must have gotten back to them somehow. At this point, I gave up trying to make sense of anything. It was more accepting and joyful that way.

"Amelia, how do I look?"

"Oh my gosh, Liz! You look more beautiful than I have ever seen you!"

Tears started forming in my eyes.

"You stop that right now, Ms. Redbird! We didn't work so hard for you to go messing yourself up before the wedding!"

Amelia and I began to laugh, saying *ok* in unison one more time.

"See you soon, Amelia! Come and find me as soon as you can. I don't know where I'm going, but I'm sure I know someone who does." I smiled and gave her a wink. I hoped that none of the people at the salon noticed my gesture. I sure didn't want to get anything started.

I began my way back down the corridor, looking way too good to be wearing the clothes that I was in. I headed back towards the front desk. Again, the front desk was abandoned.

I was beginning to wonder if Rob was as efficient as I once thought he would have been. I suddenly jumped as someone began touching me from behind.

"You almost scared me to death!"

"Sorry, I just couldn't resist. I saw on the monitor that you were headed back this way, and I just had to do that." Rob looked so young and playful, and yet there was also a maturity about the way that he was dressed that contradicted his behavior.

"Please tell me where my room is. I don't know what room number it is; I don't know where it is, and I am lost. Please help." I distraughtly requested.

"A damsel in distress. Well, I am definitely up for that task!"

He held out his hand which contained a digital room key.

"I believe that this is what you need. Now, for you to get there is another story. I have been asked to be your personal escort. Your dress is already hanging there and ready for you."

"Rob, just give me the keys. I'm sure that I can get there on my own. You and I both know that I am not afraid of big new places. If I were, you would never be here with me now!"

"Well, in that case." He seemed to be thinking it over. "Nope, that's not what I was instructed by your fiancé to do for you."

"Whatever! Which way?"

He opened the door to the room. It was, of course, the best room in the resort. I didn't know why I would have expected any less. It was large enough to look like a house. There was a foyer, a large living area, a small reading room, and a large kitchen/dining room area. I was about to go back into the bedroom when Rob stopped me right in my tracks.

"Sorry there, Lizzy, but your hubby-to-be requested that you don't even peek in the master bedroom yet. I'm assuming that he'll have something special for you in there. *Later.*" His laugh was almost like a sneer.

"Rob, you never told Scott about the fact that we knew each other in the past, did you?"

"Actually, he figured it out by remembering where I was from. He knew that we were about the same age and from the same region at least. When he asked, I told him the truth."

I turned as white as a sheet. How could he do this and why would Scott want me to be alone with him in our honeymoon suite?

"Whoa, don't look so guilty. I told him that I was a friend of your brother and that we were just like bros when you were a sophomore. I promise, that's all I said. Do you really think I want to lose my job over this?"

I took a deep breath. "Ok, no more surprises, alright, Rob?"

"I promise."

With that, he guarded the master bedroom from me as I used the guest bathroom to get dressed. I had really expected Amelia to be back to help me change, but I think that I was moving quicker because Rob was on the other side of the door. I peeked through the bathroom door to where Rob was waiting.

"Oh, come on out. For heaven's sake, it's not like you are getting dressed in what you are wearing on your honeymoon!"

"Shut up, Rob!"

I opened the door fully and couldn't help but do a quick twirl as I held the train ever so carefully.

"Wow, Lizzy. You haven't lost a thing all these years! You are still a knockout!"

"Thank you. I'm ever so happy that you are here to approve," I said with a mix of sarcasm and a hint of joy.

"Hey, I'd have married you if I ever thought I had a chance, you know!"

"Gee, I just don't know what to do. I came here with Scott, but now, seeing you after all these years, I guess I was meant for you instead!"

"You don't have to be mean, Liz. I understand that what

we had was just that. It was what we had long ago. We could never get it back. I also know that you are head over heels for Mr. Baker. I get it, ok?" He turned around like he was headed for the way out.

"Hey, wait, Rob. Look, I'm sorry. We *were* like, what'd you call us? Bros that year. I am kinda glad that you can be here to see me find happiness. Wasn't that what we both wanted for each other?"

"That's all I ever wanted for us." He came back toward me and gave me a soft hug, as to not crumple all of the hard work that everyone was working on that day. "You really are beautiful." He kissed me on the head. It was so strange. In that instant, I was back at home, and I was young again. I was so happy that it felt like it was before we lost everything. It was like I was with my father again when we were still a family. I suddenly got teary-eyed, and I began to sniffle.

"Hey now, that'll be enough of that, Ms. Redbird! You have come here to be happy and to live out your wildest fantasies with the man of your dreams. Don't you dare get sappy with me now."

"I thought that you wanted me to quit being mean. So, which is it? Do you want me to be happy or not?"

"I want you to be happy. Not tear happy, just happy, happy."

He pulled away from our embrace.

"It's time to get going! This wedding is about to wear me out! Mr. Baker sure knows how to throw a shindig!"

"Let me guess, another surprise?"

"Hey, not by me. You know that if I give you my word, I mean it. I have a feeling that Mr. Baker is used to having his own way!"

"Well, I'll just have to persuade him otherwise!"

"Good luck."

Right at the moment we opened the door to leave the suite, Amelia appeared.

"Amelia, where have you been? I had to get this on all by myself!"

"I am so sorry, Liz. They just kept me longer than I felt was necessary. I don't know why, but it was as if they were *trying* to stall."

Rob began to smile a little bit.

"Rob, what's with the smirk? Do you know something that you're not telling me?"

"I'm not going to get in the middle of this!"

"In the middle of what?"

"Well, just suppose that Mr. Baker found out that there was more between us than just friendship. You know, he could have this place bugged right now," he whispered into my ear.

"You think that he may have been testing me?"

"Hey, stranger things have happened before when rich people get married. Most of them are so eccentric that they can do anything to test fidelity before they commit."

"You better be wrong, Rob!"

I stormed out of the room past Amelia.

"Let's just go. This whole thing is creeping me out. I am not going to think that he would do something like that to me at all. That would make him a monster, and I am not marrying a monster."

We made our way to the elevator. I could hear Amelia smacking Rob. "You are such an idiot!"

I couldn't help but smile at that. She referred to him as that much of the time when we were together. It was really like old times.

CHAPTER 19

The Wedding

The wedding was booked at the Chapel of Love.

"How appropriate, huh, Amelia?"

We laughed. It was very funny that he would pick something like a cheesy chapel to get married in. Most of everything that he did was over the top and elegant. This was a side of him that I had never seen.

We carefully entered through the bride's chambers and waited to be called for the ceremony. It was already a quarter till seven. My stomach was tied in knots the longer we were waiting. I was hoping that I was doing the right thing. I was wondering if I really knew him well enough to commit my life to him. I was having cold feet.

"Help me out, Amelia! Tell me why this is the best idea that I've ever had in my life. Tell me that I am doing the right thing today."

"Oh no, Elizabeth, you will not go running and hiding from this. You will not talk yourself into thinking that you don't have the best bridegroom in the world waiting for you just outside those doors."

I never even thought about it, but she was right. She knew me better than I knew myself. She knew what to look for when I was having a nervous issue. I took a deep breath and smiled.

"You are so right, Amelia. I am so glad that he called you to be here today. He must have known somehow that I would need your help to get me through."

Before either of us could say another thing, the "Wedding March" started playing. Our door opened and Amelia was prompted to start her walk to the altar.

"Good luck!" This was all she said as she turned from me and started her ascent.

I too started to leave my sanctuary for one that was filled with loved ones, as well as strangers. I peered through the doors and saw the most beautiful chapel that had ever existed. This wasn't cheesy at all. It was stuff that fairy tales were made from.

Each of the pews were filled with white roses trimmed in pale lilac. It was what I picked out, and it wasn't. It was better. I stood in awe of what they must have been going through to get it done on time for our wedding.

I was beginning my lone ascent to the altar when someone touched my arm. I turned, and it was my father. After almost ten years of silence, my father was here. I stood there stunned. It was incomprehensible that he was here to support me on my day. I looked around for my mother. It was never like her to miss a free party, but her lack of attendance didn't surprise me. Today was about me, not her. He, on the other hand, didn't want me to be alone on the one day that you needed your father the most.

Again, it seemed like all the time of worry and anger in the past was melting right before my eyes with delight. Scott had made a miracle happen. I may not have both parents, but this was truly amazing. I decided to keep strong and held back the tears. He reached over me and kissed me on the cheek.

"Hello, Elizabeth. Are you ready to get married?"

I motioned for him to lead the way. I knew that if I tried to speak then it would all be over for the cool and calm that I was trying to portray with every ounce of my being. We walked arm in arm up the aisle.

We got married that day by a lone pastor with a quartet orchestra playing. My father gave me away and Scott said his own vows.

You are my light, Elizabeth. I will love you today and I will love you tomorrow. I told you that I will never ask for forever, but I do want forever with you. You are my heart and soul. You will be my everything till the very end of our days on this earth.

I realized then that he really did love me the same way that I loved him. You could take family, you could take past lovers, you could take friends, but the love that we shared that day was enough to sustain a lifetime of whatever was to come. As we said *I do,* there was no longer a chapel, there were no longer people around us. The earth had gone away, and all was left was heaven. We were in the misty clouds of heaven. We kissed for the first time as man and wife and ran for the door. I never said goodbye to anyone. He grabbed my hand, and we were in his car.

"Conrad, I do believe you know where to go!"

"Conrad? Is that you? We're married! We're married!"

"Yes, ma'am."

He had a pleasant smile to his voice as he spoke his last words before raising the divider of the limo. We were traveling back the way that Amelia and I had come.

"Where are we going, Mr. Baker?

"Well, Mrs. Baker, if I told you, then it wouldn't be a surprise, now, would it?"

Again, with the surprises. Actually, so far, they hadn't been so bad. In fact, if my life was spent just waiting for surprises like that, then I would be up for that for sure. I might even change my view on surprises all together.

We arrived back at the hotel and were greeted promptly by Rob. It seemed so surreal that he was here sharing in this experience with me. He handed something to Scott and headed in a different direction. Scott and I entered the elevator and headed for our room. I was wondering if we were going to have a formal reception or not.

"Wait just one second, Mrs. Baker!"

In a quick swoop, I was in his arms, and he was carrying me over the threshold of the suite.

He kissed me as if the honeymoon were already beginning. Confused about whether we were having a reception or not, I eagerly accepted his touch.

"Now, now. We will have all our lives for that! Trust me. I just have something important to show you."

He opened the door to the back of the suite that was reserved for the master bedroom and bath. There again, it was time for fairy tales. Roses covered almost every square inch. If they weren't in bouquets, they were in petal form on the floor and the bed.

"We get to come back to this tonight! Right now, I need you to go to the closet."

The closet was like a room all to itself. It was nothing remotely like the ones that were in normal hotel rooms. This was a very large walk-in closet filled with my clothes, as well as a dress I had never seen before.

"This is for the reception. I got your exact size specifications from the dressmaker and got someone to shop for you. I hope you don't mind."

"Oh, so there is going to be a reception after all!"

"Of course, why else would I invite your friends and family to the wedding if they couldn't go to a reception?"

"You have a valid point."

I reached in the closet and pulled out what I was to wear. It was an elegant evening cocktail dress. It reminded me of the one I'd worn just the weekend before to gain Scott's attention. I shrugged and thought that I could never have too many cocktail dresses. Especially if I am now Scott Baker's wife.

There was no telling what this would all entail. I knew that he was in the middle of every public appearance in Los Angeles and that I would probably be out in the mix whether I wanted it or not. I sighed and quickly took off my beautiful wedding dress and replaced it with his dress.

"Oh, Scott, I love it!" I reached over to him as I was about to get my shoes on. I was instantly thrown off of my feet and I was on the bed before I knew what happened.

"I love it on you, but I bet that I'd love it off of you just as well."

"Now, Scott, what were you just saying about the guests and not keeping them waiting and that we have the rest of our lives for that?" I began to lightly but seductively laugh.

"What guests?"

For the first time, we consummated the marriage. We spent only a few fleeting moments in wedded bliss before we had to return to our guests. As we finally entered the elevator, his long arms enveloped me from behind during the descent. I could feel his warm breath on my neck.

"I wish we didn't have to go out," I whispered back into his chest. He turned even closer towards the nape of my neck.

"Patience," he whispered back into my ear, while taking a nibble.

I wanted him all to myself, yet I couldn't help wonder what we were about to get ourselves into.

"Scott?"

"Yes, my Beth?"

"Where is the reception exactly?"

"You haven't got to tour our property yet, have you, my love?"

"You know I haven't. You've kept me impossibly busy the whole day!"

"Well, let's just say that there are rooms in the casino that are used for concerts and such."

"Just a room, right?"

"Sure, just a room."

I felt better as I was reassured that it might be more intimate than I first expected. I mean he said a room, not a hall or a theater or club. I decided that I would trust in this version of what was to come. I took a deep breath as the door opened.

We entered the *room*. There was a guard at the door checking invitations. Evidently, if you didn't have one, you wouldn't be allowed in. I stood stunned and impressed that there would ever be a case where someone would want to see me but couldn't. Most of the time, nobody wanted to see me.

I found that he told a mistruth about what kind of room it was. Yes, it was a *room*, but what he didn't explain was that there were more rooms in this room. We were really in a nightclub, our very own nightclub. People began to line up at the door to receive us.

The first person in line was Amelia. She was with Adam, of course. Then there was my dad, and in a surprising turn of events, my stepmom. I wondered if she had decided to skip the actual wedding, as I didn't see her at the chapel, but I was pretty self-consumed for good reason at the time. I smiled pleasantly and granted her a hug and continued on to some of the execs from the network.

Of course, they could take some time to come all the way here for a celebrity party. I thought of Ned briefly and what he must be going through keeping the pace as I was MIA, but it was not time for worry over things I couldn't change. Finally, out of all the people I thought I knew, Rob.

"Please, everyone, let's take our seats downstairs!" Scott knew exactly what he had planned.

I followed along with everyone else as Scott made his way

to a downstairs room. It really was the more intimate place that I had wished for all along. Even though it was past eight, we were seated for a three-course meal. It was elegantly done.

We had shrimp salads with filet mignon and steamed vegetables along with a rich five-tiered tiramisu wedding cake. It was covered in a light frosting and white chocolate roses dipped in light purple. I really didn't plan on approving of his choice of dinner or wedding cake. It was something that I felt I could have done better.

I was so wrong. I knew how frustrating it was to decorate and cater. He did me a favor by having his own master chefs from the hotel/casino take care of everything. I began to get teary-eyed with gratitude for everything Scott had planned.

"Thank you so much. I could never imagine anything better for us in my own dreams!"

"I love you, Beth, and I will show you that every chance I get for the rest of my life!"

With that, I heard a glass ting. Amelia stood to toast us.

"Elizabeth Redbird Baker has been my friend for such a long time. There is nothing that we wouldn't do for each other. When I got married to Adam, well, I found my soulmate." She started getting teary-eyed. "I just wished and wished that Liz could find the same. Then, here came Scott, a man I'd never met, who convinced me of what he wanted. From our very first conversation, it was you, Liz. You. He has convinced me, your oldest friend, that nothing but joy and happiness would abound you both from this day forward and that he's been planning this very wedding because he knew that you were his soul mate. I know that everyone isn't always lucky enough to find theirs, but thank you, Scott, for being hers. I will love you both forever! Congratulations!"

We kissed as everyone raised their glasses and joined in on the toast. I looked over to my dad and was just happy that he decided to keep any comments that he had to himself. Silence was the only thing left that he could give me on such a happy occasion. We left the downstairs dining room and moved into the room I supposed was a concert venue. There was a band and there were low lights, bright lights, spotlights, and strobe lights all in the area.

As I looked around, I saw celebrity after celebrity coming to say congratulations to Scott and me. They were his friends. I knew that I would have to get used to them eventually, so I actually joined a few for a dance. Scott didn't seem to mind a bit and just sat back at the bar and watched. It wasn't until Rob came over that I noticed anything was wrong with Scott at all.

"So, Liz, would you like to dance?"

My cheeks flushed. I nodded and took his hand. We headed for the dance floor. The tempo of the dance music slowed. We began the first slow dance we'd had since high school. His hand pulled my waist to him, and my head was automatically on his shoulders. It was only a matter of seconds before Scott interrupted our dance.

"May I cut in?"

"S-sure, Mr. Baker." Rob took a few steps back and motioned Scott to take his place.

"Thank you, Robert. That will be all for now."

Rob turned like he knew he would be in trouble somehow for the dance with me. I almost felt sorry for him.

"Please, sweetie, don't be angry with Rob. He just wanted us to catch up a bit, I promise."

"I know all about Robert, thank you very much. I hired him for his charisma. Women generally flock to him. He keeps this place running like a gem. The one thing he can't help with is the running of you."

"I thought that was why you had him watching me in our suite this morning."

He dipped me down for a long, seductive kiss.

"Let's not talk about Robert," he whispered in my ear.

Without anything else being said, I was upright, and we

continued the dance. The grandeur of it consumed me. Somehow, we were again in the past, and we were transported to a hundred years ago and all that was in the room was him. Rob was a distant memory and any answer I wanted was no longer needed. I had the answer right in front of me.

CHAPTER 20

After Party

Eventually the slow dance ended. The crowd was thinning. My dad and stepmom took off to gamble in the casino. I had a feeling that extravagance just reminded him of Mother and none of us needed those memories today. I too was all danced out. It was already 11 o'clock and seeing that I began my day exhausted, I'd had enough excitement for one day.

"Scott, sweetie, would there be any way at all that I could talk you into calling this a night? I mean, I don't mind if everyone else stays, but I would like to spend the rest of the night with you only, if you know what I mean." I looked at him with as seductive of a look as I could muster and slowly kissed around his lips. It was sad to say, but it wasn't really him that I wanted, it was sleep. I just knew that one thing had to end before the other could begin.

"Sure, Beth. I will be up to join you very soon, I promise."

"What do you mean? Aren't you going to come with me right now?"

"Not yet. I have a few guests to schmooze, if you know what I mean. It isn't every day that I get them all together like this!"

I tried to keep my head about everything. How could he seriously think about being here with old buddies and not with me up in our suite? I was a little hurt and I was getting a little angrier as I thought it over. The magic of the evening was disappearing like a cloud of smoke that covered the dance floor.

"You know what, I think I'll just hit the bar. I bet that'll wake me up a bit."

I turned and walked away and did exactly what I said I would.

"Elizabeth, wait up!"

I turned around expecting Scott to be begging for forgiveness. He was being stupid and inconsiderate, and he knew it.

"Ugh, Rob, what do you want? Did Scott ask you to assist me again?"

It wasn't whom or what I needed right now. I needed security in my decisions. How could someone change in a half an hour from someone who would lay down his life for me to someone negotiating with a business associate at our wedding reception?

"Scott did ask me to make sure I was here if he needed anything else and yes, I was watching you both for my job, but..."

"Geez, thanks so much for your assistance!"

"Come on! It's not like that! Besides, I can't help that I am still perceptive when it comes to you and other guys! If I remember right, if a guy let you walk away, then he wasn't even worth old food in the garbage. He was worse than garbage."

"Yeah, well what do you do when you just got married to someone you aren't sure about yet?"

"I'm really sorry, Lizzy. If it were still like old times, we would start to make out just to make the other guy jealous. Do you remember all the guys that we did that to? I was surprised that you never had someone ask you to marry them then. They always seemed interested in you."

"Rob, do you mind if we don't talk about the past? Just do me a favor and get me a drink."

"Lizzy, you know I don't let you drink around me."

"Do I look sixteen anymore, Rob? I mean, really."

"Suit yourself." He turned toward the bartender. "Hey, get this fine lady an Amaretto Sour." He turned to hand it to me. "There you go, it's just like its name, sour love."

I winced at his perception of tonight's events.

Instead of indulging him in banter, I abruptly downed the sweet liquid and asked for another.

"Another, please!"

I picked up that drink and it was gone as quickly as the first. I had decided that I wasn't looking to take the edge off or to get over being mad, I wanted to get wasted.

"Whoa, Lizzy. Don't you think you've had enough? Two drinks have always been your limit!"

"Another, please!"

It wasn't long after I consumed the third that I started feeling the effects. I could no longer think clearly or rationally.

"Come dance with me, Rob!"

"Elizabeth, please! You've just had over your limit. Please don't make a fool out of yourself tonight!"

I began to dance around Rob. I was grabbing toward him to come and dance with me. I had all but forgotten the distant memory of the man I'd just married who was ignoring me.

"Wait here."

"Wh-where are you going?" I started to get sad because I didn't want to get left again.

Rob left me where I stood. I leaned up against the bar and

rested my head in my hands. I was so tired. It was no time at all before two hands were coming toward me.

"Rob, you came back!"

"No, honey, it's not just Rob, it's us too." I looked up to see Amelia and Adam.

"Hey, you guys! Are you having fun at our party? I'm supposed to leave without Scott. He said that he didn't want to go upstairs yet!"

My speech was becoming so slurred.

"Come on, we have to sober you up!"

They grabbed me under each arm and escorted me away from my reception. I couldn't seem to understand why Scott wasn't with us too. I kept calling out for him the whole way to the room. I had all of my old friends, but I felt so lonely.

"You won't leave me, will you guys?"

"No, Elizabeth, Rob and I are staying right here."

"I love you guys!"

"We love you too."

I distantly heard Amelia directing Adam to go down to the party to get Scott. They were sure that this was just a misunderstanding and if he knew how I really felt on my wedding day, then he was sure to come.

It wasn't long before I was lying on my rose-covered bed with my two oldest friends by my side. I felt so safe and secure.

"Ooh! This is sooo pretty! Where is Scott? Why isn't he here in our rose-covered bed? You won't ever leave me, will you?" I somehow rolled over and began laying my head in Rob's lap with Amelia rubbing my back for comfort.

"Boy, doesn't this remind you of old times or what?" Rob commented to Amelia.

"I was really hoping she'd found happiness this time."

They were whispering to each other. They evidently didn't think that I could hear them.

"Guys, it's ok. He's just schmoozing with the important people. He said it was ok for me to come up here by myself!"

"I'm so sorry, Lizzy." That was all that Amelia could say, as she was picking rose petals off the bed.

"You know, I would totally kick his butt for you. You just say the word. Job or no job, he can't treat one of my oldest friends like that!"

"I love you guys!" That was the last thing that I could get out of my mouth before I was asleep.

I awoke with a commotion coming from around the bed.

"Get your hands off of her!"

"Shut up, man! Can't you see she's had a hard day?"

"Do you really want to go there with me, Robert?"

"How can't you know her better yet? Haven't you tried to get to know her at all?"

"What could you possibly know that I don't?"

"She doesn't like to be left alone. She likes schedules and needs people to like her! For you to tell her that you'd catch up with her later made her sad and scared! She trusted you to be there for her from now on and you just left her for the other rich people in the room. Don't you know her mother did the same thing to her when she was little?"

"How could I possibly know that was how she'd react? I know about her mom, but I really thought that was ancient history. I knew that she still didn't talk, and she was afraid that she would like to come back into her life because she was marrying into money. She's a completely independent, grown woman. She's never shown me an ounce of insecurity. Do you think that I would hurt her on our wedding day on purpose?"

Amelia began, "Well, maybe this would be a good time to pick up where you should have left off. We are going to leave you with your wife, if that's ok. Now, I was really impressed that you got this whole wedding going for her, and I don't think that you would intentionally hurt her, but if she so much as breathes a wrong sigh in the morning, then we're taking her home ourselves!"

I couldn't believe what I was hearing out of Amelia. It was

so unlike her to give threats to people.

"It's ok, Amelia." I began to sit up and try to confront everyone in the room so they would all just be happy again.

"Rob, it's time for you to go."

"Scott, I think I need to talk to you."

They all looked at me in amazement. They had no idea I was even awake, let alone conscious of what was going on.

"Honey, get some rest. We love you and will see you in the morning."

"Goodnight, Liz," Rob whispered, mouthing the words as he turned to leave.

Adam left with both of them and it was just Scott and me once again. How could this perfect day end this way? I began to cry as soon as I realized we were all alone.

"Oh, Beth, please don't be sad on our wonderful day!"

"Our day is over! It's past midnight, remember? I told you I was ready to be with you over an hour ago! Where have you been?"

"I was talking to my business contacts, just like I said." He had a mixed look of pity and confusion on his face. It never occurred to me that he never had anyone before that cared enough if he stayed with them or not. He was a man who was nearing thirty and had never been married. He probably never had a real relationship before. I thought back to Rob. He was there once again as I got myself into trouble. Where was Scott?

"Where were you?"

"I told you. I was talking with business contacts!"

"Why did you leave me?" Tears rolled uncontrollably down my reddened cheeks. I had suffered a trauma today. On the happiest day of my life, something bad had happened too!

"I didn't. I just thought that you could use some rest without me is all. You really looked tired earlier."

I covered my head with the covers and pretended not to hear him the rest of the night. I had to get away. It was only under the sheets, but if that's how I could deal, then I would. I woke in the morning to Scott looking down at me. It appeared that he had been waiting for me to wake up.

"Good morning, Mrs. Baker," he whispered.

"Good morning, Mr. Baker." I smiled back.

I could see that his tension had begun to disappear. He had something he had to say, but he didn't know how to start.

"What is it, sweetie?" I began to worry about him a little bit.

"Do you remember what happened last night?"

I reached over to kiss him.

"Yeah, we got married."

"And?"

"We went to dinner and had a party."

"How did you get here?"

I was stunned that I couldn't remember the rest of the night.

"Did you carry me to our room and make love to me all night?"

He looked at me so funny.

"Elizabeth, don't you remember anything that happened after the party?"

"Why, what happened?"

"Honey, you got wasted and fell asleep under the covers before I could talk to you at all."

"Wh-what happened?

"Let's just say that I never knew how affected you were by your mother leaving you until last night."

"Oh my God!"

I stuck my head under the pillow.

"I can't believe something bad happened last night!"

"That's between the two of us. Just promise me that today will be different!"

"What happened last night to make me turn to drinking?"

"Nothing, I just said that I needed to talk to my contacts is all. You seemed ok with it at first!"

It all started to come back to me. Why the hell was I so insecure? He'd just sworn to devote his life to me, and I'd gone off the deep end at the first sign of inattention! I began to apologize to him. I was so surprised about what I had done that I could barely look at him.

"Scott, I normally don't drink. I promise I won't touch it again!"

He reached down to kiss me on the forehead.

"I've got room service ordered. They should be here soon. Can we start over? I promise not to leave you again."

He had such sincerity in his eyes. I couldn't help but believe him, whether he was sincere or not.

"Thank you, that would be wonderful."

We sat in bed and ate our way through an egg and cheese omelet and a fruit plate, sharing a pot of coffee.

As my head began to clear, so did more of my memories of the night before. I felt so embarrassed for making so much out of a relatively simple misunderstanding. I guessed that he wasn't the only one to misunderstand. He never knew the whole story of my family history, just as I never got the whole story on his. We were two people who had made a forever commitment, and we barely knew each other.

"Why don't I go and get a shower. I think I will start to feel better," I grumbled.

"Alright. I'll be right here, I promise."

I was wondering if he was going to start handling me with kid gloves. Did he really think that I was that vulnerable? I made my way back over to him, looked him in the eyes, and smiled.

"You know, that's not who I am. I freaked out on you. I'm so sorry. You don't have to stay, I promise. If you have some business to attend to, please do."

"You are my only business this week, Mrs. Baker. I married you because I love you. I am here now because we have a first night to do over."

He reached up and pulled me to him. I lightly kissed his lips and turned to go to the shower.

After thoroughly cleansing my body, I got out of the shower feeling refreshed. I was happy to find all of my toiletries on the vanity. I tried in vain to replicate the look they made appear to be so effortless at the salon. So, I did what I knew should get his attention and made my way out of the bathroom in a towel.

"So, Mr. Baker. You said something about us making up for lost time?"

As I drew closer to the bed, I realized that he was sleeping. He must have stayed awake last night just making sure that I was ok. That wasn't good. I turned around and went back to dry my hair and get ready for the day. I figured a few minutes of sleep would do him good. I was in the bathroom about forty-five minutes before I returned. He was sitting up in the chair he'd eaten breakfast in.

"Oh good, you're awake!" I playfully skipped towards him and sat in his lap.

"Of course I am. I wouldn't want to waste a second with my new wife, now, would I? I do wish that you would still be in your towel though!"

"Funny you should say that. I came out here earlier in just that. You were sleeping on the bed. I wanted to let you sleep, so I went back in there to get ready!"

"We are really going to have to get this timing thing down with us, aren't we?"

"Yeah, I think that would be a good thing. Are you still sleepy? I mean, after last night. Well, after the commotion, I know you probably didn't get much sleep."

"Oh, I'll be just fine. I took a little nap, right? I am ready for our day together!"

He began to get up with me in his arms. I was suddenly appreciative that he was so tall and strong. He brought me to the bed for the second time since yesterday evening, but this time we never left the security of each other's arms. The morning sun waned and was forgotten. The evening began without even a notice.

We finally got to be in the middle of the honeymoon that we deserved from the beginning. We enjoyed ourselves fully and wonderfully. It was the playfulness that I longed for all along. We connected deeply in all the ways I could have ever imagined.

The rest of the week went on continuously the very same way. There was nothing like the wedded bliss that we shared. After day two, Amelia and Adam were on their way.

"Promise me, Lizzy, that at any point it goes sideways, you call us."

"Amelia, I swear! I understand that you and Adam will always be here for me. I am never alone, and you will come and get me if ever he isn't a perfect gentleman. Is that it?" I wasn't trying to take her promises lightly, and wasn't trying to be condescending, but neither of them knew what lengths it took for me to get here mentally or physically. It was my time to give something more to myself. To allow that happiness to come to my life like it'd come to theirs. So, how could they understand? They've had each other.

"Yes, Liz. Thank you for listening so intently to what we required to give our blessing to you in your marriage."

We began to laugh. Yes, it was like they were the overprotective parents I never had. With a concerted effort to prove our endless devotion to one another and demonstrate that neither was jaded by either's actions on my wedding night, they bade me and Scott farewell.

Rob seemed to take longer.

"I'll quit and take you anywhere you want to go." This was the last thing Rob offered.

"Rob, I'm not sure what the whole overprotectiveness is, but I've kinda lived basically on my own since high school. I think I'm good. Besides, who will I reminisce with whenever I come back here?"

His whole demeanor changed for the better immediately. He must have realized I wasn't going away forever to be in a castle's dungeon far away, and didn't need to be saved, but I was now free to do anything I chose. I was the wife of Scott Baker. I was in wedded heaven. Everyone could see it.

"Till the next time then, Elizabeth." He gently laid his hand over mine as we were standing at the front desk.

It was the first time he had called me by my full name. He wasn't degrading me in the least. It was as if it was his way to say he knew his place in my life and was trying to give me that respect. It didn't go unnoticed.

"Till next time, Robert."

Scott had come up behind me while I wasn't looking.

Rob took his hand away from mine to shake Scott's. I smiled as sweetly as I could. It was the only way I could say goodbye. My reckoning with the past was now over.

At the end of our week, we said goodbye to the wonderful staff. I was promised to have full privileges in the kitchen the next time I came to stay. It was everything I wasn't looking for, but it was such a wonderful feeling to know that there was another unexpected advantage. I found myself perplexed at the thought of having something so ridiculously wonderful offered to me. I was overjoyed. "Scott, did you put them up to saying that?"

"No, Beth, they know that everything I have now belongs to you as well. Yes, they were briefed at their employee meeting, but they were just trying to show you that they love you, and would like to give you something as well."

I felt a weird type of gratitude. I never approved of having someone think of me as being above them, and although it wasn't what I wanted, I appreciated the enthusiasm by those that now technically worked for me as well.

CHAPTER 21

Adjustments

Returning to LA was another story. My enthusiasm was gone. I was taken back home to find that nothing personal was to be found. Literally all my belongings were gone.

"I got them boxed up and taken over to my place."

I realized for the first time that I had never been to Scott's house. I had been to his office, I had been to his ranch out in the country, but I had no idea where we were even going to live.

"Where exactly is your house?"

"Do you mean *our* house?"

"No, I mean *your* house! You never took me there! I wouldn't know the difference if it was your house or if it was one that you bought just for us to share!"

"Now calm down, let's just get in the car and I'll show you."

The time at my house was way too short. I knew right

away that the wonderful memories I had experienced as a single successful woman on her own were over. I was just renting, but I still saw it as an accomplishment to be there.

I looked back at it for what I was sure was the last time. There are times to reminisce, and there are times to live in the moment. I realized that even with the shock of my living arrangement change, I was still happily curious about our new home.

"Is this the home you have had for a very long time, or is it brand new?"

"Beth, my wonderful Beth, you will soon see."

We were back on the interstate in his little car, making our way to a place completely unknown to me. I began to get nervous. After all the times I told him that I didn't like surprises, I really would have thought that he would have known better. I decided that it wouldn't do me any good to bring it up with him again. After the other night and my drunken escapade, the last thing I needed was to begin to demand anything from him. I would let him have his fun and hope that I would enjoy it in the process.

We pulled in front of a large golden gate with golden roses scrolled into its structure.

"Are we in heaven?" I began to tease.

"No, just a security measure. You can never be too safe in this city."

We drove through the gate as he clicked the remote-controlled doors. After going through the grand gates, we began to travel down the main drive to the house. It was an old French Gothic architecture that you seldom see in the city, with all of the elegance of a classic movie star's home.

"Oh my God! Don't tell me this is home!"

He looked at me nervously. You could tell that he was taken aback by what I had just said.

"That is why I didn't show you my home from the beginning! I knew that you would react this way!"

"Oh, I'm just kidding. Do you think for a second that I cannot see the beauty of a structure just because it is a large mansion?"

"It's not just a mansion, it's our home. Oh Beth, do you think you could ever be happy here?"

I was in awe by his uncertainty. Was he really worrying that I would think less of him for his riches rather than his quaint farm cabin?

"I could make a home anywhere with you!"

I reached over, gave him a reassuring glance, and kissed his hand.

"I love you."

"For always and forever."

He jumped out of his car and came to greet me on my side. Once again, his manners seemed from another time, as he was coming to my aid and opened the door for me. I looked at the large front doors and wondered what was inside. I had never seen anything more grand in my life.

As soon as we were inside, I noticed the same ornate woodwork and old styling as the inside of his private office at Bakersfield Towers. The whole place reeked of history.

"Oh, Scott, this is just like your office, but at a grander scale!"

"My great-great-grandfather built this years ago. It has been passed down throughout the generations."

"I can see why. I can't imagine anyone who would ever not want to live here!"

"I hope that you can always say that you feel that way!" He looked down, almost with a doubtful frown.

"Why wouldn't I, Scott? What aren't you telling me? You looked so sad when you were just telling me about this house. Please tell me about your family. You know more about mine!"

"You didn't exactly give up that information, you know!"

"Well, maybe I did and maybe I didn't, but I didn't lie to you about anything, and I am glad you know more about me now."

"Please come with me."

He led me to a small parlor-type room. There were pictures of what must have been his family members.

"Elizabeth, we are married, and I trust you with my entire fortune. You know that from the casino. Now it's time to tell you what I've been hiding about my family."

I looked back at him and tried to hide the fear in my eyes. Sometimes you don't need another shoe to drop.

He led me from one picture to another. There were many of him at varying ages, some of his mother and her family. I even saw one of Ned when he was young. He explained that throughout the years, the men in his family were always killed in one fashion or another. All of the women that were left behind always moved from the house and it was up to the male heir to keep the tradition of the family alive.

What he never told me about the ranch cabin was that it was his great-grandmother's house after she moved from this one. She built the cabin to be closer to where her husband was buried. All of those poppies would've never existed if she hadn't left this home that they built together. She left for a simpler life with a farmer in the country.

To memorialize their lives together, they got the mural in the porch painted. It was a memory that they wanted preserved, even if their family couldn't be. The same thing happened to his grandmother. His grandfather died suddenly at the hands of another, and the house was again vacant for a matter of years. It reoccurred with his father and mother. She left the house to be with someone else after his dad died.

"Ok, so heart disease doesn't run in your family?"

"Yes, it does. Only, it is disease of the heart."

"So, what's the difference?"

"It means that another man always had affection for the women in our family. Just like what happened to my great-grandfather long ago, the same keeps happening generation after generation."

"I don't think we have to worry much about me and who

238

would be so in love with me that they would kill you! I think you're safe!" I winked at him.

I didn't believe in things like he was talking about. I didn't want to.

"You know, I had your background thoroughly researched. I needed to know who you were ever in love with, as well as who loved you. If I didn't know the whole story on that part of your life, I wouldn't know who to look for as a potential killer!"

"Wh-what do you mean, researched?"

"Look, Beth, that's not important. What was important was that I couldn't find anyone but Rob in your whole history! Do you know how many people have hundreds of relationships? It was such a lifted burden when I found out you never had anyone but me in your adult life!"

I was appalled at the prospect of someone looking into my first relationship. It was something I tried to avoid even thinking of, let alone having someone bring out all of the crazy details.

"Ah, but Ned is another story. How in the world could my own cousin have fallen for my wife at the same exact time that I was? I suspect that he'll still be trying to get you to turn against me. It is just the curse of our men, I guess. It has always been my burden to carry. Do you know how hard it is to go through life knowing that when you find the love of your life, then your own life may be shortened, and your wife will find happiness with another?"

"Scott, I'm sorry, but I just can't believe what you are saying. Do you really think that Ned would take your life just to get to me?"

"Somehow, yes. I don't know how, or when, but I just know that we have been cursed all of these years with that."

"So, what? You don't want to change history? You don't want to just live life every day with me and be happy? What happens if you are wrong? What happens if the *curse* ended with your dad?"

"Do you think that I want this to be hanging over me? If you do, you're wrong. Every day, I think how wonderful it would be to live a long and happy life with the one I love the most in the world."

"Then just do it. Forget about everything and let your walls down with me. I promise, just as I promised in our marriage vows that I would be with you..."

He abruptly cut me off.

"Till death do us part. What? You don't think I know those vows inside and out. Believe me, if I am no longer around, you are not bound to honor any vows to me. We will be over forever."

"What about heaven? Did you ever think that we would always be together, because when we die, we can be reunited?"

"That is stuff that fairy tales are made of! Besides, you will be in love with that other person by then. You will have forgotten all about me."

I couldn't believe where this day was going. It was one thing to have a crazy beginning to our marriage with me getting drunk and moody. It was another for a superstition of this magnitude to be hanging over our heads.

"Well, maybe this house isn't where we should be. Maybe we should move out of here. Did you ever think that the house was what was causing this? The memories that your great-grandfather had are just returning with every generation. I'm no ghost buster or anything, but isn't that kinda like a haunted house thing?"

"Liz, this is all that I have. I mean, of my family. Things are all that I have left of their legacy. Without them, my whole history of who I am would disappear!"

"Don't be silly, Scott. That is not true. Do you know what I have left of my history? I have nothing. I left my past behind when I moved to California. Besides, my family lost just about everything when I was young, anyway. I don't have a farm to go back to. I don't have a mansion filled with my great-grandmother's furniture. I understand what you mean, but really there is almost no one on this earth that has that luxury."

"Let's just drop it for now. I just wanted to be open and honest with you, seeing as we have devoted ourselves to each other."

"Yes, we have. Now, stop sounding like you have regret!"

I reached over to kiss him. He pulled away.

"I don't make wrong choices, Elizabeth."

I gave him a perturbed look, then decided to let it go. I had to do something to relieve the tension we had going. I began to cheerfully smile.

"Whatever! Are you going to ever show me all of this monster, or what?"

He either wanted to stay in whatever mood I was in, or decided to play along.

"Of course, my sweet Beth. Come this way!" He took my hand and swung me around playfully and led the way.

We spent the rest of the day going room to room. It made me so happy when I could get him out of the mood that he seemed to get himself into when we were talking about his family history. I still couldn't grasp that he would feel that there was any truth to what he believed. How could there actually be a curse like that? It was truly insane.

We finally came to the end of our tour late in the day. We had been to the kitchen and ate some food that was already prepared by his cook. I wondered if I would ever be allowed to cook here. He took a chilled bottle of wine with him and handed me two glasses.

"Hey, I have one more room to show you."

I knew the rooms that we had been to and those we hadn't. I had been waiting all day for him to show me where we would be spending much of our married life. He led the way up the small staircase in the back of the kitchen.

"Ladies first," he instructed after we got to the top.

"Scott, I don't know where we are going! I'm already all turned around!" I laughed. "I hope you have GPS here—I think

I'm going to need it!"

"Just go. Your heart will lead you in the right direction!"

"Scott, please don't ruin this with your superstitions!"

"Please?"

He looked at me with pleading eyes. You could see it was the same way he was looking at me that day in his office. It was like he was seeing if everything fit just right. I knew that this was some sort of test, but I didn't believe in this. I was sure that I wouldn't know the right door to choose.

"Fine. But if I get this wrong, please don't divorce me yet!"

"Not a chance!"

I led him down the corridor. It seemed to look familiar. I didn't know if we had been here earlier, or if all the hallways looked the same. I hoped not. I really would need a GPS!

"Ok, this one *here* will do just nicely!"

He gave me a quirky smile and motioned for me to open the door. Though it was dark out already, I could see by the light of the moon that it wasn't a proper bedroom. It was pale in color, and I had a hard time seeing the size of the furniture.

"Where are we?"

He kept his quirky smile up as he turned on the light.

"The nursery."

I began to laugh nervously.

"Uh, I don't think that we are ready for all of that! Maybe you need to give me another chance to pick the right room. I told you that I wouldn't be any good at this!"

"Did you know that you did kind of go to the right room?"

"I understand that you may be eccentric, but please tell me that you aren't going to make us stay in this room just because I picked it first!"

He began to laugh.

"No, no! I was simply saying that there was something about this room that would lead you to the right room!"

He continued his giggle. He thought this was funny?

"You know, I think that I may be ready to lie down for a

while. Do you mind just telling me where we are going to be sleeping, please?"

"Now, don't go getting too cranky and tired yet, little mama. Look over there behind that tapestry of Little Boy Blue!"

"Scott, I am not your little mama, so please don't say that again. You are starting to creep me out."

"Sorry, I was just stating the obvious."

"What obvious?"

I was tired of his games and surprises.

"We are expecting a baby already!"

I made my way to the tapestry on the wall and moved it. Sure enough, there was a door. It was adjoining one room to another. I was too tired to argue with him or hear his crazy tales of what was to come in our lives. So, I decided not to respond. Instead, I simply opened the door and found my way by the little light brought in from the nursery light to the bed. I went to lie down and proceeded to take off my shoes.

"Just wake me up when I'm out of the latest *Stranger Things* episode, please. Hey, if you believe so hard, you know that I need my sleep if indeed I'm now magically expecting!"

He climbed over to me and laid his head on my stomach.

"You must be. I am not trying to be strange, but I promise that you are."

"Scott, we used protection!"

"That isn't one hundred percent, you know. Besides, you aren't taking birth control to back it up!"

"Ok, how would you know?"

He buried his head in my stomach, as if embarrassed.

"Good night, Scott."

"Good night, Beth. I love you."

And I believed that he did. Even though the day was one surprise after another, even after all of the openness about him knowing that I would leave him one day, I believed that he loved me.

"I love you too, you crazy man."

I went to sleep almost immediately.

CHAPTER 22

Back to Reality

I awoke to something soft trailing across my cheek.

"It's time to wake up, sweetie," he said calmly.

I opened my eyes and saw that he was waking me with a single rose in his hand.

"What time is it?" I asked groggily.

"About five in the morning. Don't you have to be at work at six?"

I sat up quickly. Work. Oh. The honeymoon was over. I had real life I had to go back to.

"You are exactly right. Thank you." I was softly thanking him not only for the rose that I just took from his hand, but also for getting it right when it came to knowing that I still had a career. I got up and started heading for the bedroom door.

"Where are you going?" he asked playfully.

"To shower. You did wake me up to go to work, right?"

"That is true, but really you have to know where the bath-room is first, and I noticed that you were going in the wrong direction," he mused.

"Is that so? Then please, lead the way!" I answered enthu-siastically.

"Right through this door."

He led me to what I had assumed was a closet. I knew that there was one outside door to the room, one adjoining the room that evidently was a nursery, and so there was only one door left. He opened the door and I realized immediately why there was only one door. There was a massive walk-in closet and changing room that eventually led to the master bath.

I was expecting everything to be totally out of date, but it looked like you could see it in a recent top design magazine. Everywhere around me seemed to be one form of granite, marble, or tile. They were all in light ethereal tones. It was one of the most serene baths I had ever seen in my life. To say that it was grand scale would be understating it.

"Oh, Scott, this is absolutely beautiful!"

"I got it remodeled for you. I made them really rush, but it still took over a week! I was so afraid that it wouldn't be done in time!"

"You really *were* confident about me, weren't you?"

"You and I were made for each other. I don't doubt that for one single second. I just want to make everything as special as I can for you. It's actually been fun. I had never put much thought about anything in my life until I met you. It was like you woke something up. Something that I didn't even know existed. I just love and adore you."

"Oh, Scott, I don't ever want to hear those words stop, I promise, but..."

"But you have to get ready for work. I know, and besides, I do too. I already took my shower earlier, so it's all yours."

"Thank you."

I watched him leave the room as I made my way into the

massive shower. I wasn't sure if I really knew how to work it all.

"You know, you are going to have to show me how to use all of these gadgets tonight!" I yelled out so he could hear me in the other room. I thought I heard him reply that he couldn't wait, but I really wasn't sure.

The water was so loud as it came out of only half of the showerheads on the wall. I leaned against the cold wall as the hot water splashed against my skin. I began to think about the whole Scott thing. He was so abrupt about everything. I was so afraid that when we were married, he wouldn't let me have my career. It wasn't that he ever said anything about it before, but seeing that he was so wealthy, did he want his wife to work outside the home?

It brought me back to the weekend. I suddenly was worried for Ned. What if what Scott said was true? What if Ned was to do something drastic to keep me as his one and only best friend, or more? I was suddenly worried about them both. I didn't want harm to come to anyone I loved—whether it was someone I vowed to love forever or someone that made my life happy by their unending friendship.

I didn't want to give either up. It was such a relief that he wasn't going to make me choose. He wanted me to be happy the way I was, not the way that he thought I should be. That was all the difference.

I quickly got dressed and headed for the studio. It was a whole week since I had graced the halls to my set. I didn't know why, but I was so nervous. I was hoping that I wouldn't run into any of the management. I just wanted to get back to work. The work that I was into about a week and a half ago. Uncomplicated, ordinary work. I was suddenly thinking about all the food that I was going to have to produce that day on the show. I realized that I was actually hungry!

In all of the years that I'd worked here, I was never hungry when I came in. Tired, maybe. But I only nibbled here and there on the products for sale. That wasn't until at least seven in the morning! It was way too early to be feeling this way. I attributed it to the overabundance of wedding cake and rich foods in Vegas.

"Ah, there she is!"

"Surprise!"

Ok, I guess that my un-grand entrance was not what everyone here wanted for me. Standing in the room were all the executives and Ned, of course. My face immediately went red, and I really had an uncanny need to leave the way I came. I didn't care how many times Scott had seemed to try to change my core behavior by surprising me unceasingly since I'd known him, my transformation wasn't going to be immediate no matter what he did. It was, however, a first step, and I was surprised for the first time to have the courage to stay. Deep breaths, I said to myself, and entered the room.

"Oh my gosh, you guys shouldn't have!"

I meant it so much more than what it sounded like. Before I knew it, my colleagues surrounded me. There were hugs going all around. It seemed like some kind of celebrity reception where there was a line of important people and others introducing themselves or exchanging well wishes. What was going on? I slowly came upon Collin Singleton, who had been in cahoots with Scott the whole time.

"So, Mrs. Baker! How does it feel to be married? Oh, you could have given us a heads-up about who you were dating. Who knew that you were such a catch? Our own Elizabeth Redbird, now Mrs. Baker!"

"Ok, ok, thank you, everyone. Please, I feel awkward enough already."

I put my head down, outwardly embarrassed.

"Besides, this was more of a surprise to me than it was to you, right, Mr. Singleton?"

Collin looked down in a bit of embarrassment himself. He knew that he had the goods on my relationship, way before I ever did!

"Please, Mr. Singleton, do tell me, how long did you know about our engagement?" I decided to turn the whole thing back to him. I figured that if he dared put me on the spot like this, then he could be right on the stage with me.

"Oh, just a while. Never you mind the particulars. You said yes!"

They could tell that I was starting to go from the look of horrid surprise to one that resembled a playful puppy with a new ball. I had managed to turn it around to them and it wasn't long before the conversation ended and the whole management team left me with Ned to do our job. They may have liked the thought of a party, but in the end show production was the first and foremost on everyone's list.

Ned and I sat back in the same seats we had been in for two years now. I was increasingly nervous about our first alone time since I'd ditched him all together and got married without giving him an invitation. I thought about how that must feel. I thought about how left out I would be if my very own best friend didn't even bother to include me on something so important. I could barely look at him.

"I am so sorry, Ned." I put my head down once again, this time from shame rather than embarrassment. I also found myself a little teary. I wasn't going to boo-hoo or anything, but I was going to need all the strength I could muster to get through this day.

"Why are you sorry, Elizabeth? What do you have to be sorry about? Aren't you happy you married playboy Baker? Isn't that what you wanted ever since that game those weeks ago?"

"I-I just wanted to make sure that things with us were ok, is all. I just don't want any hard feelings. I know I was the one who started this whole mess. It's just, well, you have to know that I am happy being with Scott!" I looked intently into his eyes, pleading my case to my best friend. He seemed to just take it in stride.

"I know," Ned responded with a reassuring smile.

It allowed me to ask the real question that was on my mind all along. "Speaking of which, did you know anything about our marriage arrangement before I did? It seems like he told an awfully large number of people." I hoped he could see the innocence in my eyes. I knew now that from the moment of that first fateful night, I'd no longer been in control of my own destiny, and I had to know how many people were in on it.

"Liz, why would he tell me? I am his direct competition. I would be the last person that he would tell. Did you think that he asked for your hand in marriage from me?"

He began to laugh softly yet uncomfortably. I didn't know what to think about the whole thing. It seemed too simple to think that he didn't know anything about it and that he was just as surprised.

"Are you mad?"

"Are you quitting now?"

"Why would I quit? Hey, quit changing the subject! Are you mad?"

"No, Elizabeth. I am not mad. I'm not happy though. Do you think that I really wanted this for you? Or for us?"

"There wasn't an us, Ned!"

"There isn't now."

I turned red in the face. I didn't want this to happen, but really how could it be stopped.

"Do you want me to quit? Is that what you are getting at?"

I looked up at him with eyes of fury. I knew how he felt. I also knew that if he wanted to, he could let go of the spark in our relationship that happened the night of the ball game. He knew that it was over for sure now. Nothing could ever bring us back to that place. It was not anything that he wanted to forget, but he needed to for both of us.

"No! I just know how Mr. Scott likes to play by his own rules. He won't let you come to work if he decides that it isn't something that he wants you to do!"

"Don't be silly, Ned. What makes you think that I am that stupid? Do you think that I would fall for some guy that was going to ruin my life or take away everything that I have worked my whole life for?"

"I don't know, Liz, you tell me."

"I'll tell you this, I don't want anything more than for us to get into the job that we are supposed to be performing right now. You know, the one that I left the lap of luxury for this morning? So, do me a favor and drop this so we can get our work done. We can hash this all out later!"

"Fine, Elizabeth, but mark my words, he'll never let that happen. Do you think that you will ever have so much as a coffee break without him trying to butt in? I don't think so. But, you know, I think that I have said my peace, and to tell you the truth, I am just happy that you haven't given over to the dark side yet. You still may have a chance of living a partially normal life."

This was one side of Ned that I'd never seen. It was a jealous cruelty. I didn't like it, and I would have called him out on it at any other time, yet I decided to let the conversation die with that. I didn't want to stir up any more than had to be. I'd set out this morning to make it clear that things with Ned and I were going to be strictly professional while we were working together and that I wasn't going to waste my time with a could-have-been with someone that didn't deserve it.

I knew that up until two weeks ago, Ned really thought that he could have a chance with me, and this showed what a strong friendship we had. But I'd realized on my honeymoon that the relationship that we always had would have to change.

As the morning progressed, the feeling of unending appetite was coming back. I devoured two servings of at least three separate foods.

"Wow, Elizabeth! I can't even try to keep up with you today! What happened last week? Don't tell me you're one of those women who try to catch a man by looking good, just to let yourself go when the honeymoon is over! Maybe you did make the right choice in guys."

I immediately smacked him on the arm.

"Snide comments are not needed, thank you very much!"

Right then and there, I realized that the tension had broken and the relationship we had always shared was still going to be there. He may have been hurt, but in all the years I had known him, cruel was never him. Even in anger, he must have decided that it was better to have me as a friend than nothing at all. Either that, or he was really just making fun of me. I didn't care. I was just happy that there was finally a turning point to our first day back together. I started tearing up again like before. What was going on with me?

"Don't look at me with teary eyes! You know that I didn't mean anything by that! Do you think that I would be able to talk?" He once again pointed to his bulky stomach. "Didn't we already have this conversation a couple of months ago?"

I couldn't help how I felt. I was just so happy to be back with my best friend. I reached over and began to give him a quick hug.

"I don't think that you meant anything by it, I swear. I just missed my best friend, that's all."

"Oh no, let's not get sappy. I just couldn't stand it."

He put his arms around me in response. Everything felt right with the world finally. I was married to the man I loved and was with the man that made me happy by friendship alone. I also had the best job in the world. All I could wish for is this to never end. This was my happy ending.

CHAPTER 23

Did I Say Happy Endings?

It didn't take too long in our marriage for Scott to be caught up with his job. Even though he explicitly swore that I was everything to him in his life, he still had an empire to run. It was almost funny in retrospect to think that Ned thought that Scott would overtake every single moment that I had to myself. Not only did he not overtake my personal life, but he also wasn't there to finish what he promised he would.

Oh, he showed me how to use the fancy showers, and even got me a map of our house so I wouldn't get lost, but we had only been married for three weeks and I already felt as alone as I did before I met him. There is nothing that made me feel special about his business trips that he swore he'd set up about a year ago and he just forgot. It wasn't important to him to take such a hard look at his schedule ever before in his life. It was me that had thrown him. I just wanted to know why he was so hurried when it came to getting me to marry him when he was too busy for a new wife.

"I think that I am going to go lie down, Scott. Work was pretty demanding today. Nothing you wouldn't understand, Mr. Baker."

I leaned down and kissed his cheek and turned to leave.

"Hey, I'm not going anywhere this week! It'll be business as usual at Bakersfield Towers, so why don't you take a day off and spend it with me?" he begged.

"First, Scott, you know that I don't take days off. Secondly, it's only Friday night. You already have this whole weekend with me, regardless. Do you think that you can stand being here with me two full days without being bored out of your mind?" I was so tired of being ignored. I almost would have rather had an argument, because it would mean he cared at least a little if it got heated. Even a fight would be better than this.

"Let's go somewhere then, dear Beth. Nothing would make me happier," he calmly requested. It was as if he knew where I was headed and knew exactly what kind of negotiations he would need to extinguish the fire that had built up inside of me. The prospect of him listening to me and bending to my will for a change made the conversation pivot back to what he wanted all along. It was time with me. Maybe he really did have those demands, I thought. My mood immediately cleared, and excitement took its place.

"Sure. I know a perfect place to go!"

I was now perched in his lap.

"Wherever would that be? Have I been there before?"

He was getting into the conversation with a fully responsive look.

"Oh, you could say that you have been there, yet it is somewhere that I have yet to explore fully."

"Oookay, where would that be?"

"Back to the old cabin by the poppies."

The look on his face told me what he was going to say.

"Why don't we go there another day? You know that I would take you anywhere that you would ever wish to go, but why don't we go somewhere new to both of us as a couple?"

I knew if I couldn't have exactly what I wanted from him, then I would make him pay for what would satisfy me in other ways. Wildest dreams, here I come!

"Ok, Europe it is!" I exclaimed.

His look became enthusiastic once again. Money was always the easy way out for him. He knew I would play right along. Who wouldn't? At least if I took him completely away from here, then I would finally have him to myself.

"Where in Europe? Was there a place that you have in mind?"

"Let's country hop! I've seen where it was possible to eat breakfast in one country and end up eating dinner in another seamlessly. I want to find the best local cuisine in each country. Austrian Strudel in the morning, maybe Portugal for Pasteis de Nata for a midmorning snack, and then to Spain for some Paella! It doesn't matter where we start! You know that pastry is my first love, so I may be going a little overboard with the first two countries, but you *did* ask!" I said firmly. "So, that is where I want to be! Small and local, not big and commercial. It has been my dream since I came to California to check out the cooking techniques of the locals abroad. I wanted to be taught where the foods originated. There is no better instruction than someone who lives in the middle of nowhere and feeds the hungry masses that come to them for a source of nourishment and celebration in everyday hard-working life."

"Your wish is my command. I'll call the office and have it set up for the morning. What time would you like to leave? You probably want to sleep in, seeing as you were already ready for bed."

"Yeah, I don't know what's wrong with me, ever since we came back from our honeymoon all I want to do is eat and sleep. I feel like a cat!"

"Well, maybe tonight will get you refreshed. I'm sorry if I haven't been giving you enough of my time the last couple of weeks. This married thing is just something that I'll have to get used to."

"Do you regret marrying me so quickly?"

"NO! Don't ever doubt my love for you, Elizabeth. I mean it. Look at me. Do not *ever* doubt my love for you. I will adore you for *eternity*."

I laid my head on his chest.

"Come on, my sweet Beth. I'll run a nice bubble bath for you. Have you even used the tub once since you moved in?"

I turned my head back and forth into his chest in response. He placed my feet on the floor, got up from his sitting chair, and took me by the hand to lead us to the bedroom. He prompted me to lie down to rest as the bath was being drawn.

"Rest."

That was the last thing that I remembered before I woke up to the smell of breakfast.

"Hey there, sleepy head! Time to get ready for the best day you've ever had in your life!"

"I thought that was the day we got married!"

He kissed me lightly on my lips and handed me a tray of the most luscious strawberries, croissants, lightly honeyed butter, milk, and juice.

"So, are these croissants from Paris?" I teased. "Also, where is my coffee? I mean, I'm impressed. I really am, but what about something to get me to wake up this morning?"

"Oh, I brought myself for that."

With those words, he showed me how one body could fully arise the other from sweet slumber to the feeling that you would never have desire to sleep again for fear of ever missing that kind of bliss. Even with those overwhelmingly pleasurable feelings, I still felt like there was an edge I couldn't quite take off. I began to unconsciously yawn, rather loudly. There was a point at which he was sure that the sound was coming from my overwhelming pleasure. It was short lived as he glanced into my eyes.

"Still tired? Maybe I shouldn't have woken you yet."

"What? It's not like five in the morning, is it?"

"How about 9:30? I have been waiting for hours for you to regain consciousness. I decided to wake you when I realized that the plane is supposed to take off for Europe at eleven."

A look of horror came to my face.

"Oh my gosh, why didn't you tell me? Tired or not, this is really my dream trip! I wouldn't be late for that for anything!"

"Don't worry; as you know, Conrad can get us there in less than thirty minutes."

"Well, I better get a quick shower! Wait, what happened to my bath last night? Oh no! I really must have been tired! Didn't you try to wake me?"

"Nope, couldn't wake you up for anything last night. If it weren't for light snoring, I would have wondered if you were alive or not. That's how deeply asleep you were!"

"I am so sorry. Here I was pouting that we haven't had any time together because of your work schedule, and I can't even stay up till ten on a Friday night. It just seems that I caught a sleeping bug when we were in Vegas. If I didn't know any better, I would think that I had a mild case of mono."

"The kissing disease? Do you really think that I would give you something? You weren't kissing anyone else on our honeymoon, were you?"

"Ha, ha. That isn't even funny and no, I don't think that you would give me a disease. I am just saying that it is particularly strange that I am this tired. That's all."

"Maybe we should visit the doctor really quickly before we go. I'm sure if you were really sick with anything, then Europe would rather that you wait to visit!"

"Ok, you have a point, but my doctor is at the other end of town. I could never get to him before we're supposed to take off!"

"Well, I have a personal doctor that will make house calls pretty quickly, if that would be alright."

"Of course, you do! What was I thinking? You can probably get a person to do anything you need for the amount of money they know that you can pay!"

"Impressed, or is it something else?"

"Just call him. Let's leave it at that!"

"Again, your wish is my command!"

He promptly left the room to make the call necessary to make sure I was free of disease. I must have looked pretty rough for him to persuade me so quickly to be doctored.

"Ugh!" I grunted as I made my way to the shower. I felt accomplished as I turned on all of the necessary gadgets to make the shower go properly. The varied placements of the showerheads brought great comfort to my body every morning, and this one was without exception. The feeling made looking to a long trip and touring a new land promising, if not completely bearable.

The excitement began to build. I was finally going to be able to taste and see everything my heart had desired. My heart swelled with anticipation. I thought surely getting into the routine of my mundane schedule would have been the cause of my fatigue and the first thing I wanted to do was to call off the doctor. But it was too late. As I stepped out of the shower, I heard voices by the bed. I peeped out into the room and realized that it was Scott, with a stranger beside him. How did he get the doctor to come so quickly? Does he have a doctor living here too?

"Hello!" I tried to seem as chipper as possible.

"Beth, this is Doctor Bertrand. I asked him to come as soon as possible."

"He was lucky enough to get ahold of me while I was in transit to make my rounds at the hospital. I was literally just about five minutes away. So, what can I do for you, Mrs. Baker?"

I immediately felt better about the questions I had about him a moment ago. I decided that I just had an overactive imagination to think that he might own his own private doctor. I also knew that I had some real convincing to do for him to clear me to go on my fantasy trip.

"Well, I guess that I've been tired lately. Pretty much since we got back from our honeymoon. I have also been really hungry. I was dieting before our wedding and I really just attribute all of this to a poor diet and just trying to get back into the routine of daily life in new surroundings. But otherwise, I am just fine. If anything, I think an impromptu trip with my husband by my side would do just the trick to make me feel better!" I just needed the doctor to hear me.

"Scott, are you feeding her badly?"

"Hey, don't look at me. It would definitely be from her job at that food shopping place!"

I looked at him disapprovingly and corrected him.

"I am the Producer of the Dessert Division at Culinary Shopper's Network, thank you very much. I am afraid that I have to say that it isn't the most nutritious food in the world. So, that is probably the bad food I am referring to. However, I have been eating my fair share of a large variety of foods all throughout the day."

"Ahh, I see. Ok, well there are many things that can cause fatigue. A poor diet is definitely one of them. Let me take a little blood and urine and I should be able to tell you a roundabout answer in a matter of minutes. It appears I caught you at an ideal time to test you before you ate. I believe I will be able to clear you and I bet it will be done by the time you get ready for your trip."

Dr. Bertrand was right. It was only a matter of minutes

before he returned with a diagnosis.

"Are you ready for children, Mr. Baker? It appears that you are going to be a father in about eight and a half months!"

That did it. Not enough time had passed to tell me something that I was completely unprepared for.

I was so happy that I was by my bed when I heard the news. I think I would have passed out if I hadn't lain down.

"I knew it! Didn't I, Elizabeth?"

He looked at me like he had won some kind of *being right* race. This was not a race I wanted him to win.

"Oh my gosh! I'm not ready for this! We haven't been married nearly long enough to start a family! What about our trip? You aren't going to tell me I can't go out of the country or something, are you?"

"Take a deep breath, Mrs. Baker. You will be just fine. Babies are born every day to those who are much less prepared. As far as your trip, just be careful. There are no ordinances against travel on early expectant mothers."

I began to panic. I began to think of my own mother. When Andrew and I were born, did she feel like she was ready? Did she even care that we were coming? Would I be like her and have the ability to disconnect from my children and want to leave them too?

Tears started welling up in my eyes and I ran from the room. The doctor might understand why I was doing this. He could probably spot panic, but I was sure that Scott did not. I ran to the nearest bedroom that had an open door and hid behind it. There was no way that I would let them find me. I didn't want to hear this kind of news. I wasn't ready. I wasn't ready. I held my hand to my mouth to prevent myself from hyperventilating or giving myself away.

I heard them outside the room as they were calling out for me in the hall. I knew that as soon as they left this wing to go into a lower level, I would probably find a new place to hide. I would need a lot of time to think this one over. That was for sure. I stopped hearing footsteps. I decided to run once again to find a better hiding place.

"Oh my gosh! You scared me to death!" I exclaimed as I ran right into Scott.

"What are you doing? Are you ok?"

"What, what?" It didn't seem like anything he was saying was comprehensible. I was too deeply in a state of panic to understand.

"Beth, honey, please, what's wrong? A baby isn't so terrible, is it? Our baby?"

"Baby. Baby," I said weakly as I slowly fell to the ground.

I was back in bed when I awoke from my instant slumber.

Scott looked to the floor. As he was getting me back to bed unconscious and calling the doctor to my side, he also called Conrad and cancelled the entire trip.

"What happened?" I still sounded so weak.

"You passed out, Beth. You passed out!"

Scott had such a look of panic on his face. I must have really given him a cause of concern for him to be this upset.

"Mrs. Baker, please eat some of your breakfast. Your blood sugar was pretty low when I tested it earlier. It happens to many expecting women. That is probably why you just took it so hard. Low blood sugar can make you irrational, as well as weak."

"Are you sure that she's going to be alright, Doc?"

His look of concern had yet to ease up.

"I am fine, Scott, I promise. It was just a lot to take in is all. I wasn't ready to hear that we're going to be parents!"

"Please, Mr. Baker, allow her to get some food into her before you do anything more to upset her. She needs the sugar to think rationally."

I sat on the bed and managed to get some of the carefully planned breakfast down, even with the lump in my throat.

"You see, Scott? I'm just fine! Can I please get dressed now so we can go?"

"I'm so sorry. It just isn't meant to be today. We missed our flight. But I promise to be right here with you the rest of the weekend."

"Then to the poppies?" I pleaded.

My pleas went unnoticed. The rest of my pregnancy was filled with moments very much like those. The fact that I couldn't seem to agree with Scott about anything and the fact that he looked at me as I would fall apart at any moment didn't help.

After the trip to Europe was immediately cancelled, I began to see the doctor much more frequently than a woman with a normal pregnancy would. Scott just felt that even though the doctor kept telling us that everything was textbook, there must be something else wrong with me and I needed some extra care.

To say that I was being driven crazy was an understatement. He even began paying me extra visits to work to see if my coloring was ok. It was ridiculous.

In fact, I nearly ran every morning to get to work just so I could get away from him. How could our short honeymoon phase turn into this so quickly? It was so much more than a doting husband and I wasn't just another thing in his life that he could control.

It carried into my work life, which was never my intention, yet it was comforting to know that Ned was still on my side.

"Liz, do you need me to talk to him or something? As your best friend, I can't allow him to upset you this way!"

"Please, whatever you do, don't talk to him about me, especially with you and me in the conversation!"

"Why not, Liz? What aren't you telling me?"

"Nothing, Ned, just take my word for it and drop it. Please."

"Something isn't right with him, Liz. You know that and I know that. Just remember that I am here for you if you ever change your mind about him or anything."

"Don't say that! Don't ever say that! He and I are supposed

to be together. He knows that and I know that. You should know that by now."

"No, Liz, I see the pain that he causes you. I see you mindlessly answering with what he has been feeding you since the moment you met! Don't you ever think what would have happened if I'd never taken you to that stupid game?"

"Oh my gosh! Would you please drop—no, drop-kick—that game night from our conversations forever! You act like that was some big defining moment that you had some control over. Yeah, we could have not gone, but on that other hand, destiny is destiny!"

"You don't talk like that, Liz! You sound like some kind of robot recording. I don't believe in destiny. I do believe in bad luck though, and his family has been full of it for years. It's not because it's their destiny, it's because they are all crazy!"

"Let's just say that you don't know everything about the situation, ok? Maybe he's not the crazy one in this relationship."

"You see, quit doing that! Quit defending him for making you think that you have something wrong with you!"

"Sorry, but as far as I have understood marriage, you are supposed to be there for your spouse!"

"So, when is he going to be there for you only and not just his interests? Let me ask you this. Do you know if you are having a boy or a girl?"

"What does that matter?"

"Boys are special to that crazy family, that's why. In fact, you don't have to tell me, I already know. You're having a boy."

"Shut up, Ned. Quit talking about my baby like it is something bad. I'm having a tough enough time thinking about what kind of mother I'm going to be without your words of wisdom!"

"Don't even begin to second-guess yourself. If he thinks that you'll be a bad mother, he'll probably get rid of you as soon as you have the baby."

"Stop!"

I was feeling exasperated by the constant bickering at home and now it had come to work. I was tired of arguing with everyone about what was best for me. I knew. I just wished that everyone else would understand.

"Look, Ned, do you think that you can handle the rest of the day on your own? I really just want to go home and get some rest."

"S-Sure Liz. Hey, I didn't upset you, did I? I really didn't mean to. I just hate to see you in pain over that guy. Look, I promise I won't even bring him up anymore, ok?"

"Thank you. Remember that tomorrow, please!"

CHAPTER 24

Baby Blues

"Elizabeth! Elizabeth? Are you home?"

Scott was crying out to me from the hall below. He knew that I was probably in bed. My car was in the garage. The car that he didn't want me to drive anymore. After that first day, he tried to stop me from driving. Not only because of being pregnant, but because it was my little silver Honda Accord.

It was *my* car I bought on *my own* long before we met. I let him know right away that he would never hinder all of my independence just because we were together. I was becoming tired of hearing him yelling my name.

"I AM IN HERE!"

I began to yell to him.

I wished he would just leave me to sit with my feet up and read my mother-to-be books, like I wanted.

"Hey, Beth, are you alright? I heard you left work early. If you weren't feeling well, you should have called, and I would have called the doctor immediately. And you drove in this state? That's it! It is no longer safe for you or the baby! Conrad will be taking you to work from now on!"

I listened inattentively to his now regular rant and responded.

"I am just fine, Scott. I just wanted some peace and quiet." I lifted the book as if to show the importance of what I was doing. "Speaking of that," I continued, "what are you going to do when the baby is here? You most certainly cannot go around yelling for me then, now can you? For that matter, what is wrong with me wanting some rest and relaxation?" I began to rant. "Don't make me bring up the fact that you were supposed to take me on my dream weekend and instead I have had nothing but trouble from you about this baby! Just do me a favor and go. I want to be alone!"

His head went toward the ground, and he looked defeated. He didn't say anything, he just turned and left the room.

I didn't see him for two days after that. They were the most peaceful days since the day I moved in. I finally felt in control of what was going on in my life, which was different from when *he* chose to stay away because of his work obligations.

I didn't know where he went, nor did I care. In the end it gave us both ample time to think about our situation. He had to realize that what I said were my needs and what he perceived to be best were two different things.

The day he returned it was with a bouquet of flowers and a solemn apology.

"Beth, I promise that for as long as we live, I will never disregard your feelings again. I understand now that you have always been a very strong person who could take care of herself. I have been a fool to think that you would need me."

"Please don't apologize. Of course, it was right for you to

worry. If you didn't worry about the woman who was carrying your child, then what kind of man would you be? Of course I need you, *we* need you! I was just having a really bad day the other day. It's been difficult for me to adjust."

"Can we please call it even?"

"Definitely."

It was like an energy in the room completely changed and we were right back to where we were when we had left off before the initial disagreement began.

"Can I take you somewhere?"

"Sure, where to?"

"Can it be a surprise?"

"A surprise from you? I can't imagine."

I smiled and he could catch the playfulness that I was trying so hard to give off.

We went down a very familiar road and I realized within about a half an hour of being there that we were headed for the hills of poppy and the old cabin on the hill. The anticipation was killing me.

"You're finally going to let me see your grandparents' cabin?"

"Hey, I told you, it's a surprise!"

We pulled up to the spot where we'd parked the day that he first brought me. I looked around and although it looked the same, there was a definite difference. The poppies had faded and now the hills were rolling grassland.

"Well, what do you think?"

"It looks bare without the poppies!"

"True, but that's not it!"

"I'm sorry, Scott, I guess that I am just slow. I don't know what you mean. It's been pretty long since we've been here. Plus, it was raining, if you remember."

"Look over there."

"Whose cabin is that? Was it here before? Is that what is different?"

"Yep. It sure is. I just had it built."

"You *just built* it? Why?"

What was wrong with the old cabin? I decided it must have been in more disrepair than I could see. I guess it would make sense, if you were an *eccentric millionaire*. Otherwise, we would be working together to fix it up and make it our own. I guess he couldn't picture me with power tools and a sledgehammer. I smiled at the thought of that. He could only see that it appeared to make me happy.

"Ok, I can see how curious you are to check the cabins out, so why don't we start with the new one and work our way to the old one."

"That's a deal."

I jumped out of the car, as well as any large pregnant woman could, and looked happily at the dirt path that led us to our new cabin.

It was so quaint. The furniture was split logs made into furniture. It was amazing how comfortable the couch was. I was sure that it was bound to be uncomfortable, as it was made of solid wood covered in cushions.

"So, is everything here new or did any of it come from the old cabin?"

"Nope, all new. This is a cabin to build our new memories in. It's not to be shared with the old memories that come with the old cabin."

"I'm always up for new memories."

I reached for him and pulled him to me. I embraced him as delicately yet ferociously as a woman in her seventh month of pregnancy could. We officially made our cabin ours, not by picking curtain colors like normal couples, but in the way we seemed to communicate best, through touch and body exploration.

He seemed to embrace the curves along with the moods. It felt like there was a new me with every day that I awoke, and he enjoyed every one of them in a new way. It was like a challenge that he was going to happily conquer.

I decided that this was one surprise I could live with and I was ecstatic to receive.

"Thank you, Scott, for everything." My heart had melted right into his.

"I love you with all of my heart, Beth. Please don't ever forget that."

"Why would I ever forget that, Scott? Our time here has been nothing but perfect. Just the way that I thought it would be if we could ever come back. Is this why we're here? Is this some kind of big apology for making me think that you might not love me enough? I'm sorry, but you didn't need to do this. The old cabin would have been fine for me. You know, normal couples might even start out in a little cabin just like that one!"

He looked down as if embarrassed by his grand gesture.

"I only wanted to make something of our own. I tried."

"I knew that you still loved me. Even when you were gone for the last two days, I knew that you would be back. Did I realize that you were gone to make final arrangements with the builders and designers? No. But you have to know that I believe with all of my soul that we were meant to be together. You know it and I know it. We feel it every day we're together. Call it fate, call it destiny, we were meant for each other. I would never doubt that." I looked hard into his eyes and continued. "I love you more than you could ever know, Scott. I just got upset because you were crowding me. I just needed time by myself. I spent nearly ten years on my own here in California. It's hard to change old habits. You know I have trust issues."

"Please, don't ever think that you can't trust me!"

"Oh, please don't misunderstand! The trust is not for you. The trust is me. I didn't know what was going on, but when I found out we were having our baby, I wasn't sure I could trust myself to be a good mom. I was worried that I would turn out like my mom. You know, she left us. She decided that she just didn't want my dad or me. You could never know how that feels. You could never know."

I began to quietly weep. Somehow, once again, this beautiful day turned into another moment of foolish despair. Scott reached over to me and brushed my hair out of my face.

"You are not, nor will you ever be anything like your mother. She is a stupid, rude, horrible woman. She never deserved anything in life. That is why she never had anything. Look at all that we have together. She would have given her life or the life of her children just to experience your life for one day. She will never know how that feels. Please, don't worry about how you will be as a mother. You will be the best. I promise. I knew it from the moment that I saw you. I could see our future too. I wouldn't be seeing a future with a nut!"

He chuckled.

"I don't think that I am nuts, just disassociated. I just want to be sure that once this baby is here, I will have the correct motherly instincts."

"Once again, I have no doubt that you will be the best mother that this world has ever known."

"Thank you."

Our talk about my fears and doubts were ended as he took me around all of the new nooks and crannies of the cabin. There were high ceilings like I would have expected in new architecture. I just couldn't help but wonder if the original cabin had the same features inside.

The more that he showed me around, the more of a need I had to go into the other cabin. I just wondered what was wrong with me. Why did I always seem to dwell on what I shouldn't? I walked silently as he guided me to the last remaining room.

"I didn't decorate this one for you, Beth."

"What is this room?"

"It will belong to our children. It is their nursery. I have a feeling that you were a little bummed out that the one at home was already so tastefully done that we didn't need to change a thing. I wanted you to have a place that you could make your own. This will be our *normal* house in the country. When the baby is born, we could even live out here if you would like."

I looked up to his sincere smile. He was looking for gratitude. I was looking for answers about a future that he didn't consult with me on.

"Can we please go to the other room and sit down?"

He led me back to the great room. As we sat, I took his hand. I wanted him to know that I was appreciative of everything that he was giving to me. I also needed to know what he expected of me to make me this great super mom.

It took only about ten minutes for our conversation to come to a head. He poured out his biggest wishes for the future. He wanted me to be here waiting for him when he came in from the long city commute. He wanted me to raise our child out here by myself. More to the point, he wanted me to leave my job.

"Scott, you don't understand! This job means everything to me. Well, without it, I would just lose my self-worth all together. We both know that it isn't about the money with me, it's about independence."

"Maybe you can go back after a year or so. I'm not saying that you can't work forever, I just pictured you as being happy to have that choice to be a good mom. Listen, I already talked to Collin at the Network, and he told me that you could take off as much time as you wanted." He began to try to reason with me. "He promised that he would take you back as soon as you decide that it's time to come back. He said that you guys have some great interns that would be more than happy to get the chance to get firsthand experience! I promise, I worked it all out for you!"

He leaned over to give me a congratulatory hug.

"Scott, ugh. Never mind then, I'm going for a walk. You just stay here."

I got up and headed for the door.

"Beth, please don't leave me here mad. I can see that you are. What is so wrong with the future that I have planned?"

I turned around to face him. I was so angry that I felt like I was going to explode.

"Your future, Scott, not ours. You never even let me in on this grand scheme that you have for us."

"But, Beth..."

"You leave for two whole days, come back and expect me to completely give up my life on your request? Not another word, Scott. I told you already. I am going for a walk alone. I'll be back in a little while. Why don't you make sure that we have a future by making lunch or something? I'll be back."

I slammed the door behind me. The thick wood planks in the massive door made a large thud that echoed through the hills. I headed directly to the path that we took that first day. Thoughts were racing the more that I walked. I wasn't able to work anything out in my mind.

I knew that Scott would never listen to me. He never did. He always made his rules up when he wanted to. He wanted me to choose him and not Ned. I did. He wanted me to get married to him on a specific date. I did. He wanted me to move from my home and move into his massive mansion. I did. He wants me to give up my career altogether and look after our child on my own. I won't!

Tears streamed down my face. In all my life, I never thought vast fields would ever make me feel so bound up and tied down. I couldn't breathe. I hadn't been this full of despair since I was a teenager and my world still revolved around my parents. The more I cried, the madder I got, until I was in as close to a sprint as I could get.

I was headed for the other cabin. I was tired of living with his rules. If he could do anything he wanted, then so could I. I made my way up to the front porch and decided not to even try the front door. I knew that he would have that locked up tight. I ran around the back of the cabin to look for the back door.

What I did find was a small light shining through the window of the cabin. I wondered if it was just the bright sunshine coming through the chimney that was causing the room to light up. I knew it wasn't due to an open window or something, because he had them heavily covered.

What other explanation could it be? I grabbed the back door handle and heard a thud coming from the way of the other cabin. Scott decided to come looking for me after all. He didn't stay true to his word. Of course, he didn't. He never did. He lived by his own rules. The rules that didn't apply to me.

I swung the back door open. I was actually surprised how easy it was to move. You would think that a hundred-year-old cabin would creak more or something, but it didn't. It gave way. I decided that I probably didn't have very long, and that I had better start first by finding that light. I knew if I could get a small answer to a small question, then all of the big ones would have a fair chance of coming out.

"Hello?" I didn't know why I felt like I had to address the house like there was a possibility that there was someone here to answer, yet that is exactly what I did. I didn't even have time to hear an answer before I could hear someone coming through the front door.

"Why, why, why? Why does this always happen, Grandmother? Why can't I ever seem to find real happiness? I gave her everything that I have to offer, and it is never enough!"

His voice was frantic. I decided to hide myself behind the rustic paneled, whitewashed kitchen door. There was nothing that I wanted more than to go around the corner and confront him. Was his grandmother here? I thought he said that she was gone also. I pushed the door just a bit so I could get behind it. It was the creaking sound that made me shiver in fear of being found. Oh, why did I have to be pregnant? My old belly would have fit just perfectly.

"Elizabeth? Are you here?"

He had a strange sound to his voice that I couldn't quite place.

"If you are in here, answer me right now!"

I suddenly realized what kind of voice it was. It was an angry voice. I hadn't heard it since the first day that he brought me to Bakersfield Towers. He was always so polite to me after that, and most of the time in the beginning, we spent our little bit of time together in a loving way. There would have been no point getting mad. We were married and we had to respect each other's differences and work ethics.

As I was contemplating everything about our relationship, something that I didn't expect came over me. It was fear. I couldn't imagine that there would ever be a day that I would have to fear the man that I loved more than life itself. What on earth was he doing that was so bad now? I tried my best to take to common reasoning and decided that he was just mad because he didn't want me inside this place.

That did it for me. I became angry back. How dare he treat me like an outsider to an important part of his life! We had been married over seven long months now! I was tired of his secrets and by gosh I was going to confront him in the very place he forbade me to go!

"What do you want, Scott Baker? What do you want from me? Ooh, are you going to be mad at me now for entering your big secretive world? Well, you should have thought about that before you built me a cabin right next to it!"

Anger flared up in his eyes. He wasn't used to people defying him, not even his wife.

"And who were you talking to? Who is in that other room, Scott? Are you hiding some family member that you didn't want me to know still existed?"

Clap, clap, clap. That was all that he did. I couldn't tell if it was to shut me up with the sound of his slapping palms, or if he was clapping because he thought I was putting on a show.

"Stop clapping, Scott! I want some answers now, or, or..."

"Or what, Lizzy? Isn't that what your old friends called you? Back when you were a nobody living in a nobody part of town living with nobody parents that had no future planned for you except that they didn't want you? Or, was it all the times in high school that you tried to fit in by letting others use you to their own advantage? Please, do tell me, Lizzy, what is a girl like you to do?"

I couldn't believe what I had just heard. It was all I could do to remain calm in my composure. I knew right then and there that I was dealing with a side of Scott I'd prayed would never come out. Ned warned me that he wasn't everything that he appeared to be. He said that he was cursed because they deserved to be cursed. It was at this very moment that I realized that Ned was right.

I didn't say one word back to him. I didn't want to give him the satisfaction of an acknowledgement for what he was accusing me of. I wasn't going to let him call me white trash and get a rise out of me. No, instead, I decided to be strong. I looked at him with large, clear eyes.

"Monster!" I screamed at I turned around to head for the back door. At this point, I didn't even want to see what was hiding in the other room. I hoped that there was no one else alive to hear what he'd just said, but I really didn't care. I was going to go back to the city if I had to walk. I would have none of this abuse. He should have known better. He should have, but he's never learned a thing. To him I was nothing but a possession.

CHAPTER 25

Old Fred

I swung the back door open and realized it was on a spring. It closed rather loudly. I heard footsteps behind me. They were coming fast, but I didn't pause for one single second. I was so relieved to be out of that cabin. I began the same sprint as when I was first heading there. This time it was in the opposite direction. I decided that I wasn't going back to our cabin either. I was heading for the only other cabin I could see on the top of the hill. It appeared that it had occupants. If I could just get to that cabin and ask them to help me. I knew that I needed help. I knew that I was never turning around, and I would never go back to Scott.

As I was quickly approaching the unknown cabin, I noticed that there were chickens in a little coop and a goat tied under a tree. There were also remnants of corn stalks that had not been plowed after the season's end. Good, it is inhabited, I thought.

As soon as I thought it was safe, I turned around to see if he was still following me. By the time that I realized that he was nowhere to be found, I was smacked squarely on the forehead by a low-lying branch of the only tree that was near the house. I fell backwards and hit my head.

I woke up to the goat nibbling on my jacket. He had already managed to gnaw a small hole in the outer layer and part of the stuffing was in his mouth.

"I hope you choke!" I said to the goat.

"Now, that's not a nice thing to say, dear! The goat was just trying to help wake you is all."

I looked up and saw a man I had never seen before. Upon first inspection, I saw that he was older with gray hair, bristly whiskers, and calloused hands, reaching out for me. He helped me up from the cold, damp ground.

"Now, why don't you tell me why such a pretty young lady was sleeping under my tree with my goat in the first place?"

He had a large, welcoming smile.

"I don't know. I was trying to get here, and I must have slipped."

"Well, by the looks of it, the knock on your head from my tree would be my guess!"

I reached up to my head and sure enough, I felt a rather large bump.

"Ouch!"

As I reached around, I found the same on the back of my head. My head was pounding. It must have taken me a minute to get reoriented and realize I had been hurt.

"Look, I know this may sound a little crazy, but I am Mrs. Baker and I just wanted to use your phone. I want to get back to the city."

"Ah, I see. Well, I'm known in these parts as Old Fred. I also noticed all the noise that was going on while your cabin was being built. I would have noticed a pretty young gal out here, so where have you been?"

"I hadn't seen it until today. My husband was keeping it a surprise."

"Ah, surprises! There always were a lot of surprises with that family."

"What do you mean?"

"First of all, easy does it. Why don't I take you inside and make you a cup of coffee, tea, or warm milk? You're making me cold!"

I did as he requested and followed him into the house. It was much more rustic than the new cabin the Scott had built. It too looked old like his grandmother's cabin. Its porch was made of rustic boards, with rails worn smooth by years of hands that had rubbed it for support. As we entered the living space, we went directly to the fireplace along the far wall. We began to watch the fire blaze as he stoked the logs.

"Ok," he began. "Now back to the Bakers! Oh, you can say that they have had their fair share of belief in all kinds of good things. I suppose that every generation expects to have what the former generation left off with. I've seen it for years. One carrying on the torch of the former one. They are funny that way. They never seem to be living life for themselves. It's like they are living it for the past."

I took in a deep breath. It was all becoming clear.

"Well, that makes sense. Scott has been showing me the past since I met him. Now that we've been married nearly a year, he still has never let me go inside that old cabin up there. He said that he built this one so that we could make new memories. He said that nothing in it is an item from the past. I suspect that I'll be coming home to a really angry spouse when I get home tonight."

I looked down.

"Oh, there, there." He took my hand and patted it with his other. "There's nothing that you could have done that couldn't be fixed, Mrs. Baker. Where is that husband of yours, anyway? I'm sure that this has all been a misunderstanding. Besides, don't you think that he'd be awfully worried if he knew that his expecting wife was knocked out in the cold?"

"Oh, he probably already knew. He knows everything that I do at all times. I can never be privy to his full past. *I* have to wait for him to return from long business trips that he promised he wouldn't have to go on. *I* even have to agree to live out here when our baby comes and quit my job!" I couldn't believe how agitated I was becoming by my newfound revelation!

"Yes, yes, that does sound much like the Bakers that I have always known. They always kept strict tabs on the ladies in their life, that's for sure. I believe that is why the former Mrs. Baker was so happy when she found someone new. Too bad she was in that horrible accident though. You could really see the light in her eyes when she talked about her new guy. Yeah, it really was too bad. I always wondered how that boy took it, losing both parents at such a young age."

"I thought that they died just a few years ago." I knew what Scott had told me so far, like I knew my own story!

"No, no they have been gone for over ten years now. Scott was raised by his grandmother Baker. The very one that owned that cabin."

I couldn't understand what he was talking about. Maybe Old Fred really was too old to keep up with time. Either way, I wanted to know what he knew, even if it *was* out of order.

"Please don't think that I am being rude for asking, but does anyone still live there?"

"Heaven's no. The inside is way rougher than this old cabin. It was here first. Why do you ask?"

"Because when he was out looking for me, I went into the cabin, you know, in through the back door to the kitchen. Anyway, he was looking for me and he started talking out loud to someone in the front room."

He began to chuckle.

"Ah, I see. Remember what I said about the past being really important to the Bakers? Well, when his grandmother died about five years ago, he buried her in the family plot, but there is a huge picture of her hanging over the fireplace. I would suspect that he was just wanting to talk his problems out loud to her."

I had a look of shame on my face.

"You know, I think I may have overreacted about everything that has happened today. I mean, maybe he does just have our welfare in his mind when he does all of these over-the-top things. But, who builds a cabin out in the middle of nowhere and expects someone to raise a child here? There's virtually nothing to do out here!"

"Oh, have faith. You *will* have me for a neighbor, after all."

He smiled as he stood up.

"I'll be right back with, well, what did you say that you would like?"

"Nothing, sir, nothing. Thank you so much for your hospitality, but I think that it is time for me to get home."

"Well, I have to say that I understand. Me and the Mrs. used to squabble like that from time to time back in the old days."

"I'm so sorry to have bothered you today. I also hope that your goat doesn't choke. I had no business passing out in your yard anyway."

I chuckled a little as I rose to get up to leave. It was suddenly hard for me to see. Before I knew it, I was out cold once again.

"Elizabeth, wake up, honey. I am so sorry. Please wake up. I promise, I'll let you do whatever you want, just please wake up."

I opened my eyes to find myself lying on the worn brown leather couch where I had just had my conversation with the old man. Scott's voice seemed to be the catalyst to waking me.

"What happened?" I inquired, dazed.

"Mrs. Baker, you stood up and you took a spell." Old Fred explained. "I caught you sure enough though. I thought for sure you were going to hit the floor. Just got lucky, I suppose!"

"He filled me in on everything," Scott corroborated. "You have been out for at least a half an hour. Beth, what was I thinking when I said that you should say out here all by yourself? I couldn't even get an ambulance to promise to get here in thirty minutes! How could I possibly take care of you in an emergency?"

"It's ok, Scott. No harm, no foul." I began to sit up, as if to show my improving state.

"What do you mean no harm?" Scott pleaded. "Can't you see what is going on here? You have been hurt and it is all my fault. What's wrong with that picture?"

"You love me, Scott, that's all. The gesture came from your heart. I know that and that is what makes it so special." I took his hand in mine to show my sincerity.

"What, your concussion?" he retorted.

"No, silly, the cabin." I ignored his condescending attitude and tried to stay loving.

"Let's just forget about that stupid cabin and get you home to civilization." He looked back at me and took his hand from mine. He took Old Fred's instead to shake farewell.

"Thanks, Fred, for taking such good care of her in my hardheaded absence."

He rose up from the floor where he was kneeling and proceeded to lift me from the sofa.

"Scott, it's ok, I can get up." My arm immediately felt sore as he grabbed it. My head was already throbbing. I really didn't want to appear to be weak.

"I believe that is what got you into trouble in the first place, Mrs. Baker." said Fred.

I couldn't believe this old coot would take Scott's side after speaking so badly of his family!

"No matter what anyone believes, I will be just fine. I am

tough, just like sour bread dough that hasn't risen properly."

I got not one laugh about my food joke. I was trying to lighten the mood, but instead the guys didn't buy one single word out of my mouth. They remained in defense mode.

"Good evening, Mr. and Mrs. Baker. It was very nice to have company. It doesn't happen very often. Please come back when circumstances are better!"

"Goodbye, Fred."

"Yes, goodbye!"

Scott swung me through the door and into his waiting car.

"Conrad! Hello!"

"Hello, Mrs. Baker, it's always a pleasure to see you."

"You also, of course."

Through my puzzled gaze at Scott, I could see that he looked a little smug.

"How did you—or how did he—know?"

"As soon as you went storming out, I knew that you would be back and when you did, you would need a ride back into town. I called for Conrad at once."

The car stopped just as we were in front of our cabin.

"That will be all, Conrad."

"Be careful going home, sir."

"You do the same."

Conrad left the car and went straight to Scott's car that we'd driven to the cabin.

"So, are we staying the night, or are we going back home to LA?"

"Well, I think that it would be best if you could at least be checked over by a doctor, and it's getting late to ask *our* doctor to come all this way. Plus, I really don't know if he's busy or not. So, why don't we just..."

"Stay here." I interrupted.

"Stay? But, don't you think..."

"That I'll be just fine, yep. I'm just dandy. Besides, it looks like it may snow. I just know that these hills will look magnificent completely covered with snow!"

"I really don't know, Elizabeth. What if there is something more serious with your condition? You know that you did pass out twice, don't you? That has to be a pretty good concussion at the very least."

"So, keep me up and make love to me. Don't let me sleep for twelve hours. Isn't that the time limit on concussions?"

"I have no idea, but that does sound awfully tempting. Except, how's your head?"

He gently touched the top of my forehead. He could feel the grooves of the tree branch that I ran into.

"Ouch."

"Yeah, you would think that I could remember hitting the stupid tree!"

"What, you don't remember what happened to you?"

There was suddenly a look of panic on his face.

"Well, I just remember looking back to see if you had followed me. That's all. When I turned around, that was all I could remember. The tree must have been right there. I just wasn't paying close attention to my surroundings. But I have to say, the last time I looked at that tree, I could have sworn it was at least twenty yards away. Oh look, that's really not important, now, is it?"

"You could have been killed!"

He lightly took my face in his hands.

I pulled away so I could look him directly in his eyes.

"It's ok, Scott. I promise!"

"I should have never taken you here!"

"Wait, Scott, why? What is with this place and you? Why are you so desperate to keep me out of this loop that you seem to have with the past?"

He kissed me lightly on the lips and then on the head where I was injured. I bent my head down and showed him that the back of my head hurt also. He once again lowered his lips to kiss my head.

"See how great of a dad you are going to be? You are already kissing away the boo-boos!"

He smiled at me genuinely and sweetly.

"Let's go home."

I decided not to argue with him. We had had enough of that earlier. In fact, I wouldn't be injured at all if I hadn't gotten so mad in the first place.

"To the castle!" I jested.

It seemed to take us forever to get home that evening. I was sure that it was going to turn dark before we got there. I was pleasantly surprised to know that the day hadn't been totally wasted. As soon as he parked the car, he was over to my side. I found it amusing that he would run around the car to make sure that I didn't open my own door and get out.

He lifted me from the car, and we proceeded to the front doors of our large home.

"You know, Scott, as far as our baby's nursery here is concerned, I do think that I want to make a few changes." I smiled.

"Oh, high priced interior designers not good enough for you?" he teased.

"Of course they are, it's just that I would like to be able to make my own personal touches to it? You know, improve on perfection!"

"Only you could improve on perfection."

"Don't ever forget it!" I winked.

We spent the rest of the evening talking about the nursery. We left all conversation about the cabin at the cabin. It was like we were starting over. We were again like young newlyweds. Nothing could get us down and we knew that we could conquer the world if we wanted to. We decided to stay up for at least ten hours after the last time that I had passed out.

It was like we were having a slumber party. We talked things through about our future. I told him that I really just wanted to take a leave of absence, and not leave permanently. I needed my career to feel whole. Not that my baby couldn't make me feel whole, it was just that I knew that there was the drive in me to keep going in society. I could never be happy being a housewife and letting my husband go out and live his exciting life without me.

"So, we need to hire a nanny? Is that what you are saying?"

"I never really thought about it before, but I guess, yeah, we do!"

I was surprised by those words coming out of my mouth. Was I a bad mother to feel happy that we had the means to hire another person to do the job that I was supposed to do? I really didn't care. I knew that with all that we had together, all of our dreams should be able to come true, not just one person over another. This was one of the few times that we fully compromised. Again, it made me resoundingly happy.

"Thank you for being patient with me today. I just was a little overwhelmed earlier, I guess."

"Let's not even talk about it. I would really like to wipe our slate clean. I love you and whatever it is that makes you happy will make me happy too."

I missed times like this with him. In the first few months, it seemed we could talk for hours. It was what we did while we weren't making love. When the business trips started, then the conversations ended.

"I am so glad that you have the whole weekend to spend with me!"

"Elizabeth, you are more important than all the money and assets I have ever acquired. You have to know that by now."

"I do. I really do."

CHAPTER 26

Loose Ends

We spent the next day and a half together, at home. He was still so convinced that I would collapse the minute that I left the house. He knew that I was taking it easy and barely getting up at all, yet he still felt the need to protect me from something.

"Well, as wonderful as this weekend has been"—I rolled my eyes—"all good things come to an end."

"What do you mean by that?" he questioned. "I told you that I would be here for you this week if you need me!"

"Well, I mean that *my* work doesn't do itself and it wouldn't be fair to Ned if I just bailed again."

"If you say *well* again! I'll tell you what needs to happen!" he turned to face me, saw the look of dread on my face, and stopped. "The only thing that needs to happen...well, is... Conrad. Yes, Conrad needs to take you to work and return you safely to home tomorrow evening." He knew he had to concede and come to an understanding, or I'd be bound to run off once again, and he didn't want me going to work with something to hold over his head to Ned.

Although I was a little groggy in the morning, I managed to collect all the will I possessed to get out of that house and go back to work for as long as I possibly could. At least Scott felt secure with my decision. He knew that I would be perfectly safe under Conrad's care.

I almost felt sorry to call for him to be there at 5:30 in the morning. For some reason, my anxiety was high for work. I attributed it to the fact that I had only a month and a half and my maternity leave would start. I really didn't want to think about that.

Scott did let me talk to Collin Singleton by myself about my leave. He knew that I had specifics about my leave that only I could do justice explaining to Mr. Singleton. After all was said and done, I knew that my job was not, nor ever would be, in jeopardy. No matter what happened with how I felt after the baby was born, I still could get my job back.

Now Ned was another story. He became increasingly angry with the whole situation when he saw the bruises on my body.

"What did he do to you, Liz?

"Are you ok, Liz?

"Do you need me to hurt him back? You know I would for you, don't you?"

I laughed when he said that. He knew right then and there that I wasn't going to take him seriously.

"What would you say to the fact that a tree attacked me?"

"I would say that it is amazing that *Mr. Baker man* could transform into a tree!"

"Oh, now that will be enough! He wasn't even there when it happened!"

"He wasn't watching after you?"

I could tell by his voice that he was serious. Why was it that everyone was always so protective of me? I was pregnant, not made of glass. I was still the same strong person that I had always been.

"You of all people should know that I can take care of myself! Are we going to get any work done today, or are we just going to go around and around this morning? I would really like to work while I can."

"What do you mean while you can? Is that idiot actually telling you that you can't work anymore when the baby comes? Oh, I *knew* he was up to something when you first told me that you were having that baby. I knew he got you pregnant to gain control of you! In fact, that is what you were talking to Mr. Singleton about, wasn't it?"

"Yes, I was."

"How *could* you?"

"Would you please stop butting in when I am trying to talk? First, yes, I am leaving in a month and a half. I will be on maternity leave. Ever heard of maternity leave?"

"Of course, but that is usually for people who are saying that they will one day return to work."

"Yes, stupid. Do you think that I would be working so hard all my life to be where I am professionally just to give it all up because I married into money? Do you really think that I am that shallow?"

"I just know your husband and how he was raised. He was taught that the women in his family were possessions, useful only for having children and taking care of the house."

"Well, evidently that ended with his mom. You know that he was just fine when his mom was going to leave and move in with another man. She was going to be remarried, you know. Do you really think that Scott doesn't tell me anything about his family's past? Besides, do you think that I would give him a choice when it came to my personal life?"

"Yeah, I actually thought that he would wear you down. Also, not to be getting into the whole *mother thing*, but you know that she was leaving him to be with that other man, don't you?"

"What do you mean, leave him? He told me he was happy for the happiness that she found. He respected the fact that she was going to give everything up to be with her new love."

"You can believe what you want, Elizabeth, but he had just turned seventeen and hadn't even graduated from high school. She was leaving the home that he had grown up in to be happy for herself. He can say all he wants, but what do you think that he really felt to be left like that? How would you feel?"

"I would feel really mad at my mom for not loving me enough to stay."

The longer that I took all the inside information about Scott in, the sadder I got about my own home life as a child. I was left too, just like Scott. If he knew all about how I was, then why would he have been so adamant about telling me that it didn't matter to him that his mom was going to leave and be happy?

"Hey, I'm sorry, Liz. You look so sad. What just happened? Did you just realize that he wasn't all that he was saying that he was all along? Is that why you are so upset?"

"Ned, just believe me when I say that it is not all about my husband. Do you really think that you know my whole past? If you did, then you would know that my own mother left my family at about that same age! Now look, I don't want to speak one single word more about this, do you hear me?"

The host of the morning show looked back at us as if we were crazy. She knew that taping was just about to begin and even though she was prepared for the show, the audience was about to come in and we would have to be completely quiet. We managed to work without talking about anything personal the rest of the morning. I was too busy with my own thoughts of Scott and myself and how we seemed to be intertwined in some kind of identical past.

Maybe Ned was right. Maybe he really did have a problem with his mom leaving. Maybe he felt like he had done something and that he deserved for his mom to want to leave him.

I knew that was how I felt when my own mom left. I was left with a haunting feeling that his family's past really did repeat itself. Why did he pick me? I was in the same dysfunctional past as he was.

Was he just trying to test fate when he asked me to be with him forever? He had to have known that I would be concerned about my ability to be a mother. He'd told me that he knew me when he first saw me. He knew me. I just wished I had had the time to know him too.

Time that morning couldn't go by fast enough. I wanted to go home. I wanted answers. I needed to know that if we were going to be a family forever, the secrets had to come out. I called for Conrad to come pick me up promptly at noon.

"Conrad, please take me to Bakersfield Towers."

I was almost shaking by the time we arrived. I ran into the building up to his office floor. He was nowhere in sight. The glass-walled boardroom that was his usual office was empty.

"Where is Mr. Baker?" I asked his secretary.

"He asked me to have you call him. He knew that Conrad was bringing you here. He found himself in a predicament with some businessmen and he had to leave."

"Oh, I'll contact him, alright!"

I left her and started down the corridor to his secret office. I wasn't going to believe that he had gone until I checked his office first. The sound of my knock on the door was so low because of the sheer weight of solid wood. It gave me considerable uneasiness to be spying on my own husband. I was relieved that the sound didn't travel. I tried the secret opening, and the door began to creak open.

"Elizabeth?"

I stumbled backwards.

"What are you doing here?"

"Shouldn't I be asking you the same thing? Your secretary told me that you were gone to a surprise business meeting!"

"Yes, well, I needed some time to think is all. Things need

to be in place when our baby arrives."

"You just took the words out of my mouth. You know, I did what you said about talking to Mr. Singleton about my time off. I have a little over a month, and I will be a woman on the loose!"

"As loose as a woman with a newborn can be!"

He began to look at me strangely.

"Yeah, well, about the whole baby thing. You have approximately five minutes to start telling me what happened with your family. I will not settle for deception and secrets anymore. I need to know everything, or I promise that I will leave with my baby. I will not raise a baby to think less of his mother."

"So, been talking to Ned, have you?"

"And your neighbor," I explained.

"So what? What did you find out about my family history? What lies did these people tell?"

It disturbed me to think that he wouldn't care what the others had said.

"Why would the old man lie to me?"

"Maybe he didn't want new neighbors."

"Oh, I doubt that and besides I'm sure that it is common public knowledge about the car crash that claimed your mother's life. Why didn't you tell me that she was leaving you at the same exact time in your life as my mother was leaving mine? The first time I ever met you, you seemed to know so much about me. Oh, I was flattered, but there was no way that you could have had this whole thing planned for us ever since the day we met!"

"Please come in and shut the door. People will start to wonder where the sound of us talking is coming from."

"See, you are just so worried about revealing your family secrets! Who cares about your secrets? What makes you more special than the rest of society?"

The shutting of the door behind me was the last thing that I knew of the outside world that day. His secrets were many, and it took him the remainder of the day to get through all of the stories. It turned out that he was superstitious for a reason.

It did seem like all of the women in the past did end up leaving the men in one way or another. Whether it was their fault or due to the death of the husband. I found out that the orders in his grandfather's will applied to me, as long as that is what Scott wanted.

At first, he was going to keep the orders, but we talked it out, he decided to trust me wholeheartedly. Before his grandmother died, they somehow found out about me because of my noon show in San Francisco. I apparently held his attention from the first time he saw me on TV. He apparently told his grandmother about me and then did a complete background check.

He knew more about me than I did about myself. She told him that I should be either perfect for him or the worst thing that he could ever come across. She knew the statistics in dysfunctional families. You either are exactly like your parents or completely opposite. In the end, he just took a leap of faith.

He also explained about the furniture in the office. It was engrained in him that every article that belonged to the previous generation was to become precious. You could never part with it. To do so would be disgraceful. He was so happy that first day I came to his office because I was comfortable on the furniture that he could never bear to get rid of.

"Ok, Scott, there is still the little subject of the cabin."

"You're right, and you know, it feels great to know that I can tell you everything."

He finished telling me that it was where his grandmother died. She loved the cabin more than anything that she owned. She didn't really like his great-grandmother, but she loved the cabin she'd built. Though I had been in the cabin, I had not seen the majority of it. The great room contained pictures of family long gone and nearly lost.

He just liked to go in there to talk to them. He evidently didn't want me to go in because it contained the last memory he had of his grandmother. It was still too raw for him to talk about, so it was easier to say that the cabin just wasn't ready to have anyone walking through it because of disrepair. All the mystery seemed to be solved. I could tell just by looking at him that opening up about it all helped to store away some of the demons of his past.

"Ok, I know I said that I was done asking questions, but why did you lie about what happened with your mom?"

"I didn't. She died in a car accident."

"No, Scott, I mean about the time or year."

"It was because we were too much the same. I just didn't want to scare you off in the beginning. I figured if you knew I had no mom at the same age you had no mom, you would catch me in my untruth."

"Maybe I would have just thought that it was fate that we got together. Do you know how freaked out I felt when I found out I was having this baby? I wasn't sure if I would be a good mother or not!"

"I told you before and I'll tell you again, I have complete faith in you. If I didn't, would we even be having this conversation?"

"Ok, and what about Ned? Is he still going to be allowed to be my friend and come over and visit me and the baby?"

"I have to say, that has been one of the hardest issues with me; however, if he hadn't meddled today, we wouldn't have hashed this out."

"I agree."

"So, basically, yes. Ned can be your friend."

He told me again about how he wished that they could be better friends too because he was his cousin. By the end of the day, I couldn't be happier. It was everything I could have ever wanted. He was so truthful. I felt so much closer to him.

"Are you ready to go home, Scott?"

"Only with you."

And we did. We left to happy days of waiting together for our bundle of joy. We returned and finished the baby's room at the cabin. That was one place that I wanted to be with my children.

My last day of work seemed to come too soon. I was on the air during the whole morning show. They dedicated it to selling all desserts that pertained to baby showers, birthday parties for children, and weddings. They decided that because of newfound experience, I could sell the items the best.

I was fresh from having a wedding, about to have a baby shower, and I could imagine all there was available for birthday parties that were to come. I could immediately see my future. I would decorate the birthday cakes. I could make the cupcakes for the school parties.

There was a large gathering at the end of the show and a sendoff for my maternity leave. I felt so special that all I could do is feel the quiet stream of tears rolling down my face. I was overwhelmed by all the love that was coming from my colleagues, as well as the fans of the network. I found it very funny that they actually ordered a cake for the party. We always had enough leftovers to have a going-away party on a daily basis. Beginning to laugh, I turned to Ned.

"I'm gonna miss you, Ned."

"Oh, sure, Liz, you're gonna go to your castle and have your prince, and your king will rule over you as a knight in shining armor."

"I think the word you were looking for is *watch over me*."

"That's what I just said."

"No, you just said he would rule over me!"

"Hey, if that's what you say, then I'm not arguing with you!"

"I'm not saying it then. You are!"

Smack!

"Hey! I'm gonna turn you in for co-worker abuse!"

"Hee, hee!" I laughed. "They'll never find me!"

We continued to laugh until the very second that we realized that Conrad was waiting there to pick me up.

"Ma'am, ready?"

"I suppose that I am."

I turned and gave Ned a hug.

"I love you, you know."

"I know. I love you too."

"Take care of yourself and that baby! Watch your back, Liz. If you *ever* feel unsafe about anything, promise that you'll call me!"

"I will never feel unsafe, Ned. I trust Scott completely. Please don't go there today. I want to remember a happy day. Besides, if you gave me advice, I could give you some. So, I say for you to find a wife while I'm gone, will you?" I snickered.

He answered only with a nervous smile. Kind of the look you get when you are on the top of the roller coaster and about to drop. I turned to leave, and he held my hand, extending it as far as we could go before we couldn't reach anymore. It was over. The first part of my life had ended. I had a whole new life with a husband and a baby to look forward to.

"I'll see you soon, Ned. Six months isn't that long, you know!" I yelled out as I traveled down the hall to the elevators with Conrad.

I didn't know if Ned heard me or not, but I pictured him with a smile. I would miss him so much, but my time now was for my new family. I could deal with him later. Besides, I was one hundred percent sure that I would be safe, and I could show him up for the worrywart that he was. He would be proved wrong.

CHAPTER 27

New Life

Soon, Michale Andrew Baker was born. I was right. The future was as bright as I had ever suspected. I did spend much of my time with little Michale at the cabin. Although Scott tried as hard as he could, he still had a corporation to run. It was true. In the end, there was no mystery. There was just love. The three of us were living our lives with complete hope of all of our dreams coming true.

We beat the statistics. Michale and I were left alone most days, but they were for us to bond. I knew that the curse of bad motherhood would not touch my generation. Scott and I weren't going to hurt each other and parenting only brought us closer.

"I can't wait for the first six months to go by. Just to tell Ned that he was wrong about you to his face would give me *so* much pleasure!"

"You couldn't have said it better, Beth. You couldn't have said it better."

Scott leaned over and gave Michale a soft kiss on the forehead and gave me a soft kiss on my lips.-

It was a rather sunny day outside. The trees were just turning into the colors of springtime. The colors of the dogwoods in bloom and the fields of poppies were so soothing. I could breathe the fresh air forever. It was all I wanted to do anymore. Just breathe. I decided to take it slow after all that had happened.

It was so beautiful. Nothing better than early spring. The rebirth of the Earth. It took my breath away. I was glad everything didn't affect how I could feel about the little things in life. I wished to have days and days of this with Michale in those fields. That was all that was left. All the big ones, the ones that I thought I couldn't get through, I did. It was so surreal thinking about them in this context.

The past. Not so distant, but the past, nevertheless. Oh, to have had that when I was growing up. There was my wish, in the back of my mind, that all would stay as simple as a soft pallet and a picnic, out in a field of poppies.

ABOUT ATMOSPHERE PRESS

Atmosphere Press is an independent, full-service publisher for excellent books in all genres and for all audiences. Learn more about what we do at atmospherepress.com.

We encourage you to check out some of Atmosphere's latest releases, which are available at Amazon.com and via order from your local bookstore:

Icarus Never Flew 'Round Here, by Matt Edwards

COMFREY, WYOMING: Maiden Voyage, by Daphne Birkmeyer

The Chimera Wolf, by P.A. Power

Umbilical, by Jane Kay

The Two-Blood Lion, by Nick Westfield

Shogun of the Heavens: The Fall of Immortals, by I.D.G. Curry

Hot Air Rising, by Matthew Taylor

30 Summers, by A.S. Randall

Delilah Recovered, by Amelia Estelle Dellos

A Prophecy in Ash, by Julie Zantopoulos

The Killer Half, by JB Blake

Ocean Lessons, by Karen Lethlean

Unrealized Fantasies, by Marilyn Whitehorse

The Mayari Chronicles: Initium, by Karen McClain

Squeeze Plays, by Jeffrey Marshall

JADA: Just Another Dead Animal, by James Morris

Hart Street and Main: Metamorphosis, by Tabitha Sprunger

Karma One, by Colleen Hollis

Ndalla's World, by Beth Franz

ABOUT THE AUTHOR

Angela Geer Gann is a writer and businesswoman based in North Mississippi. She began writing her debut novel, *Redbird in the Poppies*, in the mid-2000s as a reflection of the dysfunction after the recession. Originally from Northern Illinois, she has lived in North Mississippi for most of her life. Angela has a diverse range of interests, including literature, church, music, food, and outdoor activities. For the past 20 years, she has been mentoring youth in outdoor skills, and as a businesswoman, she supports local and family businesses in her community. Angela is married with three sons, three cats, and two dogs.

I would like to dedicate this book to my family and friends. My husband, for many hours of 'story time'; my sons, for reminding me to never give up on my dream and for endless encouragement; my mom, for letting me know 'who's the best' and that what I produced was perfect in her eyes; my brother for always having my back; my friends and other family, who may or may not be with us today, for all of your support. It is much appreciated and never forgotten. Lastly, to each and every one at Atmosphere for the finished product that is my dream.

Made in the USA
Monee, IL
11 September 2023

42413513R00177